Works by Alicia Su Lozeron --

The Un-death of Me: Life of an Asian American Woman
(2016, A Cross-genre "Fictional Memoir")

Asia-literacy and Global Competence:
Collections and Recollections
(2017, English and Chinese Versions)

Global Competence Revisited
(2019, English and Chinese Versions)

Writings in the Time of Coronavirus
(2021, English and Chinese Versions)

A Man with Immense Love
(2022, English Version)

Vignettes of a Collected Kook
(2025, English Version)

Vignettes of a Colleted Kook

Alicia Su Lozeron

Vignettes of A Collected Kook

Alicia Su Lozeron

New York, Las Vegas, Los Angeles, Vancouver, Toronto, London, Sydney

Asia-America Connection Society

ISBN: **978-1-7332039-8-2**

Vignettes of A Collected Kook

Alicia Su Lozeron

New York, Las Vegas, Los Angeles, Vancouver, Toronto, London, Sydney

Asia-America Connection Society

ISBN: **978-1-7332039-8-2**

Vignettes of A Collected Kook: Contents

Introduction

Vignettes of a Collected Kook by Alicia Su Lozeron is a poignant and thought-provoking collection of reflections, narratives, and insights drawn from the author's personal experiences. These mini-stories reveal the complexities and growth of the narrator, whom the reader comes to know as a "collected kook." The term itself suggests a person who embraces both eccentricity and mindfulness, who is quirky and introspective, capable of embracing the full spectrum of life's joys and challenges. Through this lens, the author takes readers on an evocative journey that invites them to think, to reconsider their own paths and personal evolution.

The stories, though rooted in Alicia Su Lozeron's personal life, resonate universally. They offer glimpses into the narrator's family relationships, friendships, travel adventures, and moments of quiet self-discovery. From childhood memories to the unique dynamics of adult life, the narrator's journey is not just a series of events but a process of continuous transformation — an exploration of the narrator's evolving self-identity and inner growth.

Central to the narrative is the narrator's gradual self-awareness, as she learns from her life experiences and relationships, offering reflections that are at once humorous, touching, and deeply introspective. This combination of humor and depth creates a distinctive voice that invites readers to both laugh and think deeply about their own experiences. The narrator is constantly in motion, both physically through her travels and emotionally through her growth and development, and yet she remains rooted in her authentic self. It's this balance between growth, evolution and staying true to one's core that makes Alicia Su Lozeron's narratives particularly compelling.

At the heart of *Vignettes of a Collected Kook* is a focus on *personal growth and development.* The narrator's journey is not about reaching an endpoint, but about embracing the continuous process of becoming, a process that is messy, challenging, and at times, disorienting, but always enriching. Through her experiences, readers witness her deepening understanding of herself, her relationships, and the world around her. This makes her journey feel both intimate and relatable — readers see parts of themselves in the narrator's moments of clarity, confusion, sadness, joy, and struggle.

Alicia Su Lozeron's use of humor throughout the book offers both levity and a sense of playfulness, balancing out the more introspective moments with lighthearted commentary on life's absurdities. These moments of levity make the book accessible and enjoyable, ensuring that readers are not only engaged by the narrator's reflections but are also entertained by her quirky and offbeat reflections and observations.

Furthermore, *Vignettes of a Collected Kook* is an exploration of the *cultural experiences* that have shaped the narrator's identity. Through her travel experiences, familial interactions, and relationships with people from diverse backgrounds, the narrator reflects on how culture informs both her understanding of herself and her interactions with others. This reflection on culture is not just theoretical but is grounded in lived experience, making it a tangible, everyday concern. The author also highlights how culture and self-awareness intersect in meaningful ways, emphasizing the importance of embracing diversity and fostering a sense of empathy that is essential for cultivating mutual compassion and understanding to create a more inclusive, respectful, and harmonious society.

Alicia Su Lozeron's advocacy for *cultural competence* runs throughout this collection of vignettes, as she highlights the importance of understanding and respecting different cultural perspectives. This theme is further reflected in her work with Asia-America Connection Society (AACS | 亚美合作协会), where she promotes cross-cultural understanding and communication. By engaging with diverse individuals and communities, she emphasizes the need for empathy, mutual respect, and the value of learning from others. This not only enhances personal growth but also fosters a more harmonious and interconnected world.

Her work is a call for readers to engage in lifelong learning, not just in the academic sense but as a practice of emotional, intellectual, and cultural development. Through her writing, Alicia Su Lozeron encourages her audience to be self-reflective, open-minded, and proactive in their efforts to understand others. She positions personal learning and growth not as an isolated endeavor but as something that is inherently tied to understanding and appreciating the diverse world in which we live.

As a writer and communicator, Alicia Su Lozeron blends her own experiences with her professional expertise, seamlessly intertwining personal anecdotes with global issues. Her role as the founder of AACS further underscores the importance of connecting people across cultural boundaries, a theme that runs deep throughout *Vignettes of a Collected Kook*. She demonstrates how global competence — being able to navigate and understand different cultures — is not only beneficial for personal growth but essential for fostering a more cohesive and respectful world.

The themes of *self-development*, *emotional intelligence*, and *interpersonal relationships* are richly explored. Alicia Su Lozeron's writing has a unique ability to guide readers through life's complexities, offering them tools for understanding their emotions, managing conflict, and strengthening relationships. Her work encourages readers to cultivate an open and just community, to see life through a broader, more inclusive lens, and to develop a strong sense of self that is compassionate toward others.

Ultimately, Alicia Su Lozeron's writing aims to *inspire* and *empower* readers to develop better interpersonal relationships, make sense of their emotional experiences, and engage with the world more mindfully. She uses her own personal growth as a foundation to foster a larger sense of collective well-being. Through *Vignettes of a Collected Kook*, Lozeron provides not just an introspective exploration of one person's journey but a universal roadmap for personal growth, cultural understanding, and the pursuit of a more harmonious world.

In a world often filled with division and conflict, Alicia Su Lozeron's advocacy for mutual understanding, whether in family dynamics, intercultural interactions, or broader societal contexts, remains a powerful and transformative message. Her work, both as a writer and through her professional initiatives, offers a guide to navigating life with empathy, self-awareness, and a deep respect for others. Readers are left with a sense of hope, clarity, and an invigorated sense of their own capacity for growth, understanding, and connection.

"Think Global Live Noble"–together we can build a better world!

ISBN: **978-1-7332039-8-2**

You don't have to be larger than life to be a hero,
just larger than yourself.

- Mitt Romney

I do like my rock stars to be a little larger than life.
I don't mind the earnest ones
at all, but I do like a bit of individuality.

- Elton John

Wicked Winds and Minds

Wicked winds, sometimes reaching speeds of seventy miles per hour, whipped through our DC suburban home during the transitional seasons, particularly from winter to spring. Nestled between the Shenandoah Mountains and the Atlantic Ocean, the DC, Maryland, and Virginia (the DMV) metro area where we lived was vulnerable to winds coming from both directions. Each gust carried a biting chill, transforming the ordinary into something harsh, as if even the air itself were rebelling against the quiet rhythm of suburban life.

One winter, those winds proved more than just a nuisance. Our Middle Eastern-inspired gazebo, with its intricate, malleable metal beams and soft, chocolate-colored canvas tent, became a casualty of nature's fury. The winds tore through it, bending the structure and ripping the canvas apart, sending it spiraling to the ground like a forgotten relic of some long-lost dream. My carefully envisioned Moroccan-style backyard retreat, where I had imagined sipping mint tea under the stars, quickly faded into distant memories, replaced by the harsh reality of destruction, devastation, and obliteration.

It was a sad irony. The romanticism of the Moroccan backyard I'd longed for couldn't withstand the brutal reality of the wicked winds. The gazebo was gone, leaving behind only remnants of what once was. The beauty of it all felt fleeting, as if the winds themselves had come to mock my desire for peaceful, exotic serenity.

But nature's wrath didn't end there. We had to rebuild. The new structure was sturdy, functional, and practical: a hardtop, hurricane-proofed with anchors and stakes. The romantic vision had been replaced by sensible engineering.

One day, while we were contemplating the new design and wondering what else nature might throw at us next, Mike, our neighbor, approached. He was always caring for his elderly mother, a gentle woman who spent most of her time in a small shed in their backyard.

"Where are your canvas pieces from the gazebo? Can my mother have them for her she-shed?" he asked, eager to find a use for the pieces left from the storm. He didn't ask for much, just the scraps that had been left behind in the wreckage of the storm.

"We're using some of them to cover our cars, but we can give you the two big pieces," my husband, Bobby, replied. He cherished his cars, but, in this instance, valued his neighbors even more. They were good people, after all, even if their interests and ways of life were very different from ours.

Mike, grateful, nodded. "My mother can hardly walk. The smaller pieces will be just fine for her shed."

The next day, the sun beamed brightly, shedding light on the disaster from the previous day. We left the canvas pieces out in the front yard lawn to dry, unaware of what was to come. When we checked the yard the following morning, every last piece was gone. Someone had taken them, no questions asked, no answers given.

The realization that the pieces were missing left us feeling strangely exposed. We were in a suburban neighborhood, yet the loss felt as if we were living in a world much more congested, much less predictable. People, it seemed, were just as capable of being wicked here as they were in any city. In that moment, I couldn't help but think that the anonymity of suburban life had a dark side — a place where everyone was just far enough removed from one another to make the world feel indifferent, even hostile. People might be neighbors, but they were also distant strangers, and sometimes, strangers took what wasn't theirs without a second thought.

But was it really wickedness? Perhaps it was just desperation or ignorance. The truth was, we didn't know who had taken the canvas pieces, and we certainly couldn't prove anything. For days, we lived with the mystery, pondering the situation from all angles.

Before we moved from Las Vegas back to the East Coast and settled in the DMV area, Bobby and I had often discussed our dream life. I loved the metropolis, where museums were abundant, and cultures thrived. Bobby, on the other hand, preferred the countryside, where he could have more space and avoid traffic jams. We settled in the DC suburb of Upper Marlboro/Largo, where the DC Metro reaches its easternmost point. We could easily pop into DC for a concert or play and visit Chesapeake Bay whenever we wanted. Our neighbors were typical suburbanites, neither overly friendly nor indifferent. They were quiet, mostly kept to themselves, and occasionally hosted loud Saturday house parties in their backyards.

One night, three deer appeared on our front lawn. Bobby and I were both amazed, wondering how these deer managed to live in our populated neighborhood. The woods surrounding us offered plenty of natural resources for them to feed on: fruits, nuts, and various plants. They were vegetarians, and perhaps, yard furniture thieves as well. Maybe it wasn't a person who took our canvas pieces after all. Perhaps the deer had a magical ride, using our canvases as makeshift carpets.

It wasn't until a week later that we discovered the truth. Our neighbor, the one who had asked for the canvas pieces, wasn't the thief after all. Another neighbor had accidentally crashed into our motorhome, which was parked on the curb, early one morning around 4 a.m. In the darkness, likely unaware of the minor damage she had caused to our motorhome, she had taken the canvases to cover the severe damage to her car. She didn't realize the canvases belonged to us, and we had no idea our motorhome had been struck until we began searching for the missing canvas pieces.

At first, we didn't notice the damage to our motorhome. But as we scoured the neighborhood, desperately trying to find the missing pieces, we stumbled upon a dent and a hole on the side of the motorhome. That's when the puzzle pieces started to fall into place. The mysterious canvas thief wasn't some wicked person or animal after all; she was simply a driver trying to cover up the damage to her own car. Her motives, though misguided, were not malicious.

We knew we had to confront the situation. Bobby, determined to solve the mystery, took it upon himself to review the footage from our security camera. It took him days of scanning and rewinding, but finally, he spotted the red sedan that had crashed into our motorhome, backed up, and taken the canvases away. Armed with this new information, we set off in search of the car and its owner. After driving around the neighborhood, we found the red sedan parked in front of a neighbor's house, its front end clearly damaged, the headlights broken, and the fender dented.

Bobby, always the more methodical of the two of us, walked up to the car, lifted the canvas, and confirmed our suspicions. It was our neighbor's car, smashed and covered with the very pieces of canvas she had taken.

We contacted the police, and soon we were in touch with the middle-aged woman who had crashed into our motorhome. The insurance payout barely covered the cost of repairs to our motorhome, but the time and energy spent dealing with the situation far outweighed any monetary compensation.

Through it all, we learned an important lesson about assumptions and the complexities of human nature. Life isn't just about the good or bad intentions of others. Often, the stories we tell ourselves about others are incomplete, and what seems wicked on the surface is sometimes more about circumstance and misunderstanding than anything else.

There are wicked winds and wicked minds in every community, it seems, but they can be managed. The truth is, life's challenges, both natural and human, are difficult to predict and often harder to control. But at least, with patience and investigation, we can uncover the truth and adjust our perceptions. Through this incident, I came to realize that, while it's easy to label someone as wicked, it's far more complex to understand his or her motivations. Life is full of confusion and turbulence, and we must be vigilant, cautious, and adaptable. And in the end, I learned not to overly trust or suspect people — or animals, for that matter.

In the end, we learned that while the winds may be wicked, they are also unpredictable — and that, just like with people, understanding what lies beneath the surface can help us navigate the storms of life.

Tunghai Gas Station

A tall, stodgy quadragenarian in pressed beige khakis and a navy Chinese Tang suit shirt, Mr. Li, the station manager, patrolled the gas station with a kind of unspoken authority that seemed to emanate from the streaks of gray beginning to sprout at his temples. His every step was measured, every movement deliberate, as if commanding both the space and the individuals within it. For nearly two years, while I worked at Tunghai Gas Station, Mr. Li remained a constant presence. He wasn't just a supervisor; he was the heart of the gas station, managing the ebb and flow of customers with a calm demeanor and a practiced hand. Though his attention to detail could feel smothering at times, it was never unwelcome or bothersome.

While a college student, I worked as a part-time attendant at the gas pumps, and Mr. Li would help me manage the long, serpentine lines of customers, always stepping in to divert the attention of the young men on motorcycles away from me — me with my ponytail wrapped in a crimson scrunchie — and to the other lines manned by college boys with crew cuts. His intervention often felt like an act of protection, a kind of subtle gesture in which he was simultaneously helping me and asserting his role as the unspoken kingpin of this small industrial world. His presence wasn't oppressive, but rather natural and organic, comforting in its consistency.

Mrs. Chen, by contrast, was different. She was a woman who had a no-nonsense approach to everything in life, and while she was at least thirty years our senior, she ran the mini-mart's cashier register with such energy and efficiency it was as though the whole station hinged on her. I would watch her tally and double-check every receipt, ringing up customers as they hurried through to buy snacks, drinks, or last-minute travel essentials. My role was to make sure the gas pumps were attended to, customers were satisfied, and fuel was dispensed correctly, but Mrs. Chen was the backbone of the operation. Every evening, when my shift ended, I would dutifully report my station earnings to her. She would carefully review them with a sort of maternal precision, reminding me to follow the proper company guidelines for cash deposits. Her warning that she didn't know how long she had left in life — "in case I die young," she'd often say — was often made with a touch of humor, but also a strange, sobering finality. It was an odd comment, and though it was delivered lightly, I often wondered if she had some premonition that the years she had left in this world were fewer than most could fathom.

Mrs. Chen passed away one Tuesday morning in her own bed, and I never learned the cause of her death. Was it an unexpected fatal disease? Or something else? I never asked, nor did anyone else. After her passing, the station didn't hire another cashier. Instead, Mr. Li was left to fill in, ringing up customers while monitoring us jockeys via security cameras. There were days when he couldn't come out to relieve me at the pumps. It was strange, not having him stand beside me on the narrow island of concrete — him watching me fuel tank after tank, his presence almost like a protective shadow. He didn't stare at me directly, but often glanced toward the tail end of the line, signaling for traffic redirection, or perhaps just to check on how things were running. Those inobtrusive moments made me wonder: Did I prefer this middle-aged manager paying me special attention, or would I rather be left alone to handle things myself? It was a question I found myself returning to frequently.

During those moments, my mind would wander to the crew cuts — those young college men who worked alongside me, those who still, on occasion, caught my eye. Had they noticed my gaze drifting toward their lines, and did they acknowledge the unfair load of customers I often had to manage? I knew they didn't mind helping me out, calling customers over to their lines with grins that I knew weren't entirely innocent. Though their smiles were reassuring, I could tell they were testing boundaries, trying to figure out if there could be something more than simple friendship between us. The effort to avoid any suggestion of that deeper connection, however small, made my stomach twist.

Most of the college boys and I rarely spoke outside of work. But there was one exception. Ken, a sophomore engineering major, had occasionally appeared on campus, offering me a ride to work. I never quite knew if it was out of pure kindness or if there was something else — perhaps he thought that his flashy pins on his jockey uniform were enough to pique my interest. He would power-walk toward me, arms flailing in excitement, eager to offer me a ride. At first, I was uncertain, but I accepted the offer one day, driven by the fact that it was one of the few invitations to connect. Perhaps I, too, longed for a change of pace in a new friendship.

Ken's rides became routine after that. He was relentless, and his energy was just as flamboyant as the gleaming pins on his uniform. Yet, I realized quickly that I couldn't return his enthusiasm. By the third week of him picking me up, I knew it wasn't going anywhere. I wanted to be independent, to not need to rely on anyone for something as simple as a ride to work. I showed him my prized possession, my scooter, shipped from my home to my college dorm. I proudly rode it to the station, feeling a rare sense of satisfaction in my self-sufficiency and independence. No longer would I be confined to someone else's schedule or allow myself to be steered toward an unreciprocated relationship.

Nate, another member of the crew, was quick to notice Ken's advances and made sure to keep him at arm's length. Nate was the one who was responsible for creating the gas station's quirky mottos: "DON'T LOVE AND DON'T PANIC," "DON'T SMOKE AND KEEP SAFE." He had an affinity for balancing out the chaos with dry humor. Whenever he noticed Ken hanging too close, he'd make sure Ken stayed a few lanes over, his subtle interference ensuring that things didn't escalate into something more solid or complicated.

Then there was Amy, another female jockey. She was different from the others. She had this ability to blend in and stand out at the same time. She was like one of the guys, but with a certain sharpness that came with experience. "Brother, I've been there… right there in the dating game," she once told me, the words laced with a knowing tone. "I know how you play." Her words, though lightly spoken, offered a kind of camaraderie that made things a little easier to navigate. In that small world, we found solace in each other's understanding, even if we rarely spoke beyond the surface.

The Tunghai Gas Station, located on Middle Harbor Road in Taichung City, Taiwan, was a microcosm of life beyond its borders. The station was nestled on a six-lane avenue, surrounded by curio shops, strip malls, restaurants, KTV salons, game parlors, lovers' motels, and office buildings. It was a place where the past and present collided, where the industrial grittiness of the '80s and '90s met the contemporary bustle of college students, factory workers, office employees, drag racers, and motorcycle enthusiasts. Each day, cars of all kinds passed through: sports cars, SUVs, pickups, sedans, semi trucks, station wagons, jalopies, low-riders, and high-riders. They were the transient, the seekers, the lovers, and the dreamers, all filling up at the pumps before continuing their separate journeys.

It was the gas station workers who were staying there like fixed stars. Shift after shift, we lived this strange, shared existence — managers who either paid attention or didn't, cashiers, staffers, and cleanup crews who made the mini-mart hum with life, and part-time college workers like me, who were trying to figure out what came next in life. We all gave something to the station, and we all left with something as well. The station was a place where time could feel like it stood still, even as it pushed us forward in subtle ways. Nothing was constant.

I often found myself watching the comings and goings of the people who passed through. A station full of life. I had come to work there to earn pocket money, but over time, I had developed a habit of philosophizing about the attention I received — or didn't — and observing people of all kinds, trying to understand the social landscape around me. After two years of working there, I began to crave a change. The gas fumes, the narrow island of concrete, the heat rising from the pavement — everything began to make me long for something else, something with a little more air.

Just a block away, there was the campus, where I landed a new gig working in the school cafeteria. There, I served food to college students, ate plenty of buffet meals, and listened to soft rock playing overhead. It was quieter. Cleaner. More relaxed. And yet, I would occasionally see Mr. Li when I went to gas up my scooter. I had long since formed an unfair generalization about him: that he was a satyr, half-man, half-beast, a nature spirit known for his wild behavior, who was simply drawn to women.

One day, he filled up my scooter at the same gas pump I used to serve customers. Afterward, we stood by Middle Harbor Road, away from the station, and started talking. We spoke casually, as friends do, about his wife, his son, and my studies. I saw the warmth in his kind eyes, and for the first time, I realized how much more there was to him than I had initially imagined. What I had seen as special attention from him was not simply flirtation or longing, but an expression of something deeper, a sense of connection to a shared world.

It wasn't long before I finished my university degree, and after that, I never saw Mr. Li again. Years later I realized how much I had grown from those times, from the small lessons I had learned about attention, connection, and the passage of time. The gas station, and the people in it, had given me more than I could have understood at the time.

$10K for Emergencies

I hated going to the doctor. The GP Medical Center, Advanced Dental, MedPlanet — I dreaded every visit. Terrified of MDs, DMDs, and all the medical workers in between, I often felt it was unfair to pay ten thousand dollars a year just for check-ups and teeth cleanings — even with my employer-sponsored insurance. Yes, I smoked cigarettes, and my "punishment" was enduring regular teeth cleanings. But that didn't make it any less frustrating or expensive.

On top of premiums, I had to deal with deductibles, copays, and even parking fees every time I visited a medical facility. The real culprit, though, was the middlemen, the pharmaceuticals and the insurance companies. Affordable healthcare in America felt like a myth, and it was only a matter of time before I'd give up on it altogether. The complexity, the paperwork, the endless phone calls — I was drowning in a sea of bureaucracy, and the financial burden of it all was overwhelming. Sometimes, it felt like there was no escape.

I thought it would be simple to get my teeth cleaned at the dental office near my house. How complicated could it be? I booked an appointment two months in advance, optimistic that I'd get it done in no time. At the office, I was greeted by the usual clinical smell of sterilizing chemicals, the kind that made my stomach churn. I opened my mouth wide, ready for the usual cleaning, but instead, I was subjected to the dentist's plastic digital film sensors probing my mouth, searching for imperfections and stains.

That visit didn't end with a clean smile, just more X-rays and more waiting while the office tried to figure out what my insurance would cover. I felt like a pawn in their game, caught in the endless cycle of insurance verification and paperwork. Every time I thought I was done, there was another delay, another form, another phone call.

Two months later, Dr. Agwuegbo's assistant called to tell me that my insurance wouldn't cover the cleaning. Apparently, it didn't cover my "children." The problem? I didn't have any children. I couldn't help but laugh — what a bizarre mix-up. I felt more frustrated than ever. This was supposed to be straightforward, just a dental cleaning. Instead, I found myself entangled in a web of confusing policies, miscommunications, and unending delays.

Determined, I drove ten miles farther to a dental office that boasted state-of-the-art X-ray equipment, hoping this would be the place to get things right. The dental assistant hardly spoke to me. She sterilized instruments, tied a towel around my neck, and handed me a cup of Chlorhexidine gluconate mouth rinse. I followed her instructions, but the spittoon attached to the chair didn't drain properly. I had to get up multiple times to spit in the restroom. It was ridiculous, but I powered through.

Still, I believed in the hype around this place. The reviews were glowing, and I trusted what others had said — many people, even politicians and professionals, swore by Dr. Peterson's ethical patient care. I thought that this time, finally, I would get the treatment I had been looking for.

After a long wait, Dr. Peterson's assistant took all my information. The atmosphere was so sterile, so devoid of warmth, I almost forgot why I was there in the first place. Then, Dr. Peterson finally showed up. I was ushered into a small waiting area where I stood pacing around, fiddling with business cards for the doctor and several hygienists. There was nothing else to do, no magazines that interested me, nothing to occupy my mind while I waited.

"Which hygienist should I pick?" I asked the receptionist, hoping to find something that would alleviate my nerves.

"They're all good," she said, almost too casually. "You're lucky if you can book one soon."

I checked my phone for more reviews and noticed the sign on the wall: "Silence Your Phone and Keep Your Voice Low." The sign was reflected in a mirror, and I half-expected someone to reprimand me for using my phone. So, I put it away and stared out the window, following a car down Hillridge

Street until it turned the corner and disappeared, my mind wandering.

Dr. Peterson's assistant snapped me out of my trance and, for the first time, spoke to me in complete sentences.

"We're referring you to a periodontist at Advanced Dental in the city center. It would be unethical for us to clean your teeth without a periodontist assessing the possibility of gum disease. Studies have shown it may even be linked to Alzheimer's. You'll probably need deep cleaning, and we can't do that here."

I appreciated their conscientiousness. Without it, who knows? I might have let gum disease go untreated and ended up with Alzheimer's down the line. It was a scary thought, but one that seemed so distant when I was just trying to get my teeth cleaned. I made an appointment at Advanced Dental for another two months later, convinced that at last this time, I'd get the teeth cleaning over with.

Two months went by before I, again, embarked on my journey to a dream dental office for simple teeth cleaning. I parked in a garage off Arliman Boulevard for $25 and paid a $53 copay. Then Dr. Levine looked at me and said, "No, you don't have gingivitis or periodontitis. We don't need anesthesia. You'll just need to schedule another appointment for the cleaning." My heart sank — another trip, another visit, another delay.

The cleaning would cost me another $78 out of pocket. By the time I'd scheduled yet another appointment for three months later, I was exhausted, physically, emotionally, and financially. I'd had enough. I decided I'd just wait until I traveled to Central America to get my teeth cleaned — at least there, it wouldn't be a financial nightmare. The prospect of flying out of the country, getting my teeth cleaned in a fraction of the time, and for a fraction of the cost, was starting to feel like the only reasonable option.

Medical visits in America were no better. To get Rosuvastatin for cholesterol control, I had to undergo extensive blood tests. It was time-consuming and costly. And that wasn't even the worst part. On top of that, I had to pay out-of-pocket for a phone consultation with a specialist, which my insurance deemed "necessary preventive care." What was the point of having insurance if I still had to pay so much? I couldn't help but wonder if I was ever going to get ahead of this cycle.

At the end of the day, it's $10K set aside for unforeseen emergencies. That's the amount I had to allocate each year, just in case something unexpected came up, though thankfully it never did, knock on wood. God forbid, something serious happened. I dared not to imagine what I would have to pay for urgent care, for emergency medical transportation, or for emergency room care! What would my insurance even cover? And how long would I have to fight to get it?

It felt like I was constantly bracing for the worst. The endless out-of-pocket costs, the waiting, the delays — it was all a reminder that healthcare in America was a system built to serve the middlemen, not the people. It wasn't about taking care of patients; it was about managing payments, claims, and paperwork. And I was stuck in the middle of it all, just trying to make sure I didn't fall through the cracks.

At some point, it stopped feeling like a series of individual healthcare visits and turned out to be a relentless game where I was never going to win. So, I did what I could to protect myself. I set aside $10K for emergencies and opted out of my employer-sponsored insurance plans, hoping I wouldn't need to use it. My plan was that, if I ever needed it, the $10K would have accrued some interest over time. That way, I'd benefit not only from having the $10K to cover medical expenses, but also from the interest earned.

Eventually, during one of the trips to the vacation house my husband and I own on Corozal Bay, Belize, I had the opportunity to take care of my dental health and get my teeth cleaned. I had been putting it off for a while, and since we were already in Belize, I figured it would be a good chance to try something different. Dr. Nunez was absolutely amazing — she was a breath of fresh air compared to the dentists I had visited in the U.S. Despite being an oral surgeon, she didn't carry the typical arrogance or cold professionalism often associated with that field. Instead, she was warm, welcoming, and genuinely caring about her patients' comfort.

She took her time, making sure to thoroughly clean every single curve, every fine seam between my teeth, and every hidden corner I usually missed during my own brushing. Her attention to detail was incredible. The entire cleaning process took more than two hours. She was so patient, explaining each step, and ensuring I was comfortable the entire time. The level of care and precision she put into it was unlike anything I had ever experienced in the U.S.

I went to Belize expecting just a routine dental cleaning, but it turned out to be so much more than that. It was, without a doubt, the best dental care I've ever received, and I am so glad I chose to go abroad for it. When I left the appointment, I didn't just have cleaner teeth; I had a newfound appreciation for medical professionals who genuinely take their time and care about their craft. I only wish I could find that kind of affordable care in the U.S. someday.

Alfalfa and Basil

For as long as I can remember, I've dreamed of creating a garden where every plant, herb, and flower would hold a special place in the story of my life — a garden that would not only be a visual retreat but also a sanctuary for my senses. In my mind, this dream garden always had a little bit of everything: bold flowers, fragrant herbs, fruit trees, and even some edible plants that would nourish both body and soul. Among the flowers, I imagined golden sunflowers towering above, their faces always following the sun; the striking beauty of vibrant birds of paradise standing tall like exotic dancers; white and purple hydrangeas creating a soft, romantic haze over the landscape; black orchids adding a touch of mystery; and the fiery red ginger adding a tropical flair. My trees would sway gently in the breeze, with maple trees creating a golden canopy in the fall, acorn trees providing shade, and Poinciana trees adorned with their fiery red flowers, bursting with color in the warm summer air.

But it wasn't just the flowers and trees that I envisioned. In my dream garden, herbs were always meant to play a starring role. Basil, rosemary, thyme, oregano, sage, dill, mint, parsley, and cilantro — each one would flourish in their own corner, ready to be harvested fresh for cooking. Of all the herbs, basil stood out as the most important to me. There's something about its fragrant, slightly peppery aroma, and its vibrant, green leaves that always makes me feel like I'm stepping into a culinary paradise. I imagined making fresh pesto, sprinkling basil over pasta, tossing it into a salad, or adding it to a bowl of soup, knowing it would bring that perfect, aromatic flavor to everything. More than just a culinary delight, I also believed in its health benefits. I'd read that basil contains antioxidants that can help fight free radicals, and that it was traditionally used for its anti-inflammatory and digestive properties. It became more than just an herb in my mind; it was a small but powerful ally in maintaining my health.

Alfalfa, though, wasn't a plant I had given as much thought to. While I had seen it used in sprouted salads or tucked into sandwiches, I hadn't fully appreciated the way it could contribute to my garden. Alfalfa's tiny leaves and delicate stems stood in sharp contrast to basil's robust, fragrant presence, yet there was something undeniably appealing about its simplicity. Known for its wealth of vitamins, including A, C, and K, as well as minerals like calcium, magnesium, and iron, alfalfa was an unsung hero of the plant world. It wasn't flashy or demanding, but in its quiet, understated way, it had so much to offer in terms of nourishment. I began to appreciate alfalfa's versatility, from its nutrient-dense sprouts to the way it could be integrated into a garden as both a cover crop and a healthy food source.

One morning, as I sipped my coffee, I gazed out the window at my garden, which, though still a work in progress, was already bursting with life. The morning sun illuminated the basil plants, which were growing wildly tall, vibrant, and full of promise. Their rich green leaves seemed to invite me to reach down and pluck them, promising that today's meals would be a little bit more special. As I watched, a pair of American robins swooped down, hopping eagerly among the herbs, nibbling at the fresh green leaves. Nearby, a squirrel was perched on the branches of my fruit tree, nibbling on the tiny peaches that had started to ripen. Two kittens, born under the shed in the yard, chased each other through the garden, their tiny paws darting between the plants as they playfully pounced on the shadows cast by the leaves. It was a joyful, lively scene, filled with nature's little moments of wonder.

Yet, despite the beauty and vibrancy of it all, my garden wasn't without its challenges. The robins had already nibbled the edges of my basil leaves, and the squirrels had gotten to the peaches before I could. The two kittens, eager to explore their new world, had trampled a few of my herbs in their playful escapades. My garden was still very much a work in progress, not yet the serene and orderly haven I had envisioned, but it was alive with energy and growth.

I smiled to myself at the thought, recognizing that these little disruptions were just part of the process. It felt like the right moment to harvest some basil for the fresh salad I had planned. But as I reached for the familiar leaves, I noticed something else growing in the same patch, tiny, delicate sprouts that resembled young basil. Looking closer, I realized that in my excitement, I had mistaken alfalfa buds — and perhaps a few other wild greens — for basil. Amid the garden's quiet chaos, I had unknowingly picked and gathered the wrong plant — an honest mistake.

That evening, as I prepared my salad, I felt the unfortunate effects of my mix-up. I found myself running to the bathroom more times than I cared to count, my stomach cramping with discomfort as a reminder that careful attention was required when harvesting plants. The incident served as a humbling reminder that every plant, no matter how small or seemingly insignificant, has its own identity and purpose. It was a lesson in patience, in the importance of taking the time to identify and understand each plant before reaching for it.

I took a break from gardening for a while, giving myself the space to learn and reflect. But it wasn't long before the familiar excitement of my dream garden called to me once more. My husband and I visited a mountaintop covered in wildflowers, where the air was thick with the fragrance of blooming plants, and the colors of the flowers seemed to dance in the breeze. There, among the wildflowers, I found that spark of hope and inspiration that had been missing for a while. I returned home energized and ready to dive back into my garden, eager to rebuild and refine my dream.

This time, I took a more mindful approach to my gardening, paying closer attention to each plant's needs. Basil would be the star of the show, but I also began to embrace the presence of alfalfa. It would be a gentle companion to the basil, growing beneath the shade of the taller plants. I found joy in the idea that I could incorporate both into my meals, using basil for its bold flavors and alfalfa for its health-boosting qualities.

In the end, my garden began to take on a new shape. It wasn't just about cultivating beauty; it was about understanding the balance between the different plants, respecting their unique characteristics, and learning to care for them with patience. Both basil and alfalfa had their place, each contributing in its own way to the garden's tapestry of life. The basil would always be my favorite, a staple in my cooking and a symbol of the dream I had carried with me for so long, but alfalfa would quietly and gently support me, offering its nutrients in a way that was just as valuable.

And so, my garden grew, lush with basil, alfalfa, and all the flowers, herbs, and trees I managed to plant. It wasn't perfect, but it was alive and vibrant, brimming with life, learning, and growth — just like me. The soil held the memory of every failed attempt and every small triumph, from seeds that never sprouted to blooms that surprised me with their multiple hues. I learned to welcome the weeds as part of the process, to see beauty in the wild and unruly corners. Some plants thrived where I least expected, while others faded despite my careful tending. But still, I kept planting, kept trying, kept believing in the quiet magic of patience and persistence. Over time, the garden became more than a patch of earth; it became a reflection of resilience, a strong testament to change, and a gentle reminder that growth rarely follows a straight line.

A Better Apple Picker

My sister, Wenwen, was a much better apple picker than I ever was. I realized that immediately as we stepped off the bus at the orchard, and it became clearer with every passing day. Pa and Ma had sent us to 36 Family Farm Road for the summer, located in the heart of Taiwan's mountainous terrain. It was meant to be a vacation of sorts, a way to earn our keep and get a taste of hard, honest work. But from the moment the bus began its slow climb up the mountain, I could feel the difference between Wenwen and me. The road twisted and turned like a snake, its serpentine path making my stomach churn. Each curve of the mountain seemed to mirror my anxiety. High school girls like us, along with long-term laborers who had worked the orchard for years, filled the bus. The laborers were seasoned and silent, with the calm strength of those who had spent their lives in the rhythm of manual work. Wenwen, sitting beside me, was already at ease, chatting and laughing, her presence vibrant and full of energy.

As the bus made its way to the top, I could feel the air getting thinner, cooler, and fresher. The apple orchards stretched endlessly before us, their branches heavy with fruit, their leaves catching the sun like golden coins. The sight was breathtaking, but my sense of awe only deepened my feeling of being out of place. My sister, on the other hand, seemed to step off the bus with the same confidence she always had in outdoor activities. She was at home in nature, at ease with everything and everyone. The young man sitting next to us on the bus took immediate notice of her. He was a local, perhaps in his early twenties, with the same lean build and confident gait of someone who had spent most of his life on the mountain. As he looked at Wenwen, I could see something shift in his eyes — a spark of admiration, something I wasn't sure I would ever see directed my way from this mountain man.

A-bian, the orchard owner and a skilled pomologist, could hardly contain his enthusiasm when he greeted us. A-bian had a deep love for his apples, almost a paternal affection. He was kind and welcoming, pointing out different varieties with the reverence of someone who had dedicated his life to studying them. "These Fuji apples," he explained, his voice rich with knowledge, "are our most prized. They're the ones everyone wants, crisp, sweet, and perfectly balanced. But this one," he continued, gesturing to a tree laden with apples, "this one here, the wax apple tree — oh, it's very special." He looked at the trees with such affection, as if they were family members.

Despite A-bian's warm, welcoming words, I felt out of place. I was fascinated, but I didn't know where to start. When he spoke of taste, texture, and color, I had no idea how to apply and assess the apples. I just stared at them, feeling clumsy and unsure of how to begin picking. The trees, so full of fruit, seemed daunting, almost frightening. I didn't know how to approach them, how to touch them, let alone how to climb and harvest the apples. I had never been physically gifted, and this labor-intensive work seemed like a world away from my own.

Wenwen, on the other hand, was a natural. She moved with ease and grace, practically a part of the orchard itself. She was at home here, her movements fluid and effortless as she picked apples with a smile on her face. It seemed like she could do anything: climb trees, gather fruit, and make friends with anyone, all without breaking a sweat. Her presence was magnetic. The moment we arrived, she was already chatting with A-jia, the young mountain man from the bus, laughing and making light of the work ahead. The orchard, which should have been a place of hard work and exhaustion, felt like a playground for her.

As for me, I felt like I was moving in slow motion. Every step was calculated, uncertain. I lagged behind her, unsure of where to go or what to do. It wasn't that I didn't try. I did. I tried with all my might, but I just couldn't keep up. I watched Wenwen glide through the trees, effortlessly picking apples, her hands moving with precision. I was stuck, fumbling with the baskets, unsure of which apples to pick or how to climb the trees. The more I tried, the more I realized that I was not built for this kind of labor. The work, so simple for Wenwen, was a struggle for me.

In an attempt to justify my presence on the orchard, I kept repeating to myself, "Wenwen and I hardly have time to play together during the school year. It'll be good for us to spend the entire summer working and playing together, like two peas in a pod." But I knew that this wasn't true. Wenwen had already found her place there, while I was merely trying to make sense of my surroundings. She had slipped into that new world without effort, while I was still fumbling to understand what was happening around me.

"I'm going as cuckoo as you are if you don't catch up," Wenwen teased one day, glancing back at me as she continued picking apples with ease. I could see the sparkle in her eyes, the excitement of being in a place that felt like home. She felt sorry for me, but at the same time, I could tell she couldn't help herself from being swept up in her newfound world with A-jia. I could barely keep up with her, let alone the other workers. And then there was A-jia, who confidently led the orchard workers, making everything look so easy. "I'll show you how things get done here," he said with a grin, his voice filled with the assurance that comes from years of experience. The workers here were skilled, and it showed in the way they moved, graceful and efficient.

The more I observed, the more I realized that it wasn't just the apples that were being picked. Time itself seemed to slip away for the workers, especially when they took breaks, laughing, flirting, and sneaking bites of apples straight from the trees. Their lightheartedness was foreign to me. They worked quickly, meeting their quotas with ease, and then they had time to enjoy the fruits of their labor. As for me, I was still struggling to even fill my first basket. The more I saw this effortless rhythm, the more I felt like I was missing something vital.

I started to resent the apple-picking job. What was supposed to be an opportunity to connect with nature and to exercise my tired body felt like an alien world. I couldn't lift the heavy baskets, couldn't walk the long distances, couldn't bend and squat the way the job required. Every day felt like a reminder of how out of place I was. I was sunburned and frostbitten at the same time, my body aching with the strain of physical labor I was never prepared for. I tripped and stumbled constantly, broke my nails a thousand times, and never quite got clean. But what bothered me most was the bruising of the apples. I couldn't bear the thought of harming something so beautiful, so delicate.

Wenwen, however, was a master of the craft. She picked apples with ease, as though she was born for it. "Use both hands. Grasp the apple with the palm of your hand," she instructed one morning. "Then roll the apple backward until it snaps from the tree with the stem intact." It sounded simple, but my hands didn't work like hers. I struggled to follow her instructions, my movements awkward. "I have to hold the tree trunk for support," I protested. "I only have one other hand to pull or roll the apples."

Wenwen, unfazed, continued to pick apples with a perfect fluidity, each snap of the apple coming without effort. Snap! Snap! Snap! Her hands were graceful, efficient. Everything about her seemed at home in the orchard. Me? I was terrified. I was all thumbs, too afraid of falling, too clumsy to pick even one apple without ruining it. And I couldn't shake the feeling that, in some way, I was ruining something more important than the apples: I was spoiling the connection between Wenwen and A-jia. They were growing closer, their own world taking shape, and I was just… in the way all the time.

But I worked hard. For someone who wasn't built for apple picking, I tried my best, even when my hands ached from reaching for branches that were just a little too high, or when my fingers were stained with juice and sap that clung to me like a reminder of my struggles. I watched others with ease, their movements fluid and natural, like they were born for this. Wenwen, especially. She moved with such grace, her basket always full, her rhythm flawless. I couldn't keep up with her, no matter how hard I tried. Yet, I kept pushing, driven by a silent, stubborn need to prove to myself that I could belong there. That I could contribute, that I was not just an invisible shadow in someone else's success. I wanted to belong, even if I was constantly a step behind, even if I could never pick apples the way Wenwen did. Even if my hands were slower and my basket always seemed emptier. I tried.

There was a kind of beauty in it, though, the way the orchard felt like it had a place for all of us, no matter how different our paces were. The leaves rustled as if whispering encouragement, and the scent of fresh fruit mingled with the earthiness of the air, reminding me that the effort, the struggle, was just as important as the harvest itself. Even if I didn't pick apples like Wenwen, I was still part of something, still moving through the motions, still showing up.

Then I realized how difficult it must have been for Wenwen when I was called to the school auditorium stage to accept composition awards, excellence accolades, and all the academic achievements that seemed to come so easily to me, but were just out of her reach. I couldn't help but wonder how she felt as I stood there, basking in the recognition. She had been the one quietly watching from the sidelines. While I struggled with feelings of mediocrity as a non-apple-picker, caught in the shadows of others' expectations, she too must have endured the sting of humility, and embarrassment of not measuring up academically.

Wenwen had her own form of brilliance, excelling in athletics with a natural talent and drive that I didn't possess. Meanwhile, I thrived intellectually, finding comfort and achievement in the world of books and ideas. Yet, despite our differences, I began to see how much we both carried the weight of our own personal struggles, often silently.

I began to understand that her achievements in sports were no less significant than my academic ones, just as my intellectual pursuits were no less valuable than her athletic accomplishments. We each had unique strengths and weaknesses, and those differences were not something to compare or feel diminished by, but rather to appreciate and celebrate.

What really stood out to me, though, was the realization that, despite everything, we had always been there for each other. We may have been walking different paths, facing different challenges, but the strength of our sisterhood was built on a foundation of mutual support and understanding. As long as we continued to show up for each other, through the highs and the lows, our bond would thrive, no matter what.

Our relationship was never about who succeeded more or who fell short. It was about the steady presence we offered one another, in both the joyful and difficult moments. We would always be there for each other. And that, I now see, is the true measure of success.

My Chinese Man

I'm frugal. I looked up Chinese construction ads for affordable handymen — Chinese men from all over: Guangdong, Hong Kong, Beijing, Shanghai, Shandong, Hunan, and everywhere in between. That's how I found Mr. Lu, my "Chinese man" from Beijing, to install bamboo flooring in my first house. His ad was simple, but something about it stood out; perhaps it was the no-nonsense tone or the promise of "quality work at an honest price." He didn't charge an arm and a leg, only about sixty percent of what American handymen would charge. And when I met him, I could tell immediately he was no ordinary tradesman. He was fast, meticulous, and his work was like art, affordable and exquisite art.

Born and raised in Taiwan, I speak Mandarin. Finding Mr. Lu was one of the best outcomes of connecting with Chinese-speaking people in America. Over time, I came to realize that many of the connections I made with Chinese immigrants were fleeting, often transactional. But Mr. Lu wasn't like that. He was like a miniature Buddha. He was quiet, worked from dawn to sundown, and exuded a peaceful contentment that seemed rare in the frenetic pace of modern life. He had an energy about him, calm and focused. That made him easy to trust.

In only a week, he completed the bamboo flooring in my living room, and it was perfect. He didn't ask for much, just the right compensation for his skill. His pricing was transparent and very reasonable. He deftly calculated the cost of materials and listed everything for me to reimburse him. There was no haggling, no inflated costs, just fairness. He expected a fair price for a fair day's work, nothing more, nothing less.

During the job, Mr. Lu would often take his lunch on the bench on my porch. It wasn't the hurried, distracted eating that you often see in America. He ate slowly, as though savoring the moment, taking in the world around him. I started bringing fruit to him, as a small gesture, but one that seemed to bring a peaceful joy to him. One afternoon, after handing him an apple, I struck up a conversation. To my surprise, he told me that he had once been a Beijing Opera singer in China. Even in casual conversation, his deep voice offered a glimpse into his former life on stage. In America, he had taken on various jobs, including handcraft work, to support his wife and two children. Yet it was clear as day that his passion for the arts had never truly left him.

At that moment, I realized how little I had known about Mr. Lu, even though we'd shared a week together. I had assumed that his life was simply about getting by in America, doing work that paid the bills, but it was so much more than that. He wasn't just a handyman; he was a man with a history, with dreams, with a voice that carried the weight of a thousand stories. He even sang a few Chinese operas for me. The sheer beauty and emotional depth of his voice impressed me. I was in awe, not just of his talent, but of the fact that he had been willing to share a part of himself with me. In a world where so many people are too busy to truly connect, Mr. Lu had shown me a small but profound piece of his heart and soul.

In many ways, Mr. Lu felt like "my Chinese man" in a way that other mainland Chinese people never quite did. People from mainland China often seemed distant, ideologically different from me. I was from the democratic political entity of Taiwan, R.O.C., while mainland Chinese, under the P.R.C. and communist rule, have generally shown a tendency to support strong political leaders or have appeared indifferent to, or accepting of, authoritarian authority. They felt comfortable living in a society governed by a centralized government. Not me.

There was a gap between me and most mainland Chinese, like Professor Liang, an educated colleague I once had, who once adamantly denounced her son's public high school math teacher simply because he was from East India. The teacher was a scholar, a graduate of MIT who spoke English with an

East Indian accent. He had come to the U.S. to teach math, and even though his English wasn't impeccable, he taught high school students because, in his words, it was an opportunity to give back. But Professor Liang, with her academic pedigree and years of privilege, couldn't see past the fact that he wasn't "one of us." She made dismissive remarks about his background and even questioned his qualifications, all while her son was struggling with basic math at school.

I was shocked by such bigotry, and I couldn't help but feel that many mainland Chinese people, like Professor Liang, were strangely biased. They clung to the autocrats of the past, the ideological divisions, and a sense of superiority, often coupled with racial discrimination. It felt like they had lost the essence of what it meant to be an immigrant in a foreign land: struggling, adapting, and finding common ground. I had more compassion for Mr. Lu, who barely spoke any English but worked tirelessly in a myriad of trades to make ends meet in America, than for the privileged Professor Liang, who seemed to have forgotten that she herself was an immigrant.

Mr. Lu's life was a testament to humility, perseverance, and quiet dignity. His struggles were not ideological; they were real and tangible, lived out daily as he navigated a new country, learned new ways of life, and provided for his family. Unlike the smugness I sometimes saw in those who came from wealthier backgrounds or had professional status, Mr. Lu's existence felt grounded in something more authentic. He didn't see himself as above anyone. He simply wanted to work, to do his job well, and to ensure his family was taken care of.

Amid the cultural and background differences that separated me from so many of the mainland Chinese people I encountered, Mr. Lu felt like a bridge. He wasn't just someone with skills; he was a person of depth, with a story and a warmth that resonated deeply within me. Over the course of that week, he taught me more than any lecture or academic article could. He showed me the value of hard work, undisturbed humility, and beauty in simple things. Through him, I learned that it's possible to transcend political or cultural divides. I'll never forget him, my Chinese man, whose work was affordable art, and whose presence brought a peaceful serenity to a noisy, chaotic world.

Poetry Dioramas

I taught English Language Arts in the American secondary public school system for more than thirteen years. Day after day, I embarked on a journey shaped by the rhythm of bell rings and the ever-evolving personalities of my students. Between periods, I stood at the classroom door, greeting the rush of young bodies spilling into the hallway, their voices a mixture of hope, rebellion, and youthful energy. The freshmen were like fledglings, eager and light, full of the promise of growth. The sophomores, ever the playful tricksters, spent their time pulling pranks and teasing one another, seemingly oblivious to the looming responsibilities of adulthood. By the time the juniors shuffled through, their movements were more deliberate, as if they had started to grasp the weight of what lay ahead. And then there were the seniors, walking with the quiet tension of impending decisions, anxiety lingering like a shadow as they struggled to untangle their own sense of self.

I could see the skepticism in their eyes as they looked at me, their Taiwan-born teacher, speaking to them in English. Who was I to teach them about literature, about poetry, about the world beyond their immediate concerns? But I wasn't one to back down. I loved books, I adored the intricacies of language, and I refused to accept the fatalistic notion that "kids these days" didn't care about reading or learning. The distractions of their digital world were no match for the timeless wonders that literature offered. I decided to stand my ground, believing that literature could touch their hearts, challenge their thinking, and, perhaps most importantly, give them a space to express themselves.

In that moment, when their skepticism felt the most palpable, the poetry unit arrived. I wanted to show them that poems were not just stilted verses or complicated metaphors, but lived experiences, full of captured moments of emotion and insight. So, I presented them with poems that stretched across generations and genres, from the whimsical words of Dr. Seuss and Shel Silverstein to the deep, profound expressions of T.S. Eliot and Emily Dickinson. I wanted them to experience the joy of sound in language, the sharpness of rhyme, the flow of rhythm. I wanted them to play with words as much as they played with the world.

As I introduced the concepts of onomatopoeia, alliteration, and the various poetic forms, their resistance softened. It was in the hands-on nature of the project that I saw the real magic. They were tasked with writing at least ten types of poems and presenting them in dioramas, three-dimensional representations of their work. These were no mere displays of paper and glue, but windows into their souls, their desires, their fears, and their dreams.

I recall each diorama vividly, a testament to their personalities, struggles, and even their moments of growth. Jennifer's windchime of feathers and dreamcatchers, each one cradling a poem of hope or longing, was delicate and beautiful. It spoke to her quiet resilience, her need to seize moments of serenity in a world full of chaos. Heather, ever the mischief-maker, crafted a large cardboard mailbox, each poem tucked inside as though waiting to be sent to her boyfriend. Her work was playful, lighthearted, yet carried a depth of feeling that only someone so young could express with such abandon.

Then there was James, who created a papier-mâché football field to showcase his poems about sports, ambition, and victory. His diorama was grand, bold, and brimming with the spirit of competition. It was as if his poems came to life in the center of the field, reflecting his passion for success and the desire to win, to be seen. Marilyn, with her artistic flair, designed a picture book of poems, each one perfectly aligned with the ebb and flow of her creative mind. Her work danced on the pages, weaving stories that were as visually stunning as they were emotionally and intellectually engaging.

Jesse, ever the perfectionist, placed his poems in a small plastic trash can, admitting that his writing didn't measure up to the others. It was an expression of self-doubt, an unwillingness to accept his own creativity at face value. But even in this act of defiance, I saw something powerful, a raw honesty that often goes unnoticed in teenagers. It was a symbol of the vulnerability they all held inside, a reminder that even in their harshest critiques of themselves, they were learning, growing, and trying to understand who they were.

The poetry dioramas weren't just assignments; they were explorations of identity. Each diorama revealed a piece of the puzzle that was these students' lives. I could see their desires laid out in the little details: James' determination in the football field, Heather's yearning in the mailbox, Marilyn's dreams dancing on the page. Even Jesse's discarded poems in the trash can spoke to the inner turmoil of adolescence, a struggle for self-acceptance that we all face, at some point or another.

It was a beautiful moment when the dioramas were all displayed, a showcase of vulnerability and strength, of creativity and doubt. But, as I often noticed with teenagers, their attention span was brief. For a fleeting moment, I saw them transform: more introspective, gentle, engaged with each other in a way that transcended their usual banter. They seemed to understand, at least momentarily, that learning wasn't about the grades, the rules, or the expectations of others. It was about the connections they made with themselves and with the world.

After those brief moments of tenderness, they returned to their usual selves, as if the bubble of shared creativity had popped. The jokes resumed with their usual energy, each one a quick-fire exchange meant to bring laughter or discomfort to someone in the room. Complaints about homework returned, filling the air with a familiar chorus of grumbling voices, their words laced with the unmistakable frustration of teenagers burdened with expectations they felt too heavy to bear. The eye rolls at authority resumed their regular rhythm, their disdain for rules or figures of power so instinctive that it was almost a reflex, an ingrained part of their typical daily routine.

But I knew something had shifted, however subtly. In those few instants of uninhibited self-expression, something had changed in the way they carried themselves, in the way they looked at each other and the world. It wasn't as dramatic as an epiphany or as obvious as a revelation, but it was there, in the quiet after the storm, in the brief pause before the noise came rushing back. They had stepped outside themselves, if only for a few minutes, and looked inward through the lens of poetry. They had created something tangible, something that could not be measured by grades or rules or the expectations of others. A piece of their soul had been poured into that work, preserved like a fragile butterfly pinned carefully in a collector's display case, waiting to be remembered. It was as though, for an instant, they were not just students with burdens and challenges, but creators, artists, thinkers who could take their emotions and shape them into something beautiful.

They had created something, however small or insignificant it may have seemed in the grand scheme of things — that had meaning. It had weight. It had depth. And for that brief instant, they were more than just high school students; they were thinkers, creators, dreamers. In those moments, they were unburdened by the weight of expectations or the pressures of fitting into the roles they had been assigned. In those moments, they were free.

Though they quickly slipped back into the chaos of adolescence, I held onto those precious moments with a sense of gratitude. Amid all the noise, the distractions, and the frustrations, I had witnessed something extraordinary. In those fleeting minutes, I saw a glimpse of eternity, a glimpse of what they could be if they allowed themselves to pause, reflect, and create. I saw the potential for growth, for change, for the kind of self-awareness and self-expression that can transform not only an individual or a class, but an entire community.

The classroom, once again filled with noise and disruption, was a familiar scene: voices rising and falling, papers rustling, desks shuffling. Yet, amid the usual chaos, there was something different, something electric in the air. It wasn't that the students were quieter or more focused; it was that, beneath the familiar hum of teenage energy, there was a fine undercurrent, a pulse of potential. It felt a little more alive with the possibility of change. The familiar walls, the desks, and the whiteboards no longer felt like the confines of a place where routine and repetition ruled. Instead, the classroom felt like a space where something new and unpredictable could take root, a place where ideas, like seeds, could be sown and cultivated, even in the most unlikely of conditions.

This wasn't just a space for filling in blanks on worksheets or reciting facts from textbooks. No, it felt different, as though the students were starting to see that there was more to this classroom than just the mechanics of learning. It felt like a place where minds could stretch beyond the confines of what they knew, where they could question, explore, and create. It was as though the lessons were no longer confined to memorization or regurgitation but were becoming something more fluid, more dynamic. There was an openness, a delightful sense that, at the right moment, something could bloom in a way they hadn't expected.

And I smiled, watching the subtle changes unfold around me. I knew that, even in those brief, delicate moments of creation, something was being learned, something that transcended the usual lessons of grammar, books, or history. It was something deeper, something more profound. In those few minutes of silence and reflection, the students had glimpsed a different kind of learning, one that wasn't confined to the pages of a textbook. They had discovered, even if only for an instant, the power of their own voices, their own ideas. They had connected with something beyond the immediate task at hand and realized that their thoughts could have weight, could carry meaning and make a difference.

The kind of lesson that couldn't be easily measured by grades or standardized tests. The kind of lesson that might not even be recognized in the moment but would linger long in their hearts, slowly shaping the way they would see the world. Even if they hadn't fully realized it yet, the seed had been planted. It was a small, refined thing, a spark of self-awareness or creative expression that had taken root in the fertile soil of their minds. It wasn't something that would grow overnight, but it was there, gently pushing against the surface, ready to bloom and flourish when the time was right.

The possibility of growth, of discovery, had been unlocked in them, and that was enough. It didn't matter if they didn't fully grasp the significance of what had happened. It didn't matter if they slipped back into their usual patterns, complaining about homework or mocking authority. What mattered was that, for just a few precious moments, they had stepped outside their usual routines and opened themselves to something new. The seeds of curiosity, creativity, and introspection had been sown, and even if they couldn't yet see the fruits of their labor, those seeds would grow, gradually shaping who they would become. And in that moment, I understood that this was what teaching was about, not just delivering lessons, but unlocking the potential for change, for learning, for growth, for discovery. And for that brief, fleeting moment, that was enough.

A Dull Pain

I was six when my parents moved the family from Taipei to the East Coast of Taiwan. We left behind the bustling streets and familiar smells of the city, the rapid tempo of life we had grown accustomed to, for a quieter, more peaceful existence near the ocean. Every summer, before the heat and humidity set in, my father would pull out the three small electric fans from the storage space under the tatami bed. These fans, so essential in the sweltering Taiwanese summers, would hum away through the nights, providing the only relief from the sticky air. It was a ritual I looked forward to, a small act of comfort in a life that often felt like it lacked much.

My two sisters and I shared a room, where three tatami mats were lined up neatly on a solid wood platform, taking up the entire floor. The simple, minimalist design of the room always made me feel both safe but slightly confined, as if the boundaries of our space were drawn too clearly, too rigidly. My brother had his own tatami in his room, which was adjacent to ours. The two rooms were separated by a partition wall, but the fronts of the rooms were wide open, with no doors or barriers between us. The design felt more like an afterthought, as if there was never a need for privacy or separation. We could easily hop up onto the tatami mats to sleep, read, do homework, or play.

My parents, in their practicality, had positioned the fans with a certain kind of efficiency. They kept one fan in their room, one in my brother's, and one in the girls' room, our shared space. I liked to sleep on the mat to the left, where there was a built-in desk attached to the partition wall. That spot was farthest from the fan and closest to my books. I loved the quiet there, the way I could lose myself in a book and shut out the world around me. It was my personal sanctuary, my way of avoiding the complexities and turbulence of life. I was a quirky nerd, after all, much to my sisters' teasing.

My oldest sister, Xiao Yu, liked to sneak out through the backdoor to meet boys, so she claimed the mat on the right. It was more convenient for her, positioned closer to the back door of our home, and to the more secretive world she inhabited. I never fully understood her need to escape. She was always so mysterious to me, so sure of herself in ways I could never emulate. My second-oldest sister, Wenwen, ended up stuck in the middle. She seemed to exist in a state of constant indecision, always torn between the need for attention and the desire for solitude. She developed the habit of staring at the ceiling and singing to it, her voice soft and melodic, or heading to my brother's room to play when she was bored. She was quieter than Xiao Yu, more content with the steady rhythms of family life, but still far more social than I ever was.

As for my parents, they mostly left us alone. They were there in body, but emotionally distant. Pa was a stern figure who reserved his attention for moments of discipline, and Ma was a consistent presence in the background, occupied with her health, her home, and her own routines. Pa gave corporal punishments when necessary and used military drills on all four of us, boys and girls alike. There was no favoritism, no leniency. My brother, who was always getting into trouble, bore the brunt of it. Even now, in his 50s, he's a playboy, divorced and estranged from his daughters. His life was a series of missteps, perhaps shaped by a childhood marked more by rigid discipline or excessive indulgence than by tough love or heartfelt encouragement.

Xiao Yu, on the other hand, found her love through business ventures, marrying an adventurous businessman ten years younger than her. She was always searching for something more, something bigger than the small confines of our family, always testing the limits of what she could achieve. Wenwen, the responsible one, stayed married to the same person for life. She was an early-retired accountant who took care of Pa and Ma more than any of us. She visited them every other week, cooking, cleaning, and entertaining them in ways none of us could. It was almost as though she had become the caretaker for a family that had long since stopped being able to care for itself.

As for me, I was the one they'd always left alone, living far away in America. I had distanced myself from life in Taiwan as much as I could, running from the pain of a confined existence on a small island. My family never called. If I didn't initiate a phone call, I would hear nothing from home. And even when I did call, the conversation felt cold and strained, as though I was interrupting something more important. My father would pretend to be busy emptying my mother's urinal, a task that was as symbolic as it was literal. He would then disappear from the call, as though he were avoiding me — not just in the present, but as if he had always been avoiding me, even when I was a little girl. It was as though I had never been quite his, as though there had always been a distance between us, one that never closed. All he ever talked about were the herbal medicines he and Ma took daily to maintain their health, claiming that without them, they would have died long ago. It felt like the conversation was less about my life outside of Taiwan and more about their struggle for survival or their inability to venture beyond their immediate surroundings, beyond life's limitations.

The first half of my life in Taiwan feels like a past life, a different world that I can no longer fully grasp. I can no longer understand the meaning of never seeing them often or regularly again. What does it mean to have your family so far removed from you? Perhaps it's a dull pain that's been with me since childhood, slowly permeating my present life and never quite fading. It isn't the sharp pain of grief or the immediate sorrow of loss, but something more pervasive, something that lingers in the background like an ever-present hum. It's the kind of pain that you learn to live with, that you almost forget is there until it flares up unexpectedly. It's the pain of absence, of not quite belonging anywhere, not quite being seen for who you are.

It's the kind of pain that creeps in during quiet moments when you're alone, when the world around you falls silent, and all you're left with is the ghost of a family that never quite understood you, and perhaps never could.

Another Childless Cat Lady

J.D. Vance recently referred to prominent Democrats like Kamala Harris as "childless cat ladies." Well, I'm another childless cat lady, though I'm not famous. Still, I can say that I've led a fulfilling life, filled with travel and unique job experiences that could inspire envy. Perhaps it's envy that leads some to assume that childless women lead miserable lives. But I've never had the time or energy to be miserable, either for the sake of myself or others. In fact, I strive to live in a better world, one where people are kinder. My lack of children doesn't mean I have no stake in the world; on the contrary, it drives me to work harder and be more mindful of the legacy I leave behind.

I should also clarify that being childless wasn't a conscious decision; it simply happened that way. I met my first husband, Tom, while studying English Literature at National Tsinghua University in Taiwan. Tom, an inquisitive and cerebral man, shared my passion for learning about the world. Together, we traveled widely, and that period of my life taught me to always explore new cultures, languages, political systems, and societal issues. I can't help but think that, had things turned out differently, perhaps we would have raised children who shared our curiosity, who would have explored the world with open minds. But life doesn't always unfold as we imagine or hope.

When Tom and I moved to New York City, I was pursuing graduate studies at Columbia University, and he struggled to establish a career in a new city. Whether he didn't try hard enough or simply didn't see the need to contribute equally to our life together, his emotional and financial support was lacking. This imbalance created considerable stress for me, as I juggled my studies with part-time jobs to make ends meet. There were days when the weight of it all felt too much to bear. But I didn't allow myself to wallow. I was determined to succeed, both for myself and for the life I had envisioned.

My first marriage to Tom, which had begun on a spontaneous trip to Las Vegas, ended in divorce. I moved to Las Vegas to finalize the paperwork, and ended up living there for eighteen years, spending thirteen of those years as a public-school English teacher. Teaching was my calling; it gave me purpose and joy. My students, many of whom came from difficult backgrounds, reminded me of the importance of perseverance and compassion. There were no children of my own in my life, but I gave so much to those young minds. I would never regret that.

As you can see, having children with Tom was never an option. He wasn't the family type, and although there were boyfriends after him with whom I "almost" had children, it never worked out. I had one abortion and one miscarriage. The abortion was because I was still attending college in Taiwan, and my Taiwanese boyfriend and I felt it wasn't the right time for children. Later, I was simply too old. The miscarriage was harder. It felt like the closing of a door, a door I didn't even know I had left ajar.

"I feel fine about having children outside of marriage," I told Harry, m boyfriend at that time, trying to convey that my pregnancy had little to do with the desire to tie the knot.

"I've just finished paying for Helen's college," Harry frowned and responded, panicked.

"Ah…." I sighed.

"And now another child?" Harry, who had a daughter from a previous relationship, couldn't bear the idea of taking on another round of parental or financial responsibility.

"I'm very independent," I said, sensing that something wasn't right in our relationship.

"I'm very concerned," he replied.

In the end, I miscarried. It just wasn't meant to be. Life moves on, and so did I.

Then I met my second husband, Bobby, in Las Vegas.

"I already have two children. I'm done," Bobby said, referring to the two kids from his first marriage. He had passed his time of childbearing, and I was too old to have children anyway. I understood that. We had both lived through enough to know that our paths had already been paved. We were simply walking them together.

"Most of the time, I feel fine about not having children of my own. But every now and then, I feel a pang, especially when I meet pregnant women who radiate joy," I told Bobby. It was the kind of thing that hit me at the most unexpected moments, the joy and anticipation in the eyes of expectant mothers. I could almost feel their hope for the future, something I would never experience.

My second marriage with Bobby meant that I would never have biological children, but I did gain two stepchildren. These relationships, however, weren't without their challenges.

One night, I was woken by a call from Jason, Bobby's son. "What the heck is he calling so late for?" I muttered, irritated.

"My son needs my advice," Bobby explained. Jason would call Bobby up to twenty times a day, every day of the week. It was something I didn't fully understand — this constant need for attention.

But then I realized that Bobby, too, needed his children's attention, something I'd never quite understood before. A needy son was the result of a parent who had overcompensated for past absences. He had been often on business trips before he retired in his early sixties.

Then there was Bobby's daughter, Chloe — smart, beautiful, and well-educated. But she couldn't stand the idea of sharing her father's affection. Whenever we were out — at a museum, a concert, or dinner with friends — she'd inevitably call. And Bobby would always answer, giving her a play-by-play of whatever we were doing. At times, it felt like narrating our life to her mattered more to him than living it with me.

I have no children of my own. But I'm perfectly content being a childless cat lady. I've learned over the years that fulfillment doesn't come from societal expectations or external validation. It comes from living a life that feels true to yourself. It comes from the connections you make, the joy you find in the small moments, and the awareness that we all have a role in this world. My life may not follow the typical script, but it's mine to live, and I wouldn't change a thing.

So, here I am, another childless cat lady. And I'm okay with that. In fact, I'm more than okay. I'm content, grateful for the life I've lived and the future I continue to shape, one experience at a time.

People Steal

My husband Bobby and I lived in a quiet suburb of Washington, DC, but come winter, we would escape to our Belize vacation homes to thaw out and change our scenery. The transition always did wonders for our spirits. But as time passed,

I learned an unexpected lesson about people — and the unpleasant truth that some of them steal. Small things, not enough to make a scene, but enough to gnaw at my sense of trust. The cheap small bottles of body lotions I'd bought in bulk for travel. My favorite, expensive hair clips. Beautiful, hand-crafted coffee mugs we'd collected over the years. Pieces of indigenous embroidery, clothes, solar post lights — and yes, Bobby's prized heavy-duty telescopic ladder. All of them vanished during our absence at our vacation house, as if swallowed by the tropical air, without explanation or apology.

I had been raised to be good. As a child, I learned right from wrong with an intensity that seemed to define me. In grade school, Ms. Xu, who was very pregnant at the time, gave us lessons in the value of honesty. She taught us that even the smallest theft. like sneaking a few tissues to wipe away her hormonal tears, was a breach of trust. That lesson stuck with me. Later, in college, Professor David Decker emphasized human dignity and warned us against taking anything that wasn't ours, no matter how trivial. I vividly remember his disapproving look when someone borrowed pens and didn't return them. His message about integrity became embedded in my core: even the tiniest lapse could spiral into something much worse.

And then came my job contracted with the federal government, where security clearances were part of the deal. The importance of honesty and moral uprightness was drilled in me. Even the slightest moral lapse could have grave consequences. That sense of duty stayed with me long after I left that career. It didn't matter if I wasn't actively working in the government anymore; I carried the weight of that responsibility, the burden of doing what was right. I felt deeply guilty, even when all I was doing was watching others around me struggle with their shortcomings.

The oddest part was that I felt guilty, even for people, likely cleaning crew or neighbors watching over our house, who had taken things from our vacation house. I couldn't shake the feeling that I was somehow complicit, just by being in proximity to their actions. I had spent years striving to be an example of integrity, yet here I was, surrounded by thieves — however small their offenses seemed. I wasn't the kind of person who could condone theft, and yet, I often found myself trying to rationalize their behavior for them, even if it meant holding onto that faint thread of compassion. They were still human, after all, weren't they?

In a strange way, I became both the best and worst kind of thief. I judged them harshly, wondering what could possibly drive someone to steal something so inconsequential: cheap lotions, a coffee mug, an old ladder. Was it really about the items, or was it something deeper? Something psychological, perhaps? I pictured them taking pleasure in small indulgences, their motives clouded by personal dissatisfaction, a desire to feel a sense of ownership, even over fleeting things. I found myself getting red-faced with frustration whenever I caught wind of these little violations. And it wasn't as if I'd caught anyone red-handed. I could just feel it: the discomfort that permeated when their thefts were discovered, the guilt that seemed to rise from within them as they came to terms with their impulses or actions.

But, oddly enough, some of our stolen items did return to us. After weeks of wondering, Bobby managed to retrieve the heavy-duty telescopic ladder from Ken, our neighbor. Ken's wife, in a rather embarrassed tone, explained that she had "borrowed" it to clean the ceiling fans in their house. They had never mentioned it before, but at least it was back in our house. That felt like a small victory. Yet, the sense of unease remained.

We tried to host gatherings for our neighbors, friends, and even our house staff in the most generous way possible, thinking it might somehow counterbalance the small acts of dishonesty. Our parties were grand affairs, with hand-crafted cocktails, silver platters, and food served from the china I had carefully collected over the years. I wanted them to feel spoiled. I wanted them to feel like they were a part of something special. I knew they were taking things, but I hoped they would see the kindness in our hospitality and perhaps, in some way, feel a sense of refinement, a reflection of the life we lived.

I became curious about how the locals spent their time, and so one day, during a casual conversation, I asked a few of them what they did with their leisure time in this laid-back paradise. Jane, our retired American neighbor, told me she went for regular hair, nail, and massage appointments every two weeks. She said it with an air of indifference, as if it was just the way things were. My gardener's wife, an easygoing Belizean woman, shared that she grew her own vegetables and cooked every day. In contrast, our local cleaning lady said her days were spent cleaning houses and caring for her family.

The mix of cultures in Belize always fascinated me: Mestizos, Creoles, Mayans, Garifuna, East Indians, Mennonites, and Europeans, creating a vibrant, warm community. Everyone adapted in their own way, and despite their differences, they worked together. It wasn't always perfect, but there was a certain magic in the way they all came together, blending their individualities and characteristics to create something uniquely Belize.

I asked about volunteering opportunities in the area, and Michale, an active community member, mentioned that there was a constant push to improve the local environment. Every Saturday, volunteers, including many of our neighbors, worked at the town dump. They helped pick up stray pieces of trash, supplied water and food to the workers, and brainstormed ways to improve waste disposal. The dump itself was an unsettling place, an overwhelming sea of garbage surrounded by a mix of iguanas, coatimundis, snakes, and tarantulas. Yet, the workers, unfazed by the stench and the blinding heat, carried on with determination. There was something humbling about the work they did, and even more humbling about those who volunteered alongside them.

As the weeks passed, I realized something: despite the petty thefts and minor misdeeds, the people around us were still trying to build something better. Whether it was through their actions at the dump, or their genuine efforts to create a close-knit community, there was something admirable about their resilience. They weren't perfect, but they were trying, and sometimes that was good enough.

In the end, I stopped searching for the missing things. My coffee mugs appeared back on the kitchen counter one morning, seemingly moved for some guest's convenience. I didn't care enough to investigate who took them or why. The heavy-duty ladder was returned, and I let go of the small irritations that had clouded my thoughts for weeks. The important things — the community, the people, the small but significant acts of kindness — remained.

I learned a lesson in tolerance, in accepting the complexities of human nature. Perhaps, we are all just trying to figure it out, finding our way through the flaws and imperfections, knowing that some things will be lost, and some things will come back. But what matters most is how we carry on, day by day, trying to make a difference, however small.

Friend Who Died Young

Alice became more involved with Muriel and Tim the day Wendy died. Alice, the oldest of the group, was fifty-seven. Muriel and Tim were both thirty-seven, while Wendy was just thirty-two. It had always felt, in a way, like Alice had been the observer of this younger circle, present for their gatherings but never quite fully in step with their world. She would get together with the three friends, twenty-plus years her junior, whenever Muriel insisted. There was a kind of affectionate dependence on Alice, but it wasn't the kind where she could truly feel part of the vibrant pulse of their lives. She was more like the essential guest who brought a dose of perspective and maturity to their youthful exuberance. But Wendy's sudden death changed everything.

One afternoon, they had gone out together for Chinese food. They ordered their usual, a pot of Three-Delicacies Soup, and gathered around the table, chopsticks in hand. Alice glanced at the soup pot, watching as their chopsticks circled, each trying to scoop up a piece of the fish floating in the broth. There was something about the act, the communal nature of it, that unsettled her. She thought it unsanitary to keep dipping their chopsticks in the communal pot, and her mind wandered to the etiquette of it all. Where's the ladle? Why doesn't everyone just use their own bowls? But she dismissed the thought, and instead, she smiled, playing her role of the mature, funny woman in the group — always asking questions that invited reflection, offering wisdom that came from years of life's lessons.

"What do you think makes you happy in a job?" she asked, breaking the silence while they ate.

"Money. Friends. A manageable workload. Fulfillment," came the answers, rolling off their tongues like rehearsed lines.

"Yes, a sense of fulfillment comes when you're doing something you're good at and have space to grow," Alice added, nodding thoughtfully, as if imparting some great secret of the universe. "What boundaries should be established between male and female friends?" Alice continued, probing deeper, eliciting self-reflections.

The subject wasn't far from her mind, given the subtle tension between Muriel and Tim. They were both married, but Muriel's attachment to Tim was palpable, almost possessive. She often made efforts to insert herself into Tim's world, trying to carve a special place in his heart, and Tim, for his part, never seemed to set clear boundaries. The chemistry between them was undeniable, yet no one dared address it directly.

"Infatuation often feels like rabies; love happens after you heal from it," Alice mused. "You might justify your behavior and passion, but humans need to process and elevate their emotions — it's not about moral codes, just maturity." Her voice was steady, as though she had witnessed and survived the very pitfalls she spoke of. "Maturity isn't about age. Look at Wendy. She's the youngest, but she understands the golden mean," Alice said with a smile, but her words were laced with the wisdom that comes only through time and experience.

The group sat there, eating, drinking, and laughing, feeling content in each other's company. It was a rare moment of joy that Alice cherished. But as she often did, she had to leave first. She had a long drive ahead of her, back to the responsibilities of her home. Wendy, too, had her own obligations: her husband and her little puppy waiting for her at home. Muriel, however, feigned a headache, and leaned a little too heavily on Tim, her flirtation almost tangible.

Eventually, each of them went home to their spouses, the evening fading into the night. Muriel continued to suggest meetups, and while Alice was always willing, she didn't often prioritize them. She had a full life outside of these friendships, with her husband and her own routine. She thought, more often than not, that her younger friends, especially Muriel, could learn that the world didn't revolve around them. But they were so kind, so eager to involve her, and Alice often felt embarrassed turning down their invitations.

It wasn't until the day Wendy's life was tragically cut short that Alice felt a profound shift in her connection to Muriel and Tim. Wendy, full of energy, laughter, and a future ahead of her, was suddenly gone. The car accident had happened so quickly, so violently, and then the hospital news came — she was gone. The vibrant, strong young woman, who was often the spark in their circle, was extinguished just as quickly as it had all begun.

It was incomprehensible. A part of Alice couldn't believe it. How could this happen? How could someone so full of life, so full of possibility, be taken in an instant? It was like a falling star, brief, brilliant, and then gone. Alice thought to herself that perhaps it was fate or some higher force at play, watching from above, pulling Wendy from their lives before anyone had time to understand what was happening. Wendy's death felt like an injustice, a wrong that couldn't be righted.

In the midst of the shock, Alice found herself consumed with questions about Wendy's last moments. How had her husband found out? Was it a 911 call? Had the police contacted him immediately after the accident? Was it during the afternoon, or did he find out later, late at night, or the following morning? The weight of it was unbearable, and for weeks, Alice found herself awake at odd hours, her mind racing with the many questions and emotions.

And then, Muriel and Tim reached out. They called her to talk, to process the tragedy, to grieve together. They had all shared a bond with Wendy, but now it felt as though that bond was being tested in the most painful of ways. They needed one another.

"We're so lucky to have each other," Alice said in a moment of reflection. She meant it, though the words came out more as a quiet plea to hold onto what was left of their friendship. She knew that, in time, someone would always be gone — death was an inevitable part of life — but the survivors must support each other. Friends, Alice realized, were like the insurance policies for the living.

As the weeks went by, Alice found herself drawn closer to Muriel and Tim, and the three of them spent more time together. They talked about Wendy, shared stories and memories, laughed and cried. Alice liked being with them. The connection felt deeper now, forged through their collective grief. Muriel and Tim had both become more like family to her. They'd invite her over, saying, "Let's invite Alice. She needs us." It was as if, by losing Wendy, they had formed a new kind of bond, a bond of survival, of shared experience, of the full, heavy, shared weight of loss.

Alice no longer felt like the outsider, the older observer. She was a part of something now, something more real, more lasting. She didn't need to be the wise one, the mature one, always offering advice. They needed each other in a way they never had before. And Alice realized, as she spent time with Muriel and Tim, that she had never felt more engaged, more connected, with these young people, twenty years her junior, than she did at that moment. Their energy, their fresh perspectives, and their enthusiasm for life seemed to awaken something inside her that had long been dormant. It was as if the generational gap had vanished, replaced by a shared understanding that transcended age, and for the first time in years, she felt her young friends truly seen and heard her.

Jenny

I used to work with Jenny in New York City, writing Dean's Letters for medical students who were seeking clinical rotation residencies. We were both English majors, and our shared academic background forged a bond between us. While to some, English majors might be seen as people who simply read novels, short stories, poems, and plays, Jenny and I knew that there was much more depth to our studies. When I told

Jenny that my graduate studies in English went beyond literature and delved into critical theories, such as constructionism, deconstructionism, historical and ideological analysis, feminism, Marxism, post-colonialism, and psychoanalysis — she was intrigued. I explained that these theories didn't just help us understand life but also served as survival tools, helping us navigate the complexities of human interaction and society.

Jenny admired my intellectual acumen. I suppose my being born in Taiwan, attending Columbia University, and having exposure to towering figures like Descartes, Nietzsche, Sartre, Derrida, Foucault, Kristeva, Laozi, Confucius, and Zhuangzi made me seem somewhat formidable in her eyes. But more than that, it was the way I understood the world that captivated her — an analytical approach that blended philosophical rigor with practical experience. I, in turn, admired her resilience. Despite her upbringing in a world far removed from the ivory towers of academia, Jenny had an uncanny ability to navigate and thrive in spaces where others might falter.

My own upbringing was fairly average. My parents were married, and though they weren't perfect, they provided a stable home environment. My childhood wasn't burdened with the weight of extreme hardship or dysfunction. A bit of laissez-faire parenting may have shaped me, but it wasn't something I saw as harmful. Jenny, on the other hand, had faced far more challenging circumstances. She often referred to her family as "white trash," a label that felt both self-deprecating and oddly self-empowering. Jenny had been on her own since she was thirteen, a survivor in a world that didn't offer much. Over the years, she had juggled many different gigs, from strip teasing to escorting to hustling rich boyfriends, among other unconventional endeavors. While her jobs might have seemed morally dubious to outsiders, there was a certain pragmatic brilliance to her hustle.

"You know, I don't trust Jenny. She'll do anything to get what she wants," my boss at the medical school once observed.

"I don't like her either. She doesn't seem to have any moral compass," Shailee, one of my colleagues, added, mirroring our supervisor's sentiment.

But I defended her. "Jenny may be a hustler, but she's not a mean person. I don't mind her sass. She's creative, and there's something genuine about the way she carries herself."

Jenny was always unapologetically herself. I enjoyed hanging out with her, taking cigarette breaks outside the office building while we talked about everything under the sun: work, life, relationships, our ambitions, and our failures. She often made me laugh with her playful observations about our coworkers, like when she teased Pete, another writer at the office.

"Pete is such a cutie. He's a good writer, and he often feeds us doughnuts, not donuts," she would say, clearly more enamored with his pastries than his writing capability.

"You're such spelling police!" I teased her, poking fun at her sometimes pedantic attention to detail.

"I can be proper. I'm street smart too," Jenny would respond with a grin, her smirk widening into a mischievous smile.

Her street smarts were unmistakable. I witnessed this firsthand when we went clubbing together. No matter where we went, people greeted her with warmth and affection, hugging her as if she were a long-lost friend. She commanded attention effortlessly, and before I knew it, I was swept into her world of VIP treatment. She knew everyone, and they knew her. It was clear to me that Jenny had a knack for making people feel special, even if only for a fleeting moment. The charm she exuded was magnetic, and I couldn't help but feel a certain fondness for her, a warmth I hadn't felt for any other coworker.

One night, after a long evening of partying around my neighborhood, I invited Jenny back to my East Village apartment for coffee. It was one of those intimate moments where the loud music of the night seemed to fade, and we could just talk. Jenny opened up about the men who had come and gone from her life.

"Eugene was, by far, the best I've ever dated. An art dealer by trade and a lover of beauty by heart, he ended up leaving me for a young, gorgeous art student," she said, her voice tinged with nostalgia.

I shared my own heartbreaks, "Tom was my ultimate heartbreak. A restless soul, an artist who never seemed to be at peace. I loved him, but in the end, he wasn't the one."

Jenny chuckled softly. "We're both suckers for brainiacs, huh?"

I smiled and nodded. "Yes, it's hard to find balance with those who are so consumed by their intellect. They give so much to the world, but it's hard to keep them to yourself."

Jenny thought about that for a moment, then added, "I like to scatter a bit of myself with each one of them. The fireworks each fleeting moment creates are enough to shine forever in my heart."

Her words left an impression on me. There was a tenderness behind her tough exterior, something I hadn't expected. As I looked into her eyes, I saw a spark of something real, a type of love that transcended all the chaos in her life.

I smiled in return, but that was when she leaned in, her lips brushing mine. The moment was brief, and I pulled away, asking her to leave. I was caught off guard. It wasn't the kiss itself that startled me; it was the way it made me question my own identity. I wasn't ready to confront anything beyond the boundaries I had set for myself, the neat, ordered existence I had always cultivated. My intellectual studies, full of philosophical debates and radical theories, hadn't altered my deepest convictions. I had always considered myself an obstinate snob, someone who held tightly to a certain moral code that kept me in check. Though I had shared so much with Jenny: our work, our struggles, our longing for understanding — I wasn't ready to give my heart to anyone, let alone scatter it across fleeting moments like she had.

I watched her leave that night, her silhouette growing fainter as she moved down the dimly lit street. The soft click of her heels against the pavement gradually faded, replaced by the hollow sound of my own breathing. Though part of me regretted rejecting her and pushing her away — a gnawing ache that settled somewhere beneath my ribs — I knew that, for better or worse, my boundaries remained intact.

Jenny had pressed and tested my limits, trying to pry open Pandora's box I had deliberately sealed shut. Her intentions were kind, perhaps even loving, but some boundaries weren't meant to be crossed without mutual consent. Some relations weren't meant to be built, even with those we cherished as friends.

As I closed the door, the empty apartment seemed to expand around me, simultaneously comforting and accusatory in its silence. The stack of unwashed dishes, the half-empty coffee mugs from the evening, the book splayed open on the armchair — all evidence of a life continuing, however imperfectly altered.

I leaned against the cool surface of the door and exhaled slowly. Maybe tomorrow I would regret this moment of stubborn self-preservation. Maybe in a week, I would pick up the phone and try to explain what I couldn't tonight. But for now, in this uncertain moment suspended between loneliness and resolve, I had chosen myself. And maybe, that was the one thing I could still count on in a world that constantly challenged everything else — this imperfect commitment to my own boundaries, to the quiet dignity of deciding what parts of myself belonged to me, and to me alone.

Taiwan Trip

On average, I went back to my birthplace of Taiwan every decade during the thirty-plus years I have lived in America. My most recent trip was in the year 2025. I was amazed by how much Taiwan had progressed, and I was reminded once again that my people are among the kindest and friendliest in the world.

Traveling from Taipei to Taichung, then Kaohsiung, and finally Tainan, my parents, sister, brother, husband, and I found ourselves repeatedly blessed by the warmth and hospitality of our fellow countrymen. From strangers helping us navigate city streets to local vendors offering small samples or heartfelt conversations, every moment was a gentle reminder of the generosity embedded in Taiwanese culture.

The landscape of Taiwan had changed dramatically since my last visit. Sleek, architecturally striking skyscrapers now punctuated the city skylines, while once-familiar neighborhoods were now lined with luxurious townhouses radiating opulence. The country had modernized at a remarkable pace, yet it still retained the charm and soul of its heritage. As I wandered through centuries-old temples, vibrant night markets, and along scenic coastal paths with my family in tow, I was struck by a curious blend of nostalgia and discovery. Everything felt familiar, yet somehow foreign all at once.

Though I had been away for long, slipping back into the rhythm of Taiwanese life felt surprisingly natural. The gestures, the unspoken social cues, even the distinct emotional undercurrents in everyday interactions — they all came back to me. I realized that while I had lived in America for decades, a part of Taiwan had never truly left me. It simply lay dormant, waiting to be revisited and reawakened.

Amid this emotional reconnection, I couldn't ignore the ongoing political tension. China's bullying stance toward Taiwan was more evident than ever, yet Taiwan's resilience shone through. There was strength in its authenticity, an obscure but powerful defiance rooted in identity and pride. Watching people go about their daily lives with calm determination, I felt deep respect and solidarity with the island I once called home.

The heat and humidity were just as I remembered, oppressive and energy-draining. My body responded the same way it always had; I became ill within days. But this time, it wasn't me who felt seriously ill; I left Taiwan before the sickness took hold. Despite taking precautions, my entire immediate family contracted COVID-19 at the end of the trip.

It was a terrifying experience. My father, already weakened by age, ended up hospitalized. As if the virus weren't enough, he required both a stent and a bypass surgery on his legs. The ordeal was a blur of fear, anxiety, hospital visits, and helplessness.

I had planned this trip around Taiwan with the intention of bonding, of reliving memories and creating new ones, yet I inadvertently pushed my family too far. The long walks, the packed itinerary, the constant city-hopping: all of it proved overwhelming, especially for my aging parents. Even simple strolls seemed to knock the wind out of them, and still, they kept going for my sake. The guilt I felt was overwhelming, impossible to name or contain. It clung to me like the humid summer air long after I left Taiwan, heavy, suffocating, daunting, and inescapable.

In the end, the trip was both a homecoming and a reckoning. Taiwan had changed, and so had I. There was beauty, there was pride, there was connection, but there was also fragility, regret, and the sobering awareness of time's toll. And yet, in that complexity, I found something I hadn't expected: a renewed sense of belonging. Not just to a place, but to a people, a past, and a future I now see more clearly than ever before.

The days following my father's hospitalization were a haze of worry and reflection. Taiwan's renowned healthcare system provided competent care, but the emotional weight was unbearable. Watching my once-strong father lie weak and struggling in a hospital bed felt like watching time collapse in on itself. It was as if all the years I had been away — building a life in America, chasing dreams, travelling worldwide — had suddenly caught up with me in one dull, sterile room.

My mother, ever stoic, tried to remain composed, but I could see the exhaustion behind her eyes. My sister and brother took shifts between the hospital and their homes, communicating in a mix of panic and logistical planning, something none of us had anticipated when we imagined this trip around Taiwan. I was fortunate to have a sister and a brother still in Taiwan to care for our aging parents, but I also felt immense guilt for not being there with them throughout the journey. There were moments, late at night, when I questioned whether returning to Taiwan and leaving again at a difficult time had been a fated mistake. Had I forced the trip around Taiwan as a way to reconcile with my roots, without truly considering the limits of our bodies, our health, or our age?

I had hoped to share the beauty of Taiwan with my family, to walk together through cherished memories and create new ones along the way. But instead, I was confronted with a difficult truth: nostalgia can't be relived in the same body, at the same pace, or with the same people untouched by time. We had all aged. Every single one of us. Time waits for no one — and growing old, frankly, sucks.

Still, amid the chaos of change, there were glimmers of grace. At long last, a much-needed homecare nurse was arranged to check in on my parents during the hours my brother had to work. At the very least, someone would be there to bring my father food he could actually eat. Someone would be there to remind my mother to take her medication, or to stop her from taking it too many times. Even in the corners of crisis, essential steps were taken toward securing long-term care for my parents.

Once my father stabilized and my siblings were able to bring him home, the atmosphere shifted. What had begun as a trip filled with excitement and constant movement slowed into something quieter, more grounded. My family stopped rushing from place to place. Instead, they sat together, often in silence, watching birds pass by the windows, sipping tea, and reminiscing about earlier visits, childhood memories, and the people we had met or lost along the way.

I began to glimpse something deeper in my family — through the steady stream of messaged photos and video calls. The way my brother gently adjusted our father's pillows, the way my sister massaged our mother's tired legs each night — these small gestures revealed how they carried the weight of caregiving without complaint. Though the trip was shadowed by illness, it became a canvas for compassion, so spacious that unspoken love surfaced in simple, everyday acts.

The flight out of Taiwan felt longer than usual, heavier. My husband and I had left before my father was hospitalized, but in many ways, we carried the weight of his illness with us as we traveled. The journey changed us — not just physically, having weathered sickness ourselves, but emotionally, as we confronted our own fragility and mortality. In the days that followed, our itinerary was marked by a collective silence, as if each of us were trying to pack and unpack not just our suitcases, but the emotional weight of the experience.

Even now, months later, I think often of that Taiwan trip. Not in a romanticized way, but in a real, complicated way. It taught me that going back "home" is never just about revisiting places; it's about confronting time, change, and the ways we carry our histories in our bodies and minds. It reminded me that love doesn't always look like joy or laughter. Sometimes it looks like hospital corridors, sweat-drenched clothes in tropical heat, and the furtive guilt of wanting more than what time can give.

Taiwan will always be a part of me. Not just the place, but the people, the resilience, the contradictions. I had spent years living with a version of it in my head, an idealized homeland suspended in memory. But in 2025, I met the real Taiwan again: messy, beautiful, modern, vulnerable, proud. And in doing so, I also met a version of myself I hadn't seen in years.

I'm not sure when I'll return. But I know that next time, I'll go with more humility, more patience, and a heart that understands: home is not a place to conquer with checklists and schedules. It's a place to sit with, to listen to, and to let change you, even when it breaks your heart just a little.

In the months after returning to America, life resumed its familiar rhythm: emails, work, grocery runs, quiet dinners. But something within me remained unsettled, as if I had left a part of myself behind on that island. I found myself waking in the middle of the night, not from dreams, but from memories: my father's pale face under fluorescent hospital lights, the sound of rain tapping the window of our room in Tainan, the smell of incense wafting from temple courtyards we passed in silence.

There was no single moment in Taiwan that could be pointed to as "the turning point," but somewhere along the way, the trip transformed from a family vacation into a deeply personal reckoning. I had left Taiwan at a young age full of ambition, eager to explore the world beyond its shores. And for decades, I built a life far away — married, held jobs, forged a career, adopted a new culture, and traveled to many more exotic countries and fascinating locales. But going back reminded me of the gnawing gaps between the life I had built and the life I had left behind.

It's not that I felt regret — no, my years in America shaped me into someone I'm proud to be. But I had underestimated the emotional cost of distance. The kind of nameless sorrow that comes from missing your parents' aging, your heritage slipping from you, your roots growing faint under the noise of everyday life. In Taiwan, that sorrow came rushing back with a force I wasn't prepared for.

My parents, once the providers and protectors of my world, were now fragile in ways I hadn't allowed myself to fully see. I had spent so many years telling myself they were "doing fine," so long as we spoke on the phone and exchanged pictures during holidays. But traveling with them, watching them struggle with stairs, humidity, and long days, forced me to reckon with their mortality. I could no longer hide behind the illusion that time had simply paused just because I wasn't there with my parents to witness its passage.

I began calling my family in Taiwan more regularly. Not out of obligation, but from a desire to hear their voices, to really listen, to know how they fare. We talked not just about health and logistics, but about memories. My father told me stories from his youth I had never heard before. My mother shared her fears of aging, of becoming a burden. And I let myself cry with them, for once not afraid to show how deeply I cared.

The trip had also changed how I saw my siblings. As adults, we had drifted into our own lives, contacting mostly for holidays or family events. But in Taiwan, we were forced to move as a unit again: navigating illness, making decisions, comforting each other. I saw my brother's and my sister's strength, their willingness to shoulder burdens without complaint. They bickered at times, yes — stress tends to surface old tensions — but they also sang together, laughed late into the night over silly childhood memories and bonded over the shared responsibility of care.

As for my husband, he became a silent pillar throughout it all. Though he didn't share our language or our culture completely, he moved through the trip with patience and grace — supporting my parents, learning phrases in Mandarin, trying to make us all laugh, carrying extra luggage without being asked. His dependable presence reminded me of the kind of love that doesn't announce itself loudly, but shows up consistently in times of need.

Looking back, I've come to understand that this Taiwan trip was not about sightseeing or nostalgia. It was about bearing witness — to my family, to my homeland, and to myself. It was about seeing clearly, perhaps for the first time, what it means to hold two identities, two lives, in one body. The American me and the Taiwanese me had long lived in separate rooms. In 2025, they finally sat together at the same table.

There is still guilt I carry, not just from pushing my family too hard during the trip, but from years of absence. And yet, I'm learning to forgive myself. I know now that reconnection is a process, not a single act. It doesn't happen in one trip, one conversation, or one gesture. It happens in the slow, intentional return to the people and places that formed you — no matter how long it's been.

Someday, I will return to Taiwan again. Maybe when I get to my old age in another decade, to witness again how my story began. I will walk slower. I will listen more. I will hold my parents' hands, not out of necessity, but out of gratitude — for their sacrifices, their endurance, and their unconditional love.

And when I walk through those familiar streets, I won't just be a visitor chasing memories; I will be a daughter, a sister, and a Taiwanese-American woman who finally understands what it means to come home.

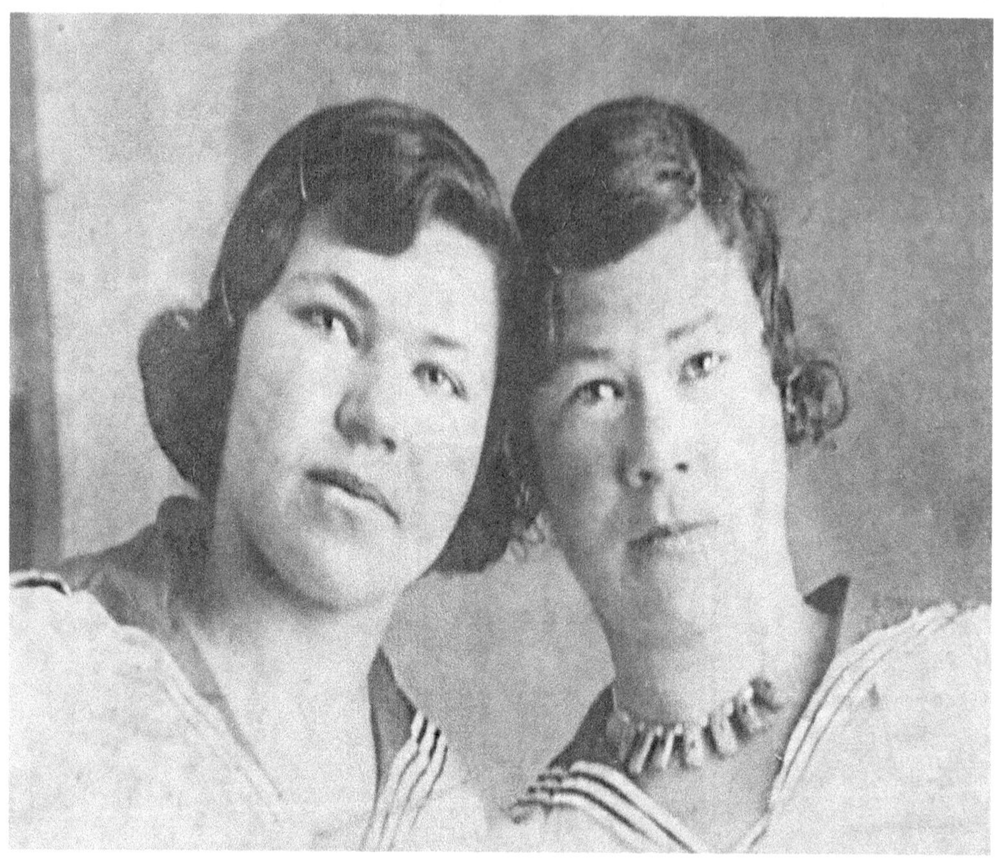

Jessica

Jessica searched for me on the internet for over thirty years. It wasn't a daily task, or even a monthly one, but every so often, she would type my name into a search bar, hoping that technology had finally caught up to fate. With the limited digital footprint I left behind, and the complications of Chinese names being romanized in countless ways, her search often led to nothing. Still, she kept looking, patiently, persistently, holding on to a hope that one day, she'd find me.

And then one day, she did.

She came across a webpage that listed an email address. It wasn't much, just a small piece of digital data, but it included a romanization of my Chinese name that looked familiar. With cautious optimism, she sent an email. It was a shot in the dark. She didn't know if it would be returned, ignored, or received by a stranger.

But it reached me.

I opened her message not knowing it would bring my childhood flooding back in a single paragraph. Jessica, my best friend from junior high, who had disappeared from my daily life but never from memory, had found me. Her message was filled with warmth, disbelief, and hope. I replied to her immediately.

We reconnected as if no time had passed. The years fell away as we caught up on our lives: our careers, families, losses, joys. We began exchanging messages regularly, sometimes brief notes with pictures, sometimes long emails. There was something sacred about reclaiming a friendship that had once felt lost to time.

Jessica was determined to see me in person. On one of her trips to the U.S. with her husband, a psychologist, she traveled from the East Coast to the West Coast just for a chance to meet. Life, however, had other plans — I was in the middle of moving from the West Coast back to the East Coast. We missed each other by a matter of days.

Still, she didn't give up.

Another time, she planned a visit to see me in the Washington, D.C. area. We were hopeful. But the trip was ultimately canceled. Amid rising xenophobia and growing instability caused by U.S. administration budget cuts and heavy tariffs, no institution was willing to sponsor her visit. It felt like the world was conspiring to keep us apart.

Time passed, but the connection remained. We shared photos, updates, memories, and dreams of finally sitting across from each other again. And then, during the 2025 trip I took back to Taiwan to visit my aging parents and siblings, it finally happened.

Jessica was living on the East Coast of Taiwan at the time. When she heard I would be on the West Coast, she didn't hesitate. She took five sections of Taiwan's high-speed rail, traveling the long northern route across the island — all during a typhoon. Just to see me.

She arrived bearing gifts: regional specialty sweets she had chosen for my entire family. When she stepped into the room, it was as if a door to the past had tenderly swung open. Her presence was both familiar and surreal. We hugged, and I felt the years collapse between us.

That afternoon, we sat with my family in Taiwan, shared a meal, and caught up face to face for the first time in decades. We cried and laughed over school memories, swapped life stories, and reminisced about the girls we once were. There was comfort in the conversation, and a placid understanding that only old friends can share.

At one point, Jessica looked at me and said something I'll never forget to recollect.

"You don't know this," she said, "but you were really important to me during junior high. I was going through a terrible time. That teacher we had, the cruel one — I was scared every day. You were the only one who listened to me. You never judged me. You didn't try to fix things. You just sat there and let me talk. You have no idea how much that meant to me."

I was stunned. I had no idea my teenage self had done anything meaningful. I thought I was just being a good friend. But to her, my steady presence had been a lifeline.

That moment stayed with me long after she left. We often think impact comes from grand gestures or monumental acts. But sometimes, it's the smallest kindnesses, the ones we barely notice giving, that someone else carries with them for years.

Jessica and I remain close now. We continue to message each other, and remind each other that some friendships don't fade. They wait. Sometimes across oceans. Sometimes across decades. But when they return, they remind you of who you were, and how even at your humblest, you may have helped someone survive. But Jessica also helped me in a personal way. She made me realize just how vital it is to nurture and maintain the relationships that matter!

Jessica grew to be an outstanding, remarkable woman, embodying the same kindness and deep concern for others that I remembered so vividly from her childhood. Even back then, her empathy, strength, and resilience set her apart. After completing her master's degree in finance, she dedicated her professional life to public service, working within the Ministry of Finance in the Taiwanese government. There, she channeled her exceptional mathematical aptitude into impactful fiscal policies and economic development efforts, always guided by a sense of responsibility toward the greater good.

Later in her career, Jessica transitioned into academia, where she served as an official overseeing international student relations at a prominent university. In that role, she combined her global outlook with her natural gift for nurturing and mentoring others, leaving a meaningful mark on countless students from around the world. Upon retirement, she embraced a new chapter: traveling extensively, engaging with diverse cultures, and ultimately settling on the scenic East Coast of Taiwan, where she continues to live a fulfilling and contented life.

I still remember the junior high school Jessica: always a leader, always driven by a genuine desire to uplift those around her. She was the kind of student who organized charity drives and took initiative without seeking praise. During this recent trip to Taiwan in 2025, reconnecting with her was a profound experience. Jessica remains a tireless advocate for social equity and justice. Her voice is strong, unwavering, and eloquent. She speaks up in political debates with clarity and conviction, championing the rights of women and marginalized communities. Fearless and principled, she continues to embody the same integrity and compassion that defined her younger years.

Jessica is my friend. I loved the spirited, thoughtful teen she once was, and I admire the passionate, fearless, wise woman she has become. I am immensely proud of her, of the life she's built, the causes she's championed, and the light she continues to shine in the world.

The Edges of Australia

While back in Taiwan, my husband Bobby and I made a point to swing over to the Southern Hemisphere, the half of the Earth tucked beneath the equator, mysterious and distant from where we had always lived. A curious traveler with a love for rare landscapes, precious encounters, and the beauty of cultures not my own, I write to remember, and to inspire others to see the world just a little differently. I would not miss the opportunity to visit the far-away land.

There's something both humbling and exhilarating about standing on the far side of the world, where the stars form unfamiliar constellations and the air carries the scent of plants you've never seen before. Until now, the farthest we had traveled was Bali, Indonesia — but this time, we ventured even farther south. The Southern Hemisphere offered more than just new geography; it offered a shift in perspective. We wandered along vast coastlines where the sea whispered stories we had yet to understand, met strangers who greeted us with the warmth of old friends, and encountered traditions rich with meaning and resilience.

Travel, for me, is more than movement; it's a way of waking up. Each unfamiliar place pulls me out of routine and invites me into presence — into noticing, into listening. In the Southern Hemisphere, I found not only beauty, but also clarity: a renewed sense of what it means to be small in a big, interconnected world. And that, I've come to believe, is the true gift of going far — to return changed, carrying a serener kind of wisdom.

Australia was an amazing place to kick off our Southern Hemisphere adventures this time around. The Australian continent had long existed in my imagination as a land of dazzling peculiarity, a place whose very remoteness seemed to magnify its allure. So it was to Sydney that we flew, our flight routed through Singapore, a necessary interlude before the continent's vast skies and the unmistakable silhouette of its iconic Opera House rose into view. That moment, with the Opera House gleaming like a cluster of seashells beside the water, was when it all became real.

Beyond the opera itself and the dazzling promenades of Sydney, we ventured outward in measured steps, each one revealing another layer of the unfamiliar. We ferried across the sparkling blue harbor to the Taronga Zoo, where the animals of Australia greeted us not behind steel bars, but within thoughtfully recreated habitats. The harbor, glistening under the southern sun, carried us farther along the Parramatta River, its bends and edges revealing glimpses of secluded suburbia framed by eucalyptus trees.

In Melbourne and Sydney alike, we traced our way through art galleries and history museums, walked miles on foot through neighborhoods and markets, and inhaled the unique blend of city bustle and coastal air. Still, we knew, as we admired the waratah's crimson blossoms along the tracks and paused for photos near lounging kangaroos, that we had merely skimmed the surface of this ancient land.

For all our wanderings, Australia remained a partial mystery. The great Outback, with its red soils and undulating heatwaves, waited somewhere beyond the urban fringe. The thought lingered: what might we have found had we driven into the interior or flown over the serrated ridges of the Blue Mountains? What wildness lay in the deserts and gorges, in the places where no roads intruded, and the Milky Way spilled brighter across the sky than anywhere else on Earth?

At Taronga Zoo, we stood inches away from emus with their piercing orange eyes and watched koalas nestling in eucalyptus branches like curled-up dreams. These weren't merely animals; they were emblems of a continent that had evolved in isolation, where marsupials rule and birds need not and cannot fly. The *Telopea speciosissima*, the New South Wales waratah, bloomed defiantly along a nondescript street corner, its fiery petals stark against the dry foliage around it. Even the mundane felt marvelously foreign and exotic.

There were moments, quiet, unremarkable ones, when the strangeness of being so far from home would settle gently around me. Sitting at a café near Circular Quay, sipping a flat white as ferries pulled in and out, I'd look up at the unfamiliar birds flying overhead. Not pigeons or sparrows, but massive, slow-flapping ibises that wandered the city alongside seagulls like locals, heads tilted and prehistoric in their appearance. It was these little encounters that left a mark, not the grand attractions, but the subtle disruptions of what I thought I knew.

The flora stayed with me most vividly. Australia wears its wilderness like a second skin, even in its cities. There were eucalyptus trees whose scent hovered in the dry heat, banksia flowers that looked as though they had arrived from another planet, and grevilleas that twisted and unfurled like coral turned inside out. These plants were not there for decoration. They were survivors, each one evolved through fire, drought, and time. I remember marveling at how beauty and resilience could coexist so closely in one leaf, one bloom.

And then there was the sense of scale, a physical vastness that pressed in silenttly. On the plane between Sydney and Melbourne, I looked out the window and saw nothing but flat, endless terrain, an ochre canvas brushed with traces of green. For long stretches, there were no roads, no farms, no signs of human touch. Just land. Untamed, unclaimed, unconcerned. That kind of openness humbles you. It rearranges something inside.

I found myself wondering what it would be like to live there, not in the cities, but in the spaces in between. To wake up with the call of magpies echoing through dry trees. To learn the rhythms of bush life, to understand the land not from the outside but from within. There's a difference between seeing a country and knowing it; we had done the former. As tourists, we had merely glimpsed its edges, felt its presence.

We left Australia with our bags a little heavier: souvenirs, Australian shirts, of course, but also small shells from Manly

Beach, a packet of lemon myrtle tea, seven fridge magnets I would add to my collection of magnet boards at home. And inside us, there lingered something harder to define: a sense that the world was stranger and more intricate than we had allowed ourselves to believe. That there are places whose mystery and magic cannot be cataloged by museums or contained in photographs.

Australia gave us that mystery in fragments, enough to stir our imagination, to pull us toward the unknown. I think we will return one day, when time allows and our curiosity is ready again to wander farther. Maybe we'll rent a camper van and drive into the Outback, or trace the coast north toward Queensland, where the rainforest meets the sea. Maybe we'll sit speechlessly under the southern stars, listening to the desert breathe.

Until then, I'll hold on to the memory of that sunburnt land, where even the ordinary seemed enchanted. A place where the earth tells old stories, and the exotic isn't just spectacle — it's life, lived deeply, in every leaf, feather, and ripple of water under the harbor bridge.

I remember the way the light slanted differently there, thick with dust and gold, casting long shadows that whispered of space beyond space. The air itself carried a rhythm, a pulse that spoke in cicada song and creaking gum trees, in tides that moved with spatial grace. People walked with an ease born of open skies and red soil, their words clipped but their silences expansive, like the landscape itself.

There was truly magic in the mundane: in roadside fruit stalls, in the screech of cockatoos at dawn, in the way the ocean breathed against sandstone cliffs. Even the rain or the sunshine seemed sentient, wrapping itself around you not just as weather, but as a presence, as though the land were drawing you closer, inviting you to listen.

And I did listen — because that land doesn't shout, it hums. Softly, insistently. With memory. With spirit.

So, until I return, I'll carry it with me. The scent of eucalyptus in the morning. The flicker of lizards darting across sunlit rocks. The feeling that, for a while, I had stepped not just into another place, but into a deeper understanding of the world and my place in it.

And that is something you don't forget.

Not ever.

Sam, Kiwi Ingenuity, and the Māori Haka

While I felt very small in a vast and strange space such as Australia, where the land stretched endlessly and the skies seemed to press down with a foreign intensity, in New Zealand, I was transported out of the present to a time older and deeper than my existence. There was something ancient in the red dust of the hills and in the echo of waves crashing along the islands — a reminder of timeless immensity and the fleeting nature of our humble human lives.

From Australia, my husband and I traveled on to Auckland and then to Wellington, drawn by a shared fascination and reverence for the legendary landscapes that brought *The Lord of the Rings* to life. What we found exceeded even our most vivid imaginations. Endless hills, mist-cloaked valleys, and mirror-still lakes unfolded before us like pages from a myth. Each turn in the road felt like a step into a living story, raw, wild, and extraordinarily breathtaking.

Yet it wasn't just the timeless land that moved us; it was the people. We were struck by a population so proud, so original in spirit, that their deep connection to place and heritage radiated from every conversation and encounter. The persistent Kiwi ingenuity, practical, humorous, rebellious, met us in everyday gestures, while the fierce and rhythmic pulse of the Māori Haka seemed to echo from the ground itself, vibrating in our chests. It was more than a performance; it was a presence. And in that presence, something rooted and everlasting engraved itself in our memories. A feeling that we had stepped not just into a country, but into a story — and we would carry its rhythm with us always.

Wellington was a city that seemed to transform us into quaint 18th-century locales. The Pegasus bookstore, filled with dog-eared volumes and the scent of old pages, was like a portal to another era. Retro vintage record stores and clothing boutiques lined narrow, cobblestone-like streets, blending seamlessly with historic pubs where laughter and music spilled out like echoes from the past. Even the movie studios, bustling with creativity and modern film production, bore an intimacy that spoke of deep artistic ancestries. High-rises and contemporary cafés stood beside buildings with ornate facades and weather-worn signs — an urban landscape where modernity didn't erase history but stood side by side with it, like old friends.

It had so many charms that I suspected one could only witness in an isolated, yet also well-composed land such as New Zealand.

Beyond the realms of Middle-earth, beyond the epic cinematic landscapes, it was the people who truly moved us: their openness, resilience, and understated pride. The extinct giant Moa, the elusive nocturnal kiwi, and other exotic creatures we encountered in zoos and museums became more than natural wonders; they came to symbolize a nation that treasures its uniqueness and honors the stories that shape it.

We hiked the rolling hills, gazed into crystal waters, and stood awestruck watching the All Blacks perform the Māori Haka on live TV, a ritual so powerful and alive that it left goosebumps on our arms. In Auckland, we explored Waiheke Island, one gem among New Zealand's constellation of islands — savoring its wines, vistas, and serenity. But perhaps most special of all was reconnecting with Sam, a dear friend I knew from my early twenties in Taipei.

Sam welcomed us like family. She drove us around Auckland, sharing the rhythms and quirks of local life as only a true local could. We visited Ambury Farm on the south side of the city, a pastoral scene of sheep, volcanic rocks, and wide skies. At One Tree Hill, where the lone obelisk stood solemnly atop ancient volcanic earth, we began to trace the roots of the Māori, the proud Polynesian people whose ancestors had journeyed across the Pacific from Taiwan 5000 to 6000 years ago. I stood there wordless, the breeze brushing my face, and felt an inexplicable kinship, as if something buried deep in our shared ancestry stirred awake.

Although I had no trace of indigenous blood in me, the tie felt real and exhilarating. There, on that sacred land, among histories that stretched long before modern memory, I sensed our interconnectedness. We were not so different, only branches growing in different directions from the same ancient tree. In that moment, I felt grounded and grateful, bound by invisible threads to those around me. More than ever before, I appreciated my friends and family, their stories, and the time we shared. Travel, I realized, doesn't always take you away; it often brings you home.

After leaving One Tree Hill, our conversations with Sam lingered in our minds. She spoke about moving to New Zealand with her partner — a Chinese–New Zealander of mixed heritage whom she met in Taipei. She reflected on her own bicultural identity and how local identity is constantly evolving: shaped by tradition, challenged by history, but never static. Her stories were filled with gentle humor, sheer resilience, and a kind of strength that was unspoken yet ever-present. Through her eyes, I saw not only the beauty of the land, but also the complexity of its soul.

One evening, she took us to a restaurant tucked away on a side street in Ponsonby. It wasn't anything grand, but it served kai Māori, traditional Māori food with a modern twist. We shared plates of hāngī-cooked meats, kumara, and rewena bread, and drank local wine as the sun melted into the harbor. That meal, so savory and rich with meaning, became a full celebration of all that we were experiencing: new tastes, old roots, our shared story and enduring friendship.

Later, we took a ferry ride out into the Hauraki Gulf. The water stretched endlessly, a glimmering mirror of sky and cloud. I remember leaning into the wind, watching the city recede into the horizon as dolphins swam briefly alongside us. For a few moments, time dissolved. The past, present, and future seemed to blur into one continuous current. I thought about how far I had come: from Taipei to Australia, to these distant islands at the harbor of Queens Wharf in New Zealand. And yet, I didn't feel far from anything. Instead, I felt closer than ever to what really mattered.

New Zealand was not just a destination on a map; it was a place of inward transformation. It challenged my perceptions and softened my boundaries. It reminded me that cultural heritage is not confined by bloodlines, but lived in empathy, in reverence, and in the willingness to listen. It showed me that nature could be both wild and tender, and that cities could hum with creativity without losing their roots.

As we prepared to leave, I carried a numbing ache. Not of sadness, but of fullness, a kind of emotional gravity that comes from being deeply moved. On our final morning in Wellington, we walked along the waterfront walk in the early light. The gulls cried above us, and the breeze smelled of salt and promise. I looked at my husband, who had shared every step of this journey with me, and felt an overwhelming gratitude. We had not only traveled across oceans, but across time, through myth and memory, through friendships old and new, and through parts of ourselves we hadn't yet known.

Leaving New Zealand, I felt different, not altered in a dramatic way, but subtly realigned, like a compass nudged closer to its true north. Something inside me had further expanded: a greater curiosity, a deeper patience, and a renewed belief in the invisible threads that bind us to people, to places, and to the stories that give our lives shape.

And so we flew onward, not just toward our home in America almost nine thousand miles away, but toward a future subtly reworked by the land of the long white cloud, Aotearoa. A place that had, if only briefly, folded us into its story.

New Zealand lingered in my mind, not just as a memory, but as a rhythm, a presence that surfaced unexpectedly in the smallest moments. The scent of sea air could transport me back to the harbor in Wellington. A patch of moss in the park might evoke the damp forest trails of Waiheke. Even the sound of wind brushing against the windows sometimes echoed the breath of the open knolls above One Tree Hill.

Travel had always meant discovery for me: new places, new people, new experiences. But this time, the discovery was more complex. I hadn't simply seen new landscapes; I had witnessed the profound harmony between people and the land they belong to. I had come face to face with a culture, the Kiwi worldview, that honored ancestry, community, and the sacredness of nature in a way that both humbled and inspired me.

And I began to question the stories I carried, about identity, belonging, progress, even time. In our fast-paced, forward-driven lives, we rarely pause to look back, to trace the roots of who we are and where we come from. In New Zealand, surrounded by oral traditions, ancestral lineages, and landscapes that felt ancient and undisturbed, I was reminded that the past is not behind us; it lives with us. It breathes through rituals, through language, through the telling and retelling of stories that anchor us to meaning.

Sam's voice would come back to me often, her laughter, her casual way of folding history into a conversation, as if these thousand-year-old migrations were just yesterday. She had helped us see what was invisible to the eye: that heritage was not only something inherited, but something actively lived and passed on. It wasn't stuck in textbooks or museum walls; it was present in every act of respect, every moment of recognition, every bridge built between cultures.

I also realized how much I had changed as a traveler. In my younger years, I had chased sights, checked destinations off a list, and tried to absorb as much as possible in a short amount of time. But this journey taught me the immeasurable power of stillness, of staying long enough in a place to let it change you, to listen instead of just look. The best parts of New Zealand weren't the postcard views, though they were magnificent. They were the moments of connection: watching high-school students playing a rugby game, hearing a guide speak about the stars in Māori cosmology, or standing barefoot on black sand, watching the tide come in and out, feeling both small and held by something vast and ancient.

New Zealand became a mirror, a place where I saw parts of myself reflected back in unfamiliar ways. The migrant spirit that brought Polynesians and Europeans across the oceans so long ago reminded me of my own ancestors, and their restless drive to seek something new, something better. The respect for elders and the sense of collective identity resonated deeply with my Taiwanese roots. And yet, there was also something entirely new in what I learned from the Kiwi way of life: the gentle humor, the egalitarian mindset, the deep, almost instinctual relationship with the environment.

Back home, I began to carry these lessons into my daily life. I tried to speak with more intention, to notice the land beneath my feet, to reach out to old friends with more regularity. I found myself revisiting the values that had once felt distant or abstract: community, humility, respect, reverence — and trying to live them more fully. It wasn't that New Zealand had given me answers. Rather, it had helped me ask better and more authentic questions.

I would sometimes close my eyes and see again the low clouds rolling over the hills of Wellington, the birds wheeling over the harbor, the carved wood of a Māori *wharenui* shimmering with stories. I would remember how my husband reached for my hand as we stood in silence on a lookout point, both of us knowing, without saying, that we had touched something sacred.

Perhaps, in the end, that is what travel offers us at its best — not escape, but return. A return to our senses, our histories, our shared humanity. A reminder that the world is wide, yes, but also, miraculously shared and interconnected.

And if you're lucky, a place like New Zealand doesn't just change how you see the world, it helps you see yourself more clearly, too.

The Banal America

Ta-Nehisi Coates argues that while "violent exploitation" of human beings can be seen throughout history, it does not excuse America's actions, especially because the country believes itself to be exceptional — the greatest and noblest nation ever to exist. This self-perception holds America to exceptional standards. We can no longer ignore the country's double standards, which affect not only African Americans but also other marginalized groups such as immigrants, transgender individuals, and those who hold differing opinions. It is time to truly and honestly make America "great again."

In his powerful critique of American exceptionalism, Coates confronts the nation's self-image as a moral ideal while exposing the violence and exploitation that have been ingrained in its history. The concept of American exceptionalism, the belief that the U.S. is morally superior and uniquely virtuous, creates a dangerous blind spot. It allows the country to minimize or ignore its flaws. While Coates acknowledges that "violent exploitation" has existed throughout history, he argues that America's sense of its own greatness requires it to live by stricter standards, leaving no room for denial of its injustices.

To make America truly "great," we must hold the nation, and its system of three branches of government, accountable to the ideals it claims to uphold. This requires confronting the hypocrisies that continue to exploit and marginalize groups like African Americans, immigrants, LGBTQ+ individuals, and others who remain excluded from the promises of equality and justice. By addressing these systemic issues, America can truthfully rise to a higher standard, acknowledging its past wrongs while striving toward a future where it genuinely lives up to its lofty ideals.

These "double standards" are not random but are embedded in the very systems of power within the U.S. The three branches of government, which are meant to balance power, have often perpetuated inequality. Legislative policies, judicial rulings, and executive actions have disproportionately affected marginalized communities, reinforcing the gap between the nation's ideals and its reality. Coates calls for a reimagining of these systems, not just as tools of governance, but as moral institutions that must be held accountable to justice.

The need for "radical honesty" is crucial. Reckoning with America's past is not just about acknowledging historical wrongs but also confronting the ongoing manifestations of these wrongs in contemporary policies, practices, and cultural attitudes. This confrontation is essential for moving beyond the blind spots created by the narrative of American exceptionalism, which often ignores or minimizes the lived experiences of marginalized communities. The power structures within the government itself must be scrutinized and reformed to fulfill their true function of upholding justice.

This reimagining of America requires reshaping the nation's identity so that it not only claims greatness but actively works toward justice and equality. Coates' challenge is not just to America as a political entity, but to the collective conscience of its citizens. Only when ordinary people demand change, when they insist on the values of equality and justice, can the nation move closer to the vision it has long proclaimed for itself.

In sum, to truly make America "great" again involves more than returning to past ideals. It requires an overhaul of systems and a direct confrontation with the country's history and present inequities. Only through such profound reckoning can America hope to embody the greatness it claims to represent. To achieve true greatness, the country must engage in a radical honesty and confrontation with its history. This confrontation would not only benefit the marginalized but would fulfill the promise of America itself, making it "great" in a way that benefits all its citizens as well as the entire world.

Achieving true greatness would require a reimagining of systems, ensuring that the ideals of justice, equality, and liberty are extended to all, especially those historically excluded. This is a call to both political and cultural action. To truly make America great again doesn't mean returning to a past ideal but confronting the systemic issues that prevent the nation from reaching its highest potential. Such transformation would not only benefit marginalized communities but would also fulfill America's original promise. This reimagining of America would be one where greatness is achieved through justice, living out the nation's founding principles, not just claiming them. America must face its contradictions head-on and work toward a more equitable society. Only through this process of truth-telling and transformation can the nation hope to become the great, just society it aspires to be.

Aging

“What could they be doing together all the time?” the husbands of the two sisters asked each other under the palapa.

“Nothing good can come of those two. Probably plotting to go out late at night after we go to bed,” Yee, the older sister

Wenwen's conservative husband, grumbled. He was against dancing at clubs.

"They're adults. No worries," Bobby, who had confidence in his wife, Yunyun, said with a smile.

Across the outdoor dining palapa, the sisters wandered by the bay, lost in their own world. They forgot their chores, their bills, and even their husbands. Their heads bobbed in rhythm with the waves, laughing, talking, agreeing, and making grand plans for future vacations. Waves would catch them off guard, pushing them back and forth, until they lay flat on the water, surfing with the fish in the bay.

The sisters were always actively shopping, cooking, washing, touring, and living fully in the present. They compared different communities: Consejo Shores, Mayan Seaside, Moonlight Bay, Consejo Landing, and Wagner's Landing. They visited the Free Trade Zone and local wood carvers, always on the hunt for the perfect home furnishings. Meanwhile, their husbands sat quietly together, occasionally commenting on the fine weather, the turquoise bay, and the whereabouts of the sisters. Bobby played tunes on his guitar, and the two men would pick up the rhythm of their conversation, like flies on the wall waking from their siestas, returning to their endless murmurs.

In the afternoons, couples in the neighborhood gathered to drink beer, gossip, talk politics, and kill time. The ice cubes in their drinks were the only things that ever dissolved, while everything else remained unchanged, too inflexible to evolve.

What did change, however, was time itself. People had come and gone: Don died in his sleep, Bill succumbed to an infection, Ronnie battled terminal cancer, and their aging wives sold off properties to return to America and Canada. Wenwen and Yunyun were in their sixties. They, too, had grown older, regretting the decades spent apart. Wenwen had cared for their parents in Taiwan, while Yunyun felt guilty for living in America and Belize, not visiting Taiwan often. Their time together, at Yunyun's Belize vacation house during vacations, became especially precious.

"When people around you die, you start to feel unprotected from death," Wenwen said quietly.

"Yes," Yunyun sighed. "We need to live fully while we can."

They spent their days golfing, socializing with other snowbirds, and swimming in the ocean. At night, they joined their husbands under the palapa to watch the starry sky.

One evening, as Yunyun and her husband were watching TV before bed, Wenwen knocked on their door. She wanted to discuss plans for the next day. Wenwen had spent most of her life in Taiwan and rarely traveled unless accompanied by her husband. In contrast, Yunyun, who had explored many countries and cultures, felt a twinge of guilt.

"We've been all over the south, but we can revisit with you guys," Yunyun gladly offered.

"Let's go deep-sea fishing," Bobby said with enthusiasm. "I'll get the boat ready first thing tomorrow morning."

"Will it be safe with all four of us in the boat?" Wenwen asked, concerned about capacity limits.

"Plenty of room," Bobby assured her.

"You can be a world traveler now. You're your own woman," Yunyun said encouragingly, smiling.

"Good morning, folks!" their neighbor Judy hollered as she passed by Bobby and Yunyun's vacation house.

"Yes, another fine day! We're going fishing in Blue Bay. What's new with you?" Bobby called back.

"My sister is visiting too! We're picking her up at the airport," Judy said with a bright smile.

"Great! Hit us up later!"

An impromptu gathering of expats was underway, and the two sisters and their husbands quickly filled their day, returning just in time to gather with friends in the neighborhood.

"Doesn't your body feel better after stretching it out over the ocean?" Bobby asked, clearly invigorated.

"I feel so alive!" Yunyun agreed.

"Let's toast to rejuvenation!" Wenwen said with a grin.

"Here's to living fully. Work is overrated," Yee added.

Neighbors complimented the sisters on their youthful looks, their sun-kissed faces, and their accomplishments. Wenwen and Yunyun returned from the gathering feeling more connected than ever. Wenwen threw her arms around her sister, and they shared a warm embrace.

"You're so smart and beautiful. I'm just the good one," Wenwen said. "Thank you for a wonderful day!"

"Do you remember when we picked apples for Boss A-bian during summer vacation in high school? You were the smart one," Yunyun said with a laugh. "You're the loved one, while I'm the one always blamed for not staying home."

"You're always missed and loved, even during the toughest times," Wenwen said.

"I understand why our parents loved you most. You were always there, caring for them."

"I envy your adventures around the world and your life in America. I've been like a frog in the well, seeing only the limited sky."

"You're retired. You have time to explore the vast sky beyond!"

Wenwen, once the office worker who had missed out on adventure, now yearned for the thrills she had never known. Yunyun, who had spent her life chasing distant horizons, longed instead for undemanding trips and quieter, simpler joys. Yet whatever their hearts desired, they found comfort in each other's presence — a sister to confide in, to reflect with, to argue and laugh beside. No matter how differently they had lived, they had always been walking parallel paths. Most of all, they shared the hope of new experiences still to come.

Even in later years, there is room for transformation, for connection, for new chapters. Adventures still called to them — not the wild, untamed quests of youth, but gentler ones: a spontaneous trip, a shared discussion, a new recipe, a long-forgotten song sung off-key in the kitchen. These were adventures of a different kind, taken not with youthful vigor, but with grace, perspective, and a sense of humor about the aches, pains, and creaky joints that came with every step of the way.

And in those steps, slow, careful, but forward all the same — they found something they hadn't known to look for in their younger years: the joy of becoming, again and again, in the company of someone who had seen different versions of you and loved them all.

Unwanted Kiss

Lucy had always regarded her brother-in-law with indifference. He was an older man, her sister's husband, and she saw him as nothing more than a fixture in the background of her family. But no matter how cool or distant she was, he kept coming back. Every weekend, like clockwork, he would ask her oldest sister to cook a meal for Lucy, inquire about her college life, and even go as far as picking her up from the dorm and taking her back at the end of the weekend. He always came bearing gifts for her birthdays, sometimes offering to take her out on special excursions, treating her like a daughter, or perhaps something else — Lucy could never quite comprehend, let alone understand

For four years, while Lucy attended college near her sister and brother-in-law's home, he played the role of protector. A subtle, awkward thread woven into the fabric of her life. Every time they spoke, he asked about her studies: whether she had met any interesting people; if she'd found a new boyfriend; if the food in the cafeteria was better or worse than before. He seemed genuinely interested in her life. At first, Lucy dismissed him as just a concerned relative. He was friendly enough, a bit overbearing at times, but nothing to make her uncomfortable — until that Sunday evening when everything changed.

It was just another Sunday dinner at her sister's house. The family gathered around the TV, settling in for their usual night of watching soap operas. Lucy, feeling exhausted from a long week of classes and assignments, voiced her desire to leave early.

"I'm so tired of this show," Lucy said, stretching her arms. "I'm going to change into some comfortable pajamas."

Her brother-in-law, who had been sitting nearby, glanced at her with what seemed to be an unusually concerned look. "You look tired. Let me give you a back massage before you go upstairs. It'll help you relax," he suggested, his voice soft and soothing.

Lucy, caught off guard by the attention, wasn't entirely sure how to respond. She had never seen her brother-in-law in quite this way before. But she nodded, half-heartedly, figuring it wouldn't hurt to let him help. She didn't want to seem rude. "Okay, just a bit. Thank you very much," she replied, a little unsure but not fully suspicious.

What happened next, however, would haunt her for a long time. As he helped her with her overnight bag, his hands lingered on her shoulders. It felt oddly intimate, like something a partner might do, but she brushed it off as nothing more than the casual touch of a family member. He was just trying to be nice, right? But then, as he held the bag, he pulled her toward him, unexpectedly wrapping his arms around her. She froze. Before she could even react or process the situation, he leaned down and pressed his lips to hers in a soft but undeniable kiss.

Lucy's heart stopped. For a moment, her mind was blank. She had never imagined something like this would happen, especially not from him. In her confusion, she stumbled backward, pulling away with a sharp intake of breath. Her eyes widened in shock and disbelief. She couldn't understand what had just transpired. She hadn't even registered the overwhelming surge of anger or disgust, just the paralyzing confusion that clouded her thoughts.

Without a word, without looking back, she grabbed her bag and fled out of the house. She didn't care who saw her, didn't care if anyone tried to stop her. Her legs moved on instinct, carrying her away from the place that had, until that moment, felt like a safe haven. She didn't stop running until she reached the dorm, her heart racing in her chest, a million thoughts tumbling through her mind.

What should she do now? Should she tell her sister what happened? Should she explain what had transpired, even though the idea of confronting her brother-in-law felt terrifying? Or should she just disappear, make up some excuse as to why she stopped visiting, and try to put the entire episode behind her?

The guilt gnawed at her. Was she overreacting? Was she just being too sensitive? But deep down, she knew the answer. No. What he did was wrong. She had been violated, not just physically, but emotionally. The weight of the betrayal settled heavily on her shoulders, and the idea of going back to that house, of seeing him again, was unbearable.

In the weeks that followed, her sister's life seemed to spiral in a different direction. She remarried — an abrupt change that didn't seem to fit with the woman Lucy had known all her life. Meanwhile, her brother-in-law's life unraveled in other, more public ways. The calm, quiet façade he had worn for years cracked when he was caught harassing one of the teenage players in his game parlor downstairs, an incident that led to his departure from the family's life entirely and abruptly. His absence, although it should have brought relief, only left a cold void behind.

Lucy never told her sister. Part of her wanted to, wanted to scream the truth so that everyone could see the kind of man he was. But another part of her, perhaps the part that still wanted to protect her family from the hurt and shame of such a revelation, kept quiet.

Her sister's new marriage brought an unsettling sense of finality to the chapter of her life with her first husband that had once been filled with such hopeful normalcy. Lucy could never see her former brother-in-law the same way after the unwanted kiss. And so, she moved forward, though the memory of that night lingered, a scar that would always remain hidden beneath the surface.

Patrons

Outside every storefront in New York City, people gathered, walked, rambled, and talked. Tourists, residents, and bums alike shared the same sidewalk. From my café's glass-walled panels, I could see all sorts of people, and I made an effort to greet each one with a bright smile, hoping to light up the entire space. Some were enticed to come in, grab a cup of coffee, use the Wi-Fi and restroom, and continue with whatever kept them busy that day.

I could never decide which was worse: the patron who pretended to stumble upon my café for the first time, just long enough to use the restroom and grab a quick bite to go; or the regulars who parked themselves all day with a single cup of gourmet coffee and a laptop. My restroom felt more like a public charity project than a customer amenity. I was the one footing the bill for cleaning, supplies, and sanitation. And bathroom costs were just the beginning. I lived in constant fear of complaints from my neighbor about the noise, either from my patrons or the music I played. Meanwhile, the cash in the register barely covered my outrageously high rent. My customers, in all their quirky glory, had the power to either make or break the day.

"Keep the change, darling."

"You have good taste in music."

"I love your décor. It's so exotic and charming."

"Where were you yesterday? Your barista doesn't make the same kind of crema like you."

"Where's Sara? I like her giving me extra servings on the house."

One time, David Duchovny came in and sat at the corner table for a couple of hours. On the street, they were shooting a movie for days. Many nights, rockers from the nearby CBGB club would come in to unwind. My café was never dull.

Some patrons came for the ambiance, lounging in the worn leather armchairs that had cost me a fortune but gave the place that lived-in feel I'd always envisioned. They'd curl up with books or sketch in notepads, ordering just enough to justify their occupation of prime real estate. Others belonged to the morning rush crowd: corporate professionals distinguished by sleek timepieces and restless sighs, dropping twenty dollars on specialty drinks and artisanal pastries without so much as a glance, before vanishing back into the concrete jungle.

There was the aspiring novelist who claimed the same table by the window every Tuesday and Thursday, typing furiously and occasionally looking up to study the passersby with intense concentration. I wondered if any of us had unwittingly become characters in his manuscript. The elderly couple who came every Sunday after church, sharing a single slice of cheesecake between them, reminiscing about when this neighborhood was something entirely different.

The musicians were my favorites — broke but generous with what little they had, often offering to play on slow evenings in exchange for dinner. They brought life and soul into the space, turning my humble café into something magical for a few precious hours. On those nights, the place would fill with locals, tourists drawn by the music spilling onto the sidewalk, and even the occasional celebrity slipping in through the private back door.

The celebrities never bothered me much. New York code demanded I treat them like anyone else. But their presence added a certain cachet, whispered about by regular patrons who'd casually mention to friends, "You know, I saw Ethan Hawke at my coffee place last week."

My baristas became part of the theater — Sara with her vibrant tattoos and encyclopedic knowledge of coffee origins; Miguel, whose latte art became famous; and Zoe, who knew every regular's order by heart and all the neighborhood gossip worth knowing.

The rhythm of the place followed the city's pulse: frantic mornings, contemplative afternoons, and evenings that could be either quietly intimate or unexpectedly raucous. Through it all, I watched New York life play out in miniature within these walls: business deals, breakups, blind dates, job interviews, reunions, and creative collaborations.

One patron asked me, "Why are you moving to Las Vegas?"

"I used to have a stable income from my marketing job at a brokerage firm on Wall Street," I replied. "I needed that stability — and the lower cost of living. But most importantly, I need to establish residency there to divorce Tom."

"Are you going to open another café there?"

"No," I said. "No more cafés."

I moved to Las Vegas and started teaching public school English. The predictable hours and steady paycheck were a world away from the beautiful chaos of my New York café. Sometimes, though, when facing a classroom of students, each with their own stories, quirks, and potential, I recognized the same human tapestry that had once flowed through my doors in Manhattan. Different patrons, same humanity.

Bipolar Boyfriend

He approached our meeting point with a ramrod-straight posture, taking long, purposeful strides around the roundabout. When he sat across from me, his shy smile and downcast eyes gave him a reserved air. I found myself instinctively trying to draw him out.

"What's a typical day like for you?" I asked.
He pulled out a magazine featuring him in a sleek blue suit, managing a crew of construction workers. The article described

him as a meticulous and responsible manager, a hands-on leader. But what did a write-up really reveal about someone? The writer had embellished his importance, and the magazine, advertising his company as the best among local contractors, felt more like a business pitch than genuine praise.

But what captivated me was his vulnerability, his bashful demeanor, his passion for the cosmos. I could close my eyes and listen to him reminisce about his hometown in Montana, where his family didn't even have clean running water. They would gather to wash clothes in the river and lie on the grass, staring up at the endless blue sky. At night, he'd point out constellations, tell me stories, and drink until he was completely plastered. He was a functional alcoholic, but in those moments, I had never felt more spiritually connected to anyone else.

He was so elated that I was his girlfriend. No one else seemed as happy as he was to spend time with me. We got lost in conversation, drinking and chatting until the early hours of the morning, making love, and falling asleep together with his beloved Labrador, Lessie, curled up beside us.

The next day, we went to work separately, but he would call me after, his mood shifting. He'd talk about how busy work was, how his parents needed money again, and how one of his friends was in trouble with meth.

He was always happy to see me. He made me feel like the most important person in the world. And yet, there were times when he would need to "take care of something," and I could hear the tears in his voice.

We loved each other deeply, and before long, we decided to move in together. But when the day finally came, he never showed up to help, despite all his promises. I arrived at his place alone, confused and unsettled by the air, thick with the stench of tobacco and alcohol. He appeared to be talking to himself, his words unraveling like a tangled, endless story. And then I saw her, the woman he was talking to. His new female roommate. She had moved in that very same day.

When I confronted him, his eyes glazed over, perplexed. "Why are you here again?" he asked, his voice detached and hollow.

His woman roommate looked as puzzled as I felt. She clutched her suitcase, backing toward the door: "I will let you two talk."

"I'm supposed to move in with you today, remember?" I said, throat tightening. "We have been planning for a month!"

Recognition flickered across his face, followed by horror. "No, no, that's next month. You've got it all wrong." His confidence was absolute, as if my reality was the mistaken one.

Later that night, he called me sobbing. "I don't know what happened. I forgot. I'm so sorry. Sometimes I lose track of time, of plans." His voice cracked. "Please don't leave me."

His doctor adjusted his medication the following week. Bipolar II disorder, they said. The extreme highs that made him passionate and vibrant, followed by crushing lows where he'd disappear for days. The periods of disorder and confusion, the impulsive decisions — it all suddenly made sense.

I stayed, learning to navigate his cycles. When he was manic, I'd find him cleaning the entire house at 3:00 a.m., planning elaborate business ventures, or spending money we didn't have. During depressive episodes, I'd coax him to eat, to shower, to remember he was still the man who knew every constellation in the night sky.

Some days were beautiful. We'd hike with Lessie, his arm around my waist, both of us laughing as the dog bounded ahead. Other days, I'd come home to find him staring at the wall, whiskey in hand, unreachable.

"Do you regret staying?" he asked me once, during a moment of sobriety and clarity.

I thought about his passion, his vulnerability, how deeply he loved when he could. I thought about the chaos, the unpredictability, the times I cried alone.

"No," I answered truthfully. "But it's not easy."

He nodded, understanding. "I'm trying," he whispered.

"I know," I said, taking his hand. "We both are."

The relationship with my bipolar boyfriend was neither perfect nor simple. It ended when he brought his female roommate back without any advanced discussion or warning. Our relationship mirrored his moods, intense and overwhelming at times, then fragile and withdrawn at others. I loved him for his genuine curiosity about the universe, a quality worth fighting for, even on days when he couldn't remember where we were or who he wanted to be.

Some days, he would speak about black holes with the fervor of someone trying to understand his own darkness; other days, he barely spoke at all. I learned to recognize the stillness before the crash, the way his voice would thin out like smoke before disappearing completely. I stayed through the highs that made me feel invincible and the lows that made me question if I was enough to anchor him. Maybe I wasn't. Maybe no one could be.

The second arrival of his roommate, unannounced, abrupt, wasn't just the final straw; it was a reminder that I had always been living on the edge of someone else's shifting reality. He didn't see how it broke something in me, how it confirmed a fear I'd carried for months: that in his ever-expanding universe, I was just a satellite, circling but never aligning or landing.

Loving him taught me how deep empathy could go, but it also showed me the cost of losing myself in someone else's storm. I still wonder if he ever noticed the silence I left behind.

Otherness

After over thirty years in America, I came to terms with my own Zhongbuzhong, Xibuxi — Chinese but not Chinese, Western but not Western. I didn't seem to fit in anywhere. For so long, I had tried to make sense of my place in this vast, diverse country, and yet the more I attempted to define myself, the less I felt validated by a particular label. It was as if I existed in a perpetual state of being caught between worlds, never fully belonging to one or the other.

At 2:00 a.m. in Reagan International Airport, I found myself alone in the terminal, sitting at the café bar, working away on my laptop, the soft hum of airport announcements in the distance. The lights in the corridors were dimmed, casting shadows that made the space feel even more isolated. All shops, stores, newsstands, restaurants, bars, and eateries were deserted, their metal gates tightly shut and locked, leaving behind only the faint scent of stale coffee and disinfectant products. I couldn't go through security into the ticketed terminals yet, as the TSA agent on duty that night had barred my access. Too early.

His gaze lingered on me for a moment, scrutinizing the yellow undertone of my East Asian skin. His suspicion was palpable. He wasn't sure if I spoke English, and his assumption, rooted in the biases of his own culture, made his words unnecessarily loud and slow.

"Ma'am, can I help you?" he asked, each word dragged out as if I might not understand him.

"My flight leaves at 7:00 a.m. Can I go in now?"

"No, you cannot. The gates are all closed," he replied curtly.

"I'm TSA Pre-checked," I said, my voice steady, but even the certainty of my status didn't seem to matter.

"Don't matter," he answered, switching back to his usual idiolect, one that spoke of finality, of exclusion.

There was a moment of silence, and then the only person who acknowledged my existence in that ghostly, deserted terminal was a cleaning lady, who kindly pointed me to an empty chair. Alone, surrounded by the eerie quiet of the airport,

I wrote, read, and dozed off occasionally, the hours slipping by in the limbo between night and morning. My tired body needed rest, but the restlessness of my mind would not allow me to fall into complete sleep.

I wandered around the airport, stretching my legs, my thoughts drifting back to my years of travel. I thought about all the times I had journeyed to different countries and had been embraced by strangers. In those moments, I was one of them — spoken to in their native languages: Hola, Konnichiwa, Aloha, Sawadika, Nihao, Xin Chào, Merhaba, Anyoung haseyo, Asalaam alaikum, Selamat siang, Shalom, and so on. Each time, they spoke to me as if I belonged, their voices warm with the hope of connection. Yet, despite the effort, it was always clear from that first greeting that I wasn't one of them. My appearance, my mannerisms, my way of being were foreign to them, no matter how much I tried to blend in. They either switched to English or gave up trying altogether, choosing the universal language of assumed difference.

"What's your nationality?" That question was the most annoying.

What is nationality, I wondered. Where was I born? Taiwan. Where was I from? Taiwan, Asia, and America — New York, Las Vegas, and DC. Where did my heritage stem from? Taiwan and America. What was my citizenship? American. I was everywhere and nowhere. None of these places could fully define me.

"You don't look Chinese," even Chinese people would say, their words tinged with surprise or perhaps confusion.

And so, the questions would always come, endless and unyielding:

"Are you Polynesian?" No.

"Are you Filipino?" No.

"Are you Hispanic?" No.

"Are you biologically 100% Taiwanese?" Yes.

"Are you mixed?" No. My parents were both Taiwanese. But was I mixed because I married two Caucasian men from North America?

It seemed that my appearance defied simple categorization. My features were considered beautiful but unusual for an East Asian: a pretty face, large eyes, full lips, a head of loosely curled dark brown hair. My not-so-petite frame could pass for an American-born Asian, but my fluency in multiple languages only added to the confusion. In a world that craved easy labels, I was a walking contradiction.

Culturally, no one knew where I belonged either. I studied world cultures long enough to teach world literature, English Language Arts, and Chinese Mandarin, but in every culture, I was still foreign-looking and foreign-sounding. No matter how much I tried to assimilate, I stood out as someone who wasn't quite the same. It wasn't just a cultural gap. It was an emotional one as well.

It bothered me that I could not obtain top-level security clearance for federal employment simply because I was deemed "too foreign." My Americanness seemed to go unrecognized. It felt wrong, unjust. I had loved this country, built a life here, paid my taxes, and followed the rules. Yet, I was still doubted — an American who wasn't considered American enough. It felt especially unfair when figures like Edward Snowden, who betrayed his country, were granted top-secret clearance, and when a man of questionable character could waltz into the highest office in the land. Meanwhile, I, an upstanding, law-abiding American woman with the expertise to serve my country, was excluded.

Okay, to be fair, I was American enough to teach English and Chinese to Americans. The American ways were mine; the Taiwanese ways were mine, yet nothing was fully mine. I was a mix of both, but neither was all me. I was a collection of identities, a mosaic pieced together from various corners of the world, yet none of those pieces fully captured the essence of who I was, who I could become.

Only one thing about me felt truly mine: the otherness within me. It was the only thing that belonged to me entirely, an identity forged in the cracks and folds between cultures, a place where I had learned to exist despite the world's attempts to define me.

Eventually, after what felt like an eternity, I finally made it through TSA security and found my way to a restaurant. I sat down to have a full breakfast at the airport, my stomach growling in relief. The Ethiopian waitress who greeted me was incredibly warm, her smile genuine. There was no hesitation in her voice when she asked me if I wanted coffee or water. In her eyes, I was just another traveler, just another person in the world. It was the first time I felt welcomed that night, and the warmth of her kindness felt like a balm on my tired soul.

As I sat there, sipping my coffee, I realized that, in that moment, I didn't need to explain myself. I didn't need to define my nationality, my culture, my history. I was simply a traveler, sharing space with other fellow human beings. For once, the world felt a little cozier, and I felt a little more at ease.

In that cozy corner of the airport, I felt something rare, something beautiful — an understanding that I was not defined by the labels the world had tried to place on me, but by the connections I made and the people who saw me for who I truly was, not what I looked like. For that brief moment, I wasn't just someone caught between worlds. I was simply me, a world citizen, belonging everywhere and nowhere.

The morning sunlight streamed through the terminal windows as my flight to Taipei City was announced. Two hours until boarding. I watched travelers hurry past: businessmen in crisp suits, families with sleepy children, college students with overstuffed backpacks. Each person seemed to move with such certainty, such belonging.

My phone buzzed. A text from my goddaughter, Amelia. "Safe travels! Don't forget to bring back lots of pineapple cakes!"

I smiled. Amelia, with her blonde hair inherited from her American father and brown, almond-shaped eyes with epicanthal folds passed down from her Mexican mother, carried her mixed identity with a grace I had never quite managed. She wore her dual heritage like a comfy sweater, effortlessly embracing both sides, while for me, multiple cultural identities had always felt more like an ill-fitting costume.

The café began to fill with the morning crowd. Across from me, an elderly Chinese couple argued softly in Mandarin about their connecting flight. I understood every word, but hesitated I offered them help. Would they see me as Chinese enough to be trusted? Or would they notice something off, something about me that wasn't quite "one of them"?

An announcement in English, then Spanish, then Mandarin, echoed through the terminal. In the Mandarin version, I counted three tonal errors. It made me smile — like me, the official airport announcer lived in between linguistic worlds.

I pulled out the manuscript I'd been working on, essays about teaching global competence. My editor in New York had called it "fascinatingly multicultural." As if my life's work could be condensed into such a neat hyphenation.

"Excuse me, is this seat taken?"

I looked up to see a middle-aged man gesturing to the chair opposite mine. Something in his accent caught my attention.

"Not at all," I replied in English, then, taking a chance, added, "Qing zuo. Qing zuo."

His eyes widened with surprise and delight. "Ah, ni hui shuo zhongwen! Taiwanese?"

"Yes," I said, feeling that familiar mix of pleasure and unease. "Though I've lived in America most of my life."

"I could tell from your accent — Taiwanese, but with something else." He switched effortlessly between Mandarin and English. "I'm from Kaohsiung originally, but I've been in California for thirty years. Software engineer in the Silicon Valley."

"I work at Foreign Service Institute," I offered. "Teaching Chinese to foreign service officers."

"The perfect bridge-builder!" he exclaimed, seeming genuinely pleased. "We need more people like you, especially now."

Bridge-builder. I'd thought of my in-betweenness that way, as a connection, a liaison. We talked for nearly an hour, about Taiwan's changing identity, about life in America, about the strange comfort of airports around the world— these liminal spaces where everyone is simultaneously coming and going, belonging nowhere and everywhere.

As we said goodbye, he handed me his business card. "If you're ever in San Francisco, my wife runs a cultural center. They'd love to have you visit and share your experience."

I studied his card: Dr. James Chen, Ph.D. Another hybrid name for a hybrid existence.

Boarding my flight later, I found myself seated next to a young White woman buried in a Chinese language textbook, struggling with characters. Without thinking, I pointed to one she'd been staring at.

"That's 'qian' — it means 'money'," I pronounced the syllable distinctly. "Second tone. The tone goes up, like you're asking a question, saying 'What?'."

She looked at me with such gratitude it was almost embarrassing. "Are you a teacher? My professor at UCLA is amazing but I still struggle with getting the tones right."

"I am. At FSI." I explained what my job entailed.

"That's so cool! I'm studying International Relations, focusing on U.S.-China relations. It's so important now with everything happening."

For the next hour, I helped her practice pronunciation. There was something healing about it: using my in-betweenness as a gift. When we landed in Los Angeles for my connecting flight, she thanked me profusely.

"You explained it better than my textbooks. It's like you understand both sides perfectly."

Waiting for my final flight to Taipei, I called my husband Bobby before the long journey.

"How's the airport marathon?" he asked.

"Surprisingly enlightening," I replied, watching the diverse crowd around me. "I've been thinking about what you said last Christmas, about how being exposed to diverse cultures gives you a wider view."

"Embrace your inner cultural ambassador. Be safe!" he had high hopes for my trip to Taiwan.

"I think I'm starting to see that I can belong anywhere."

"That's what I always said about you — that you could walk into any room in any country and find connection."

The thought of reconnecting with my Taiwanese family and friends warmed me up. As they called for boarding, I gathered my things, feeling the weight of my passport with its American eagle, the Kobo Reader with English novels and Chinese poetry books in my bag, the jade pendant my mother had given me, the FSI ID badge in my purse. Layers of identity, once jagged pieces that didn't fit together, now beginning to form something new — a mosaic rather than a divided self.

Perhaps otherness wasn't about being less than whole, but about being more than one thing. The spaces between identities weren't empty after all, but filled with possibility, with perspective, with the unique wisdom that comes from seeing the world from multiple vantage points.

I boarded the plane to Taipei, not as someone returning home or as a foreigner visiting, but as myself, complex, contradictory, and finally, comfortable in the in-between.

Days with Chloe

The first time I arrived at Chloe's parents' penthouse in Manhattan, the sky was so bright and blue that the apartment walls reflected the sunlight in a stunning display, almost like the aurora borealis. The ten-bedroom penthouse had panoramic views of the city's iconic skyline, the Empire State Building, the Chrysler Building, Central Park, and the Hudson River — all framed perfectly in the backdrop. The floor-to-ceiling windows were open wide, yet the space still exuded an elevated sense of privacy and exclusivity. Polished hardwood floors, sleek marble countertops, custom cabinetry, and state-of-the-art appliances screamed wealth and prosperity.

I liked the formal dining space the most. That's where Chloe would sit in her crib, reaching out to those around her, asking to be picked up. That's also where Melissa, the cook, would be preparing meals, filling the room with the aromatic scent of spices simmering away. The dining area was large, with an elegant chandelier hanging overhead and a polished mahogany table that seemed too grand for its intended use. In that space, Chloe looked small, like a delicate flower in a vast, opulent garden. I remember the days when I would watch her reach her tiny hands toward people, eager to be held, as if the world around her was something to be both explored and adored.

Chloe's connection with her mother was strong, and in those early days, Mary, her mother, was always there, always present, often speaking in a calm and soothing voice, her gestures tender but full of purpose. She would sit beside Chloe, watching her play, always attentive, never rushed despite the endless demands of their lifestyle. It was hard to imagine someone with so much material wealth, surrounded by servants, with so many resources at her disposal, could ever feel lonely, but I began to realize that was precisely the case for Mary.

Sometimes, I would travel from Manhattan to Princeton, New Jersey, to visit Chloe when Mary took her there for a break from the hustle and bustle of the city. The New Jersey house had a more traditional, opulent interior with rich textures, chandeliers, and grand staircases. It didn't have concierge services like the penthouse, but the housekeeper was always there, ready to greet guests and offer assistance. The house felt timeless, like a place where generations had lived and loved. Chloe seemed happier and more talkative in the comfort and luxury of the vast house. It was as if the sprawling space allowed her to stretch her legs, explore the world on her own terms, and maybe, in a way, feel more at ease.

"Nainai, nainai," she cooed one afternoon, reaching for a snack as she sat on the plush rug. Her wide eyes were filled with innocent wonder as she looked up at me, waiting for me to respond. Her desire for comfort was simple yet undeniable: a bottle of milk, a warm hug, the assurance that someone was always there with her.

"Mama mashang huilai," I responded, smiling softly. "Mama will come soon." I said it with an affection I had developed over time, as if Chloe truly understood every word, every subtle inflection in my voice.

Chloe was supposed to learn Mandarin with me as her tutor. Mary had insisted on it, wanting her daughter to speak her father's native language, Mandarin, despite the ease with which she could learn English from her mom and Spanish from her nanny. At three years old, Chloe was already balancing three languages, learning English from her mom, Spanish from her nanny, and Mandarin from me.

Chloe's learning journey was fascinating. She was like a sponge, soaking up whatever was around her, yet her affection for Spanish was undeniable. She would babble in a mix of the three languages, often stumbling over the Mandarin phrases but speaking fluently in English and Spanish. Still, there was something distinctly special about the way she would light up when she heard her father's voice, especially when he would return home after long stretches of business trips.

Her father, a wealthy commodity trader, was often absent, and though he had the ability to buy anything Chloe might need or want, it was clear that he couldn't buy the time and emotional presence she craved. It was Mary, though, who truly dedicated herself to Chloe's growth, leaving behind her prestigious career as an attorney to become a full-time stay-at-home mom. She had attended Columbia University, and in moments of reflection, she would tell me stories of her competitive days in the legal world. I was a graduate student at Columbia at the time, and though she seemed to want to help me cope with my academic pressures, it felt as if Mary's own internal struggles were subtly bleeding into her desire to keep me occupied.

Despite the extravagant lifestyle and every material luxury Chloe had access to, there was a void in their lives. Mary often shared her frustrations with me about her husband's busy schedule, revealing that the only time she truly felt connected with him was when they were on a plane, side by side, holding hands, escaping their busy lives. These moments were few and far between, but they were the ones she clung to, almost like a lifeline.

Mary's days were spent in a blur of car services, shopping, dining out, or preparing for Chloe's enrollment in an elite nursery school. Chloe, more often than not, was left with me and her nanny while I tutored her, but I could sense Mary's reluctance to leave her daughter with anyone. I think, deep down, she didn't want Chloe to be surrounded by too many strangers, despite the household staff and the constant bustle. Mary was always looking for some semblance of normalcy, something that could tether her to a simpler time, but the weight of their lifestyle often kept her from finding that peace.

One day, I tried to engage Chloe in a game, suggesting we build a Lego house together and learn about the different rooms of a house in Mandarin. "Gai Legao fangzi," I said cheerfully, trying to make it fun.

"Buyao! Buyao!" Chloe yelled, throwing her hands up in a playful but firm refusal. Her reluctance to engage with Mandarin was evident, and I couldn't help but smile at her stubbornness. She had already mastered the art of saying "no" and seemed to use it more than any other word in her Mandarin vocabulary.

"¿Qué pasa?" Chloe's nanny intervened with a gentle laugh.

"¡No quiero!" Chloe responded rapidly in Spanish, her words almost a jumble, but she spoke with such certainty, her face scrunching up in a mix of frustration and defiance.

I couldn't help but laugh at how easily Chloe slipped between languages, her mind already able to compartmentalize them, refusing to speak Mandarin unless her father was present. It became a game of cat and mouse, with me trying different tactics: Legos, puzzles, number hunts, drawing — all in Mandarin, but I would be lucky if I could get her to utter even five Mandarin phrases.

It was a strange, fascinating dynamic, and I often wondered how much of it was due to Chloe's natural inclination toward English and Spanish, or whether she was simply holding on to her connection with her father, whom she adored and whom she could understand and communicate through Mandarin.

Years later, after I had moved on from my time with Chloe, I heard from Mary again. Chloe had grown up, moved away from New York City, and had become fluent in English, Mandarin, and Spanish. She was working as a trader, just like her father, and it was impossible not to feel a strange sense of pride when I heard of her success. Despite my fleeting role in her early life, I couldn't help but think back to the days when she was just a toddler, sitting in the sunlit penthouse, speaking in a jumble of languages, asking for comfort and connection in a world that seemed too large for her.

In the end, Chloe had found her own path, navigating the complexities of language, culture, and family, much like her parents had before her. And though I may have only played a small role in her story, I knew that the days we spent together would remain a part of me, as a reminder of the ways in which we are shaped by those we meet along our life journeys.

For Xuewei

I know Xuewei as a bright and promising professional. She was one of the youngest fellow teachers in the Chinese Mandarin Section at FSI, yet she consistently demonstrated both maturity and dedication beyond her years. I applaud how, at such a young age, she was not only accomplished but also understood the importance of maintaining balance in life. Xuewei brought a steady, supportive presence to her students and fostered a pleasant, engaging atmosphere in every session she led and every meeting she attended. She was truly remarkable — her presence lit up every space she entered.

It was a complete shock to me when such a beautiful life was taken so suddenly in a car accident that made no sense to anyone. My disbelief eventually gave way to immense sadness, especially as I had the time and space to process this tragedy privately (I was on a two-week leave when the incident occurred). I share the same sense of devastation with my colleagues over Xuewei's sudden passing. The pain and ache only began to subside as we took comfort in knowing that her family and close friends were supported by the entire staff, who offered an overwhelming wave of condolences that, in some way, brought solace.

The grief I feel, along with the sense of collective strength from my colleagues, speaks to how deeply Xuewei was loved, respected, and admired. Coming to terms with this loss is difficult, but we must continue our work to honor her memory.

Grief doesn't fade with time; only a sense of acceptance remains. What else can we do, except accept that Xuewei is now at peace? Where else can we go, except forward and upward? Knowing that we share a common goal and mission, we must continue with courage, striving to be our best for the living. I believe this is what Xuewei would have wanted: for us to live life to the fullest and work together toward our common purpose. While the vibrant, strong young woman — so full of life — was gone in an instant, like a shooting star, the traces of her brightness will continue to shine on forever, forever etched in our hearts.

我认识的雪薇是一位聪明、前途光明的专业人士。她是美国国务院外交学院中文部最年轻的老师之一。我很佩服她在这么年轻的当时就不仅有成就，而且懂得生活平衡的重要性。她对每个学生都保持稳定教导的态度，并为教授的每堂课和参与的每次会议与团聚带来愉快的氛围。雪薇照亮了她所进入的每一个空间。

如此美好的生命突然在一场不幸的车祸中被夺走时，我感到非常震惊。我的疑惑继而转成了沉重的悲伤，特别是当我有时间和空间私下处理这场悲剧时更显苍凉（事件发生时我正休假两周）。对于雪薇的突然去世，我和同事们都有同样的悲痛。知道她的家人和密友得到了全体工作人员的支持，痛苦才得以开始逐渐消退，只愿全然的哀悼能在某种程度上为人带来安慰。

我所感受到的心痛，以及同事们集体形成的力量感，都显示了雪薇是多么深受爱戴和钦佩。接受这一可贵生命的丧失是很困难的，但我们必须继续努力，才能切心纪念雪薇。

悲伤不会随着时间而消退；只会余存一种莫可奈何的接受感。除了接受雪薇现在已处于平静天堂之外，我们还能如何自处？除了往前走、向上推进之外，我们还能置身何地？针对共同的目标和使命，我们必须继续勇敢地努力迈进，为生活做出最好的贡献。我相信这就是雪薇想要的：让我们过着充实的生活，为我们共同的目标而努力。那个充满活力和生机的坚强年轻女子，像流星一般转瞬即逝，但她的光辉将永远闪耀，永远铭刻在我们每个人的心中。

Respectfully,

Alicia Su Lozeron (苏明采 Ming Cai Su, Ming Tsae Su)
Chinese Language and Culture Instructor
FSI/SLS/EAP

Of Sorrow and Joy

Life is a delicate dance, a rhythm that sways between joy and sorrow, an endless ebb and flow, like the unrelenting tides of the ocean. As Kahlil Gibran so eloquently put it, "Your joy is your sorrow unmasked. And the selfsame well from which your laughter rises was oftentimes filled with your tears." This duality of experience, joy and sorrow intertwined, is a universal truth that each of us lives and feels in our own unique way. For me, joy became most apparent when I realized that the very things I had, the ordinary and the mundane, were in themselves the source of my happiness. However, this joy was often tempered with a bittersweet sorrow, a sadness rooted in the simplicity and banality of my existence, in the everydayness of life that seemed both ordinary and fleeting.

My days were largely shaped by routine — the rhythmic monotony of commuting and work that filled my weekdays. Evenings were spent in quiet company, watching TV soap operas with my husband, a shared ritual that weaved a sense of comfort into our otherwise busy lives. At night, I would half-sleep, my eyes glued to the screen as I watched live-streamed sports games, my athletic partner by my side, while I simultaneously buried my nose in a book. On weekends, the cycle continued, though in the form of house chores, cooking, and the rare weekend getaway or vacation, a small escape from the otherwise predictable tempo of life.

Yet, within the simplicity of it all, I discovered profound joy. One of my most cherished moments of happiness arose whenever I donned my black leather jacket and red full-face helmet and mounted my motorcycle. The act of slipping into that gear was a quiet rebellion, a defiance of the role I usually played in society. There, in the contrast between my work attire and the boldness of the protective gear, I found exhilaration. The controlled rumble beneath me, the wind rushing past my face, and the thrill of the road ignited a sense of freedom I could not find anywhere else. In those moments, I wasn't just a commuter or a wife or a worker — I was a rider, an individual alive with a pure purpose of moving with the wind.

But even in the joy, there lingered sorrow. When my husband encouraged me to "speed up and follow the traffic flow," I could not help but hesitate, burdened by a fear of speed that I could never fully conquer. "I'm tired and can't keep up. Slow down," I would reply. The fear, the sorrow of not being the kind of person who thrived on adrenaline, swelled within me. I longed to be a fearless adventurer, a daredevil unburdened by caution. Yet, I was not. And in that sorrow, I was compelled to face the reality of my own limits.

This sorrow grew heavier when I observed the fragility of nature in my own backyard. One day, after a storm, I saw that the bird's nest in the possum pine tree had disintegrated. My heart ached as I stood before the remnants, yet I could not help but marvel at the resilience of the bird that had gathered pieces of torn cellophane to build such a delicate home. "Look at how the bird gathered all those torn pieces of cellophane from the grill wrapping to build her nest. Marvelous!" I would tell guests who visited, fascinated by the bird's ingenuity. Even in destruction, there was beauty, and that beauty carried with it a deep, indescribable sorrow.

In my quest for fulfillment, I tried hard to transcend the ordinariness of my existence. I wanted more, always more — a higher purpose, greater achievements, and recognition. I sought ambition, pursued bigger jobs, and chased various versions of happiness that promised fulfillment. I believed that smart, capable people should never settle for their circumstances, that life could be more if only I could push further, climb higher. Yet, despite all my striving, I never found the satisfaction I craved. I was always restless, always searching for something beyond what I had.

Books, writing, and learning were my lifelines. Through them, I sought to explore the world, to unravel its mysteries, and to make sense of my place in it. I traveled far and wide —

across America, through the jungles of Cambodia and Thailand, along the bustling streets of Vietnam, China, and Japan, and into the heart of Indonesia, Malaysia, and the Arabian deserts of Abu Dhabi. I read voraciously, immersing myself in the works of authors and critics who challenged my understanding of identity, culture, and history — Edward Said, Julia Kristeva, Michel Foucault, Simone de Beauvoir, Gayatri Spivak, John Irving, Amor Towles, and Susan Sontag, among many others. Their words shaped my identity, shaped my perception of the world.

The reader and writer within me were always in pursuit of knowledge, always searching for clarity, for ways to improve not just myself, but the world around me. Yet, despite my journeys and intellectual pursuits, there was always a feeling of a vague, persistent discomfort in not being able to shine in the way I wished. I often felt too shy to reveal my true self, too uncertain of my place in the grand narrative of life.

Writing brought me joy, but it also brought a sense of loneliness. My joy was found not in external recognition, but in the act of writing itself, in the process of trying to capture my thoughts and emotions, of seeking clarity and understanding. It was in the act of creating something that reflected my inner world. Yet, that joy was always tempered by the understanding that my words, like my thoughts, would never fully reach the outside world in the way I had hoped. There was sorrow in that realization, a sorrow that came with accepting the limitations of my own writing, my own voice.

Eventually, I found peace in self-publishing. There, in the wonderful space of being a writer with no external expectations, I could breathe freely. It was a humbling joy, the kind that doesn't need validation, the kind that acknowledges both the joy and the sorrow of the journey. My joy was reflected in my own personal journey — an intimate exploration of my own thoughts, emotions, and aspirations. It was a joy rooted in the acceptance of both the ordinary and the extraordinary, the moments of joy and sorrow that define us all.

In the end, joy and sorrow are not opposing forces but two sides of the same coin, each giving depth and meaning to the other. Life is richer for it — the dance of joy and sorrow, the ebb and flow of emotions that shape who we are. And in that dance, I find peace, knowing that I am both the dancer and the dance, forever moving with fluidity.

A Lone Wolf

I was always ill-suited for social interactions by nature. My tendency to retreat into myself set me apart from the crowd, and I could never quite figure out why I felt more comfortable in solitude than in the company of others. It was never about being shy or introverted in the traditional sense; it was simply that I found peace in my own thoughts, in the quiet space of self-reflection. I felt most at ease when I was alone — reading, writing, reflecting, learning, exploring, and creating. These activities nourished my soul and allowed me to feel connected to something larger than myself. The hustle of the outside world, with its constant chatter and expectations, often felt extraneous to me.

My husband once called me a "kooky Gap-kid-size woman," scolding me for not being fond of talking on the phone with family or friends. He was, in his way, affectionate in his critique, but his words made me acutely aware of the way I was perceived by others — quiet, quirky, different, perhaps even a bit distant. I often felt like I didn't quite fit into the usual boxes that people like to put one another in. Edward, a close friend from my Wall Street days, once described me as a "lone wolf" after I left my corporate job to start my own business. His words were not without praise, though — he acknowledged my quirky need for autonomy and the courage it took to step away from the comfort and security of a familiar path.

Yes, I was a loner, a solitary traveler on the road of life, greedy for my own space and time. My insatiable desire to study, to understand the world, and to experience life on my own terms often left me feeling like an outsider in many places. I craved adventure, often putting distance between myself and the people I loved. My parents, especially, were perplexed by this. They could never understand why I refused to stay home, why I didn't adhere to the typical patterns of family life. To their horror, I desired to study further in America and fell in love with an American expat in Taiwan. The relationship made no sense to them, and they were left questioning why I chose to forge my own path, one that so often took me far from home and out of their reach.

In my early twenties, I backpacked alone across neighboring countries, never tethered to any one place for long. I became the black sheep of my family, someone who valued the freedom of exploration over the traditional values they held dear. And yet, as I journeyed from one place to the next, I often found myself in situations where I neither fully belonged nor could fully blend in. I was always a step removed, an observer of life rather than a participant in the easy camaraderie that others seemed to slip into so naturally. I was both an insider and an outsider, always searching for a sense of belonging that remained elusive.

Yet, despite my fierce independence and preference for solitude, I began to realize that I needed others. It was a realization that caught me off guard — how could I, someone so invested in my own world, possibly need anyone else? But the truth became undeniable: no matter where I traveled, I found myself forging connections. I made friends and engaged with locals, learning about their lives, their cultures, their dreams. With each encounter, I discovered a piece of the human puzzle I hadn't yet seen. I began to appreciate the beauty of human connection, not as a crutch or a necessity, but as a meaningful complement to my own journey.

In every job I held, I adhered to social etiquette, blending into the professional world like a calm, collected chameleon. I was capable of navigating the social landscapes of various environments, from corporate offices to creative spaces, adapting without compromising my individuality. I was both odd and grounded, a daring straight-shooter who embraced both boundaries and freedom. I could hold a conversation with anyone, whether it was about marketing strategies or the meaning of life. My moral complexities were paradoxical — I was both deeply introspective and outwardly engaged. I reveled in the contradictions that made me who I was, understanding that they were a part of the tapestry of life itself.

My contradictions, I came to realize, were not flaws but integral parts of my journey. I wasn't searching for a perfect formula or a prescribed path. I was engaged in a deeper exploration of life — a mindfulness that stretched across all the layers of my experience. I had a fascination with human emotions, the raw and untamed energy that guided people through their lives. I wondered about the potential for transformation in each person I met, the way they could reconcile their talents, dreams, obligations, and personal histories. It was this complexity — the juxtaposition of hopes and fears, growth and stagnation — that intrigued me most.

In truth, I was just trying to make something meaningful out of this life and this world. I wasn't interested in the superficial trappings of fame or success, nor was I motivated by the shallow chatter of gossip. I longed to understand the deeper layers of experience in both myself and others. The world, vast, diverse, and endlessly fascinating, was worth paying attention to. The people in it, with their quirks, contradictions, and dreams, were worthy of thoughtful observation and understanding.

And it was in this learning, in this understanding, that the lone wolf discovered what truly mattered: humanity itself. In the end, it was the shared human experience, the joy and pain, the triumphs and losses, that made the journey worthwhile. It was the companionship of others, those brief moments of connection, that anchored me in a world that often felt overwhelming in its complexity. Despite my independence and desire for solitude, I discovered that interdependence was essential, and that humanity was the truest companion on the road ahead.

Best Mangoes I Never Had

I sought out spaces that would open doors to escape, reflection, and renewal. My search for these openings offered me the social mobility I deemed essential for my sanity. Whenever possible, I traveled. We had purchased a vacation home in Belize so my husband and I could snowbird from Washington, DC, seeking refuge when the bitter cold of North America became unbearable.

Our vacation home sat across from a park that led to a bay full of marine life: jackfish, tarpon, snapper, hogfish, grouper, and sawfish. Manatees swam in the bay, and amphibious sea turtles, alligators, and iguanas came ashore through the mangroves to greet us. Poincianas, palm trees, and mahogany trees dotted the seashore park, while my front yard boasted a colorful display of fruit trees and vibrant flowers: a massive mango tree, a Nani fruit tree, two prolific lime trees, coconut palms, fan palms, Bougainvillea, Plumeria flowers, hibiscus, and other tropical flora.

Of all the trees, the massive mango tree in my front yard was the most celebrated among our community of American and Canadian expats. Botanists, zoologists, restaurateurs, bar owners, kayakers, sailors, retired admin workers, and digital nomads, who formed the backbone of our neighborhood, gathered each summer to pick mangoes. Their gardeners and cleaning ladies would often collect dozens, and even the locals praised my mango tree as the best in the area. Everyone in our Belizean neighborhood loved my mangoes.

My husband and I typically stayed at our vacation house in Belize during the winter, missing the mango harvest. However, we often heard stories about the tree's magical, delicious fruits. Conversations with neighbors left us with vivid images of mangoes hanging heavily from the branches, their juicy flesh untouched as we were rarely there in the summertime. Our mangoes felt like a distant curiosity, much like the wildflowers that grew along the road leading from the township to the émigré community — untouched, yet ever-present. Year after year, these flowers returned, resilient, despite the road never being paved, only grated and smoothed after each monsoon.

I often considered it a break from my life in America. Although I missed the endless flow of flora and fauna in my tropical paradise and never tasted the mangoes on my Belize mango tree, I accepted that it came with its own cycles of growth and decay, like the universe I would never fully grasp, small as I was. I marveled at how the plants in my yard had flourished every time I visited Belize. When I returned to America, I would tell people I'd been recuperating peacefully by the bay, before the snow had melted from the ground.

The irony wasn't lost on me — owning what everyone claimed was the most magnificent mango tree in the area, yet never experiencing its fruits. Those mangoes had become legendary in my mind, their sweetness, juiciness and texture described so vividly by neighbors that I could almost taste them. Each winter, as we settled into our tropical escape, I would gaze up at the lush branches of the mango tree, trying to imagine them heavy with fruit.

Sometimes I wondered if the mangoes were truly as extraordinary as everyone claimed, or if their reputation had grown through shared community storytelling. Perhaps there was something magical about fruit you never taste — it remains perfect, unblemished by reality. The mangoes became a metaphor for me, for possibilities unrealized, for experiences just beyond reach.

Our cleaning lady, Maria, would shake her head and click her tongue when we mentioned missing mango season again. "Next time, you stay longer," she'd say, making a promise to save some for us if we ever extend our visit into summer. The local fisherman who sold us fresh catch would ask, "Still never tried your own mangoes?" with a mixture of amusement and disbelief.

One winter, I brought mango seeds to our house in Belize from some especially delicious fruit I'd bought at a local market in the DMV area. I planted them beside our existing tree, hoping for a second chance — maybe one that would bear fruit during our winter visits. The gardener chuckled, gently pointing out that mango trees take years to mature, and even then, the timing probably wouldn't align with our stays.

The untasted mangoes served as a reminder of life's peculiar arrangements: how we can possess something wonderful without ever fully experiencing it. Like distant stars whose light we see but can never touch, my mangoes remained beautiful abstractions, existing in stories and imaginations, their legendary sweetness preserved in the collective memory of our little expatriate community.

Each year when we locked up the house to return north, I would stand beneath the mango tree and promise, "Maybe next summer." The tree, indifferent to my schedule, would continue its cycle, offering its bounty to others while I was away, teaching me lessons about my small existence, about impermanence and the beauty of letting go.

The mango tree stood as a silent witness to my comings and goings, its roots deeply anchored in Belizean soil while I drifted between two worlds. In those moments before departure, I would place my hand on its rough bark, feeling the ancient pulse beneath my fingertips. The tree had existed long before I claimed ownership of the property and would likely outlive me by decades. Its branches would continue to extend skyward, its fruit would ripen and fall, whether I was there to witness the process.

This realization was both humbling and liberating. My absence did not diminish the tree's purpose; if anything, it fulfilled it more completely by nourishing the community I had come to love from a distance. The gardeners who tended the property, the neighbors who gathered the fruit, the birds and insects that found shelter in its canopy, all formed a complex ecosystem that thrived regardless of my presence or absence.

In the DC area, surrounded by monuments built to commemorate human achievement, I would sometimes find myself thinking about my mango tree, standing sentinel by the Caribbean Sea. The contrast was striking — here were structures designed to defy time, to immortalize human names and deeds, while my tree simply existed, unconcerned with legacy or remembrance, perfectly content in its temporality.

My mango tree taught me to hold my possessions lightly, to recognize that ownership is often just an illusion we maintain to feel secure in an uncertain world. Those mangoes were never truly "mine" to begin with; they belonged to the moment, to whoever was present to appreciate them when they ripened. There was a strange comfort in this knowledge, a release from the burden of trying to control or contain experiences that were meant to be shared.

As I aged, I began to view my life through the lens of this understanding. Like the mangoes I never tasted, many opportunities would come and go without my participation. Some doors would open when I was looking elsewhere; some seasons of abundance would coincide with my absence. And yet, the world would continue its beautiful unfolding, with or without my witness.

I slowly came to understand that missing out is not always a failure, but often simply part of being human. There's a quiet grace in accepting that life doesn't wait for our readiness. It moves to rhythms larger than our calendars, offering its gifts on timelines not always aligned with our reach. For every moment I missed, another opened up for someone else. For every opportunity I passed by, I found myself seeking fulfillment in a different way.

There were times when I stood still while everything bloomed around me, and I felt the ache of invisibility. But in that stillness, I also discovered the beauty of witnessing rather than possessing, of being a small part of something endlessly vast. I began to carry my regrets not as burdens, but as gentle reminders that life is not meant to be fully captured, only touched, however briefly, in the passing.

And so, I walk forward, not with urgency, but with reverence. The mangoes will ripen again, likely during our absence. And there will be other blooms in the yard of my home in America. The world will go on offering its fruit, its doors, its light, and I will continue learning how to see, even if I do not always arrive in time to taste.

Bosses

One of my former supervisors was, in my experience, both abusive and discriminatory. As an English Language Arts teacher of Taiwanese descent with a non-American accent, I was frequently subjected to mistreatment that I believe was rooted in racism and prejudice. He would enter my classroom unannounced multiple times a day, insisting that my lesson plans be laid out on my desk so he could scrutinize whether they aligned with my teaching in real time. Both he and the school principal claimed these visits were part of a broader effort to help teachers refine their instructional methods and prepare for various classroom situations, but the frequency and tone of his visits suggested otherwise.

"Mr. Thompson will be joining us for this class period. Let's see which team wins." I smiled at the class and my boss, Mr. Thompson, but my eyes were ice-cold.

"Mrs. Lozeron has the best plan. Please listen." Mr. Thompson yelled at the boisterous scholars, demanding they stay in their seats, raise their hands to speak, and speak only when permitted.

I created a classroom disciplinary plan to enforce school rules and expectations, posting the plan, seating chart, and group rotation schedule on my classroom wall, just so everything was "in writing," in addition to my verbal instructions. But that wasn't good enough. Mr. Thompson insisted that no student would abide by the rules unless I became a "royal nasty," a bully to the students. He stood by this conviction, behaving like the biggest tormentor on campus everywhere he went, intimidating both teachers and students alike.

I was traumatized by Mr. Thompson's ghost-like appearances on campus, his booming yet far from sonorous voice barking orders, and his cynical criticisms of everything I did or did not do. "Why are you calling each student to your desk to examine his performance data? Why didn't you share student data to encourage student learning growth?" From him, I learned nothing but the kind of fear that makes people weak. I was afraid of him, and I was unsure of the educational system's true consequences. To me, Mr. Thompson was nothing more than pure evil, eviscerating any semblance of hope.

Mr. Thompson's toxic, authoritarian leadership used fear to maintain control. His actions, seemingly rooted in personal biases and a lack of empathy, created an environment where I felt anxious, powerless and demoralized. His constant surveillance and unrealistic demands captured a leadership style that stifled creativity and destroyed creativity and confidence.

The days I saw his silver Lexus pull into the faculty parking lot, my stomach would knot instantly. I'd check my lesson plans twice, three times, scanning for any detail he might criticize. The other teachers understood without words — we'd exchange glances in the hallway that communicated volumes about our shared dread. Some days, I would rehearse my lessons at home, standing in front of my bathroom mirror, anticipating his interruptions and preparing rebuttals to criticisms.

Once, during a novel unit with my sophomore class, Mr. Thompson stormed in just as a student was sharing a particularly vulnerable piece about her immigrant parents. He cut her off mid-sentence to lecture me about proper annotation techniques. The girl never volunteered to read aloud again. That afternoon, I sat and cried in my car before driving home, questioning whether teaching was worth this systematic humiliation.

My colleagues suggested I file a complaint, but the principal was Thompson's longtime friend, their offices connected by a private door that was almost always open. The few teachers who had complained in the past found themselves with the most difficult class assignments the following year. So, I kept my head down and developed a second self: a performer who could smile thinly while being belittled, who could nod appreciatively at nonsensical criticism, who could apologize for imaginary infractions.

The irony was that my students' test scores were improving under my guidance. My classroom management, despite not conforming to Thompson's "royal nasty" approach, resulted in fewer disciplinary referrals than other teachers. Parents requested my advice for their children, and former students would stop by to thank me years later. None of this mattered to Thompson. In his world, control was the only measure of success, and my refusal to break student spirits as he had broken mine was an unforgivable act of rebellion.

Another boss of mine, Joe, adored me. He was meticulously fussy, always quick to notice if I was even slightly late for a meeting or event. He frequently asked me to speak or share at team gatherings, his eyes often scanning the room in search of me. Though we spoke only occasionally, there was an undeniable sense of attachment. I felt ambivalent about his attention. On one hand, I believed it took a discerning eye to recognize unique talent. He saw something in me — like a Chollima, the mythic winged horse that could travel a thousand li (about 310 miles) in a day — the finest among his subordinates. On the other hand, I found myself avoiding his gaze, thinking I was too swift and too elegant for a mere mortal like him.

"It boggles my mind how Joe appreciates you," a co-worker said, clearly feeling jealous.

"Why on earth are you saying that?" I feigned ignorance.

"Don't you see it? He always asks about you."

"Well, he doesn't really know me."

"At least, he sees your capability."

"I don't think he has any idea what talents I have."

That's how I felt: Joe was nice to everyone, but he paid particular attention to me. While I was comfortable around him, I didn't feel that my potential was truly acknowledged or developed. He didn't nurture me; instead, he hypocritically advanced his own reputation by being a "nice" boss. While Joe had positive intentions, he lacked the depth needed to truly develop my potential. His leadership was superficial; kindness alone didn't translate into real mentorship or empowerment.

Joe's office door was always open, a physical manifestation of his self-proclaimed "open-door policy." His walls were adorned with motivational posters featuring eagles soaring over mountain peaks and teams of climbers reaching summits. He collected inspirational quotes like some people collect stamps, deploying them in emails and meetings with religious fervor. "Remember, team, as John Maxwell says, 'A leader is one who knows the way, goes the way, and shows the way.'" He would beam after such pronouncements, expecting appreciative nods.

At school functions, Joe would place his hand on my shoulder, introducing me to executives from other departments. "This is my star performer," he would say, though he had never once observed my work in detail or asked about my process. The praise felt hollow, disconnected from any meaningful understanding of my contributions or capabilities. It was as if I were a trophy he could display, proof of his excellence as a manager of talent.

When I completed projects ahead of schedule or developed innovative solutions, Joe would claim partial credit during leadership meetings. "We came up with this approach together," he would say, though our collaborative sessions had consisted of him nodding vaguely while checking his phone as I outlined my ideas. Later, he'd email me a generic "Great job!" with no specifics about what had impressed him.

I once approached him with a proposal for a development program I wanted to pursue. It would require a modest investment, some days away from school and some flexibility in my schedule. Joe listened, smiling continuously, then said, "That sounds wonderful. You're exactly the kind of self-starter we need around here!" But the approval never materialized, and when I followed up, he seemed surprised I had expected concrete action to follow our conversation.

His superficial support was, in some ways, more insidious than Mr. Thompson's direct hostility. At least with Thompson, I knew where I stood. Joe's leadership style was a mirage, promising nourishment but delivering empty calories. His need to be liked translated into a form of management that prioritized appearance over substance. He was beloved by executives for maintaining a "positive team environment," but under his guidance, true growth was unattainable.

Then there was Leo, another boss who admired and tried to befriend me. He showed an even more intense level of attachment than Joe. At a company party, he planted a kiss on my mouth. Had he not been tipsy, I would have accused him of harassment. Leo blurred the line between professional admiration and personal boundaries. His actions seemed to reflect a more personal attachment, but he lacked respect for boundaries and professionalism. Despite the incident, I didn't consider Leo unkind or malicious — he was harmless, and I liked the fact that a boss liked me.

Outside of the bosses who hated or loved me, I barely remember any others. They simply left no impression on my life.

Leo's office was a shrine to casual corporate culture: a foosball table crammed beside his desk, a mini-fridge stocked with craft beers, walls plastered with photos of team-building retreats where he invariably had his arm around someone's shoulder. He dressed like the magazines told him successful marketing executives should dress — expensive jeans, button-downs with subtle patterns, designer sneakers that cost more than my monthly co-op payment.

"We're a family here," Leo would announce at the start of every all-hands meeting. He insisted on Friday happy hours that stretched long into the evening, where attendance wasn't mandatory in name but was clearly tracked in practice. Those who left early or skipped these gatherings altogether found themselves subtly excluded from important conversations the following week.

Leo's attention made me uncomfortable long before the kiss incident. He would text on weekends with questions that could have waited until Monday. When I spoke or presented at meetings, his eyes never left my face, his attention so intense it felt like a physical weight. He remembered details about my personal life I had mentioned only in passing: my favorite wine, a book I'd enjoyed, my nickname, the name of my childhood friend.

The kiss came at a marketing campaign launch celebration. We had secured consistent revenue growth, and Leo had ordered champagne for the office. As the evening progressed and most colleagues had departed for home, he cornered me near the elevators, swaying slightly, eyes unfocused.

"You're the reason we celebrate," he slurred, though I had played only a minor role in the campaign. Before I could respond, he leaned in, his lips grazing mine. I stepped back, making a joke about his champagne consumption, desperately trying to normalize the moment rather than acknowledge its inappropriateness.

The next day, Leo acted as if nothing had happened. But something had shifted in our dynamic. I began declining one-on-one meetings, insisting on having others present. I stopped sharing personal anecdotes, keeping our interactions strictly professional. If he noticed these changes, he never mentioned them. Perhaps in his mind, the incident had been innocent, forgettable, the kind of meaningless interaction that powerful men have always been allowed to dismiss.

What troubled me most was not Leo's behavior, though it was certainly problematic, but my own response to it. I had minimized the transgression, made excuses for him, worried about damaging his reputation or creating workplace tension. I had prioritized his comfort over my boundaries. This pattern felt familiar — a lifetime of accommodating male authority, of smoothing over uncomfortable moments to maintain harmony, of questioning my right to feel violated.

The best leader and teacher is the one who draws subordinates or learners out, encourages them, coaches them, praises them, and guides them along a path to success. Leadership isn't just about authority but about creating environments where people can thrive. I had yet to encounter a supervisor who embodied this ideal. Instead, I taught myself. I was my own boss.

In the absence of true mentorship, I became my own guide. I set ambitious personal benchmarks and celebrated when I reached them. I sought feedback from peers whose judgment I trusted rather than waiting for meaningful evaluation from above. I studied leadership books not to collect quotable soundbites like Joe, but to understand the principles that create environments where talent flourishes.

In organizations ostensibly structured to nurture professional growth, I had found the greatest development by turning inward. My most significant lessons came from observing what not to do, from identifying the gaps in my supervisors' approaches and filling them with my own explanations and solutions.

Perhaps the greatest insight I gained from my parade of discouraging bosses was this: leadership is not a title but a practice. It requires continuous learning, genuine curiosity about the people in your care, and the humility to admit when you've missed the mark. It demands the courage to set high standards without resorting to fear or complacency, and the wisdom to recognize that different individuals require different approaches and considerations.

When I eventually found myself in leadership positions, these experiences informed me of every decision. I vowed never to make someone feel as small as Mr. Thompson had made me feel, as overlooked as Joe had made me feel, or as uncomfortable as Leo had made me feel. I committed to seeing the people who reported to me — truly seeing them, their unique talents and challenges, their aspirations and concerns.

The best leaders, I realized, don't create followers; they create more leaders. They don't demand respect through intimidation or superficial praise or inappropriate familiarity. They earn it by demonstrating integrity, by showing genuine interest in others' development, by recognizing potential and creating conditions where it can be fulfilled.

Until I encountered such a leader, I would continue to be that person for myself. And perhaps, someday, for others who found themselves adrift in the same leaderless wilderness I had navigated. The journey had been lonely at times, but it had forged in me a resilience and self-reliance I might never have discovered under more nurturing conditions. For that unintended gift, I could almost thank my parade of discouraging bosses — almost, but not quite.

Recurring Bad Dreams and the Journey Toward Self-Acceptance

There were nights when I would sleep soundly, with nothing more than the faint murmur of my subconscious drifting through my mind, but there were other nights when I would wake with my heart racing, soaked in sweat, and gripped by an overwhelming sense of dread. These were the nights when I dreamed of math — more specifically, when I dreamed of math tests. I could feel the weight of them long after I had opened my eyes and found myself lying in the safety of my bed. The echoes of my panic, the crushing feeling of inadequacy, would linger as though my very soul had been pinned down by the terrifying specter of failure.

In these nightmares, I would find myself sitting at a desk, paper scattered before me like an open battlefield. The questions on the test were impossibly complicated, full of equations and formulas that had once been foreign to me. I would stare at the paper in horror, unable to recall a single formula, my mind a blank slate. My breath quickened as I frantically searched for some semblance of understanding, but it was as if the very concepts of math had betrayed me. The numbers and symbols on the page swirled in a dizzying, incomprehensible dance, like a cruel game where the rules had been lost.

In that moment, I could almost hear the laughter of the universe. If Einstein himself had appeared beside me, he would have seen me as an absurdity, an intellectual void. I was the product of a brain that could navigate the complexities of the humanities with ease, but was paralyzed by most things even vaguely related to mathematics. The world of formulas and rigid structures left me floundering. My mind rebelled against its limitations, and the nightmare played out in endless cycles of failure, of freezing in place while the clock ticked away, audibly condemning me.

As a child, I had always been drawn to books, to the worlds of history, literature, and art. I lost myself in stories and ideas, consumed by the vibrant array of cultures, philosophies, and perspectives that spanned across centuries. Math, on the other hand, felt like a distant planet, its gravity non-existent for me to grasp. I wasn't bad with numbers, having learned to calculate quickly on an abacus when I was little. I could do simple arithmetic in my head, computing sums and differences with ease. But as soon as I encountered anything more complex — algebra, calculus, geometry — I lost my patience. The problem wasn't that I couldn't understand math; it was that I never really tried to understand it. I ignored the homework, skipped the practice, preferring the company of the written word to the cold precision of numbers or formulas.

In many ways, I had convinced myself that math was an irrelevant distraction, a weakness I could afford to ignore. But the nightmares, years after my formal education had ended, told a different story. The horror I felt when confronted with a math test wasn't just fear of failure; it was a deep-seated anxiety about the limitations I had chosen to accept. It was as if I had become afraid to face something that, in the grand scheme of things, didn't even matter that much to me. Still, the perfectionist in me — the part that couldn't tolerate inadequacy — demanded mastery, even in areas where my interest was minimal.

But these nightmares weren't only about math. There were other dreams, dreams that reflected a much deeper, more existential fear. Sometimes, I found myself running through endless hallways, desperately seeking an escape, but no matter how hard I tried, I couldn't find a door. The walls closed in on me, and I was suffocated not by physical space, but by the emotional weight of the situation. In these dreams, the faces around me would morph into those of people I knew intimately: my family, my friends, my loved ones. Their expressions were filled with anger, indifference, or frustration. It was as though I had been abandoned by the very people I loved, trapped by their inability, or unwillingness, to offer support for a way out of my confinement, or my path to freedom.

It wasn't just the physical space that constricted me; it was the emotional space. I was cornered by expectations I had placed on myself, by roles I felt I had to fill, by the nagging pressure to be everything to everyone. The fear of suffocation wasn't only about being trapped in a room; it was about being suffocated by the idea of living a life that wasn't my own, a life where I was stifled by the weight of others' desires or the limitations I had set for myself. I feared losing my own purpose, becoming a shadow of what I truly wanted to be.

I've always been someone who values freedom — intellectually and emotionally. The thought of being trapped in a mundane, predictable life has always terrified me. It was never about wealth or status; it was about purpose. I needed to feel that my life had meaning, that I was using my talents and passions to make a difference, even if that difference seemed small or personal in the eyes of others. I feared that if I didn't pursue my dreams with conviction, I'd be swallowed by the expectations and routines of daily life. The suffocating dreams I often had were reflections of that fear, a fear of drifting toward a life devoid of passion and fulfillment.

But it wasn't just the suffocating dreams that haunted me. There were others that seemed almost trivial, yet they too carried deep emotional weight. One recurring theme in my nightmares was the desperate need to use a public restroom. The urgency of the situation was palpable — my body would ache with discomfort, but I couldn't find a restroom in time. When I finally did reach a restroom, there were always people ahead of me in line, blocking my path. The fear that I wouldn't be able to relieve myself in time, both physically and emotionally, was overwhelming, to say the least.

These restroom dreams felt like a metaphor for the things I was neglecting in my life. I had emotional needs, desires, and ambitions that I was ignoring, telling myself that I didn't have time for them, or that they didn't matter. The long waits in line, the sense of powerlessness as I struggled to reach the bathroom in time, symbolized how I was putting off addressing my own needs — whether they were creative, intellectual, or emotional. I was putting others before myself, and in doing so, I was preventing myself from reaching the emotional relief I craved.

As I reflected on these recurring nightmares, I realized that there were patterns emerging, patterns that connected the anxiety I felt in my waking life with the fears that surfaced in my sleep. The math nightmares symbolized insecurity and fear of failure, while the suffocation dreams reflected my longing for freedom and self-expression. The restroom dreams were a reminder that I was neglecting my own emotional needs, allowing myself to become overwhelmed by external pressures. These dreams were not just random, disjointed fears; they were signs that I was struggling with the tension between self-acceptance and perfectionism, between independence and conformity.

The more I examined these dreams, the more I began to understand them not as haunting, inescapable nightmares, but as messages. They were calling me to embrace my limitations, to accept that I didn't have to be perfect at everything, especially in areas that didn't truly resonate with me. They were urging me to prioritize what mattered most: my passions, my need for intellectual and emotional freedom, my desire to create and explore.

I realized that, in many ways, my dreams were offering me a path forward. The key to unlocking the suffocating grip of these nightmares lay in accepting that I couldn't do everything, that it was okay not to excel in every area of life. The freedom I craved was not about escaping the pressures of life but about making choices that aligned with my authentic self. I didn't need to be a mathematical genius, but I did need to find fulfillment in the things that made me come alive: writing, reading, exploring the humanities.

The nightmares, frightening as they were, had served a purpose. They revealed the places where I was holding myself back, clinging to perfectionism and fear. They exposed the tension between my longing for freedom, the guilt I carried for choosing a life centered on myself, and the fear of being trapped by the mundane — by expectations, routines, or other people. In their unsettling way, the nightmares taught me that true freedom isn't found in escaping life's pressures, but in facing them with courage, self-care, and self-compassion.

I began to understand that waking up from these dreams wasn't just about escaping the fear or guilt; they were a call to action, a wake-up call to start living more authentically. It became clear that the nightmares weren't merely obstacles to be overcome or illusions to be dismissed, but instead, they were powerful signals, urging me to pay attention to something deeper within myself. They were a reminder that true freedom couldn't be found by merely avoiding fear or running from discomfort, but by confronting those emotions head-on and making deliberate, conscious choices that I need to be comfortable with.

The answers, I realized, were not buried in the nightmares themselves, but rather in the choices I made when I was awake — how I responded to the challenges life presented, how I treated myself and others, and how I aligned my actions with my inner values. I began to see that I had the power to change, to evolve, and to build a life that reflected my true self. The freedom I so desperately sought wasn't about escaping the things that scared me, but about embracing who I truly was — with all my strengths and limitations — and making peace with the imperfect, evolving journey I was on.

This was the ultimate release, the real escape from the suffocating grip of fear or guilt. It wasn't a sudden, dramatic transformation, but rather a gradual process of waking up to my own truth, of living with intention, and of allowing myself the space to continuously grow. In doing so, I found a sense of freedom that no dream or nightmare could ever take away, a freedom rooted in authenticity and acceptance.

As long as I live authentically, pursuing what I'm passionate about, I can live up to my dreams.

Bongo Drum, Ukulele, Guitar, and Piano

The bongo drum quickly became my new love. Ever since my husband and I started spending winter holidays at our vacation house in Belize, I've been captivated by this Afro-Cuban percussion instrument. The rhythmic patterns, the vibrant beats, and the way the sound connects to the soul have an undeniable charm. I knew little about its origins in Eastern Cuba, but I quickly learned how the bongo drum became popular across the Americas, particularly in Latin America, as its syncopated rhythms seamlessly blended with various musical styles. This instrument has a rich history, from its use in religious ceremonies in Africa to its eventual migration to Cuba, where it evolved into a prominent component of Latin jazz and dance music. I was drawn to the way Latin music fused with jazz and other genres, from bachata to Latin rock. The beats of the bongo are so jolly and cheery that I often felt happy whenever I heard this type of music in the Caribbean neighborhood. It was as if the lively sound of the bongos was inviting me to join the celebration.

Bongos consist of a pair of open-bottomed hand drums of different sizes: the larger hembra ('female') and the smaller macho ('male'), joined by a bridge. The difference in size creates a distinctive pitch, with the hembra providing a deeper tone and the macho delivering a higher, sharper sound. I loved the way they're played with bare hands, held between the legs. There's something intimate about how the player's body connects with the instrument — each tap and slap resonates through the fingertips. The portability of the bongos made them even more alluring. I imagined myself carrying the instrument around, ready to join impromptu jam sessions with friends and strangers alike. The rhythmic possibilities felt endless, and the more I played, the more I understood that I had to get better at it to truly embrace the joy. I wasn't just learning an instrument; I was learning to feel the music in a deeper, more instinctive way.

Another instrument I grew fond of was the ukulele. I had always been charmed by its cheerful, playful sound, but it wasn't until I had more vacation time in the tropics that I truly fell in love with it. I played thousands of songs on it and always felt like there wasn't enough time to play more. The ukulele, of Portuguese origin, was brought to Hawaii by Portuguese immigrants in the 19th century, and it quickly became woven into the cultural fabric of the islands. It's an instrument that invites easy playfulness, and the ukulele's joyful strumming was the perfect companion for the laid-back island atmosphere of Belize. I loved the varied tones and volumes that different sizes and constructions offered: soprano, concert, tenor, and baritone. Each ukulele has its own voice, with the soprano being bright and sweet, the concert adding warmth, the tenor offering a deeper resonance, and the baritone having a rich, mellow tone that almost echoes the sound of a guitar.

Part of the joy of playing the ukulele came from how easy it was to learn, especially compared to my brief forays into guitar and piano. I had always admired guitarists, but my own attempts usually ended with sore fingertips and frustration over tricky chord changes. The ukulele, by contrast, felt forgiving and accessible. Its smaller neck and fewer strings made it easier to handle, and the learning curve was far less steep. I could strum along to my favorite songs with minimal effort, which brought a sense of instant gratification.

The piano, on the other hand, had always felt like a slow, methodical climb, each note a test of patience and muscle memory. The ukulele was a breath of fresh air: simple, yet full of creative possibility. While guitar and piano demanded more discipline and time, the ukulele was about enjoying the process, not racing toward perfection. It became a joyful escape, a reminder that music doesn't have to be difficult to be meaningful and beautiful.

I sang along with the island strum or more technical strums, happy as a flea. The term "ukulele" is believed to come from the Hawaiian words uku (gift) and lele (to jump), which is said to describe the joyful and lively nature of the instrument.

In Hawaiian, the word roughly translates to "jumping flea," an amusing analogy that captures the ukulele's light, hopping quality. While I may have been insignificant as a flea in terms of virtuosity, I was still incredibly happy with my music. The ukulele became my little companion, whether strumming by the sea or playing along to the rhythm of life. There's something about the simplicity of the instrument that speaks to the soul, and I cherished every moment I spent with it.

The guitar was an instrument I had a complicated relationship with. It was always in the background of my musical journey, never quite as accessible as the ukulele, but always alluring. The guitar's deep, resonant sound could convey so much emotion, from tender ballads to energetic rock anthems. My first encounters with it were difficult, filled with sore fingertips and clumsy finger placements. The calluses that formed on my hands were a constant reminder of the discipline the guitar demanded. Unlike the ukulele, where the strings felt soft and the chords felt within reach, the guitar required more strength and finesse. But over time, I developed a deeper respect for it. It was an instrument that demanded patience, but in return, it gifted me with the ability to create a full, layered sound. The guitar became a challcngc I wasn't ready to give up on, even though it would take time for me to overcome it. Each new chord I mastered brought me closer to the music I had always dreamed of playing.

I had always loved the sound of the piano — the way it could evoke both elegance and raw emotion. But when it came to playing it, I struggled. The sheer complexity of it was overwhelming at times. Unlike the more tactile nature of the ukulele or the guitar, where you could easily feel your way through the music, the piano required a different kind of coordination. My fingers often fumbled on the keys, and I felt like I was trying to piece together a puzzle that I just couldn't solve. However, there was beauty in the struggle. Each lesson, each new piece I tackled, felt like a victory. The piano had a way of teaching me patience, of reminding me that true mastery required practice and persistence. While it was more demanding, it was also more rewarding when the music finally came together for me.

In the end, each of these instruments taught me something different. The bongo drum was all about rhythm and freedom, the ukulele about joy and simplicity, the guitar about perseverance and depth, and the piano about precision and expression. Together, they formed a colorful mosaic of musical experiences, each one adding a layer to my understanding of music. Whether playing alone or with others, I knew that music was a gift that I would treasure for years to come.

As I moved through different seasons of life, these instruments became reliable companions. In moments of celebration, they amplified my joy; in times of solitude, they offered comfort and release. Each note I played became a thread in the fabric of my personal journey, stitching together memories, emotions, and discoveries. The discipline of practice, the thrill of performance, and the immense satisfaction of creating something beautiful — all of it deepened my appreciation not just for music, but for the process of learning and growing.

Now, whenever my fingers brush across the keys or strum a familiar chord, I'm reminded of how far I've come, not just musically, but personally. These instruments gave me more than music; they taught me patience, creativity, confidence, and connection. And though I may explore new sounds and styles in the future, the foundation they've given me will always remain. Music, to me, is not just an art form; it's a lifelong conversation, one that I'm still joyfully learning to speak.

Teachers: The Backbone of Society

Teachers should be among the most celebrated people in the world. Unfortunately, they don't always get the credit they deserve. The immense commitment and sacrifice that teachers make on a daily basis often go unnoticed, leaving their hard work and dedication unappreciated. It's not easy. I don't even know how teachers manage it day in and day out. Personally, I found it to be overwhelming, emotionally and physically taxing. Yet, despite the exhaustion, teachers continue because we care deeply. We invest everything we have in our students' futures, no matter what the toll it takes on ourselves. My husband often says that if he were a teacher, there would be injured bodies in the classroom. "They couldn't pay me enough to do it," he jokes. While my pay wasn't great, I was fortunate to be among the highest-paid teachers in my district, thanks to my degrees, credentials and seniority. But it wasn't about the money. It was about the impact on the students.

I vividly remember how my students would either drive me insane or leave me in awe. Despite arming myself with a toolbox of strategies and a parade of antics, I often felt that I fell short of the job's expectations. As a teacher, I had to wear many hats: curriculum designer, lesson planner, presenter, actor, assessor, tester, grader, comedian, psychoanalyst, event coordinator, activity host, classroom decorator, inventory manager, and above all, babysitter. But somehow, I survived and made my mark.

My students at the secondary school level were especially challenging. They were at that delicate stage in life when everything felt like a crisis. Puberty's hormonal changes manifested in their physical development, mood swings, teenage angst, and constant self-centered anxiety. While I did my best to guide them and instill a love of learning, there was only so much a teacher could do. Adolescence was a storm, and they had to weather it themselves. In the end, some of my students went on to become remarkable people, while others remained in the grip of their personal struggles. But as teachers, we are happy even with the smallest shift in a single student, whether it's in knowledge, character, or human connection. That's what keeps us going. That's the light that shines through the exhaustion and the chaos.

My college students and adult government officer trainees, by contrast, came from diverse backgrounds. Some were sophisticated thinkers, capable of researching and analyzing complex issues with depth and insight. Others, however, resembled grown-up versions of uncertain teenagers, often in need of reassurance and guidance at every step. Regardless of their strengths or shortcomings, each brought a unique set of life experiences to the classroom. Together, they reflected the broader world — full of individuals carrying their own problems, hopes, dreams, setbacks, and accomplishments. In many ways, teaching them felt like navigating a microcosm of society itself.

While teaching in America is a profession that requires a special combination of resilience and optimism, it is a respected and revered position in Taiwan and many other Asian countries. In those places, students look up to their teachers as masters, and society places a great emphasis on education. But not in America. Here, the education system needs reform. Simply getting rid of the Department of Education is far from the answer. We need substantial change and deep investment in our educators. Teaching requires an extraordinary combination of skills, emotional resilience, and dedication. Teachers should be treated like the professionals they are, not be seen as people who simply "can't do anything else." It's disheartening when some teachers display childish behavior that mirrors that of their students, perpetuating the damaging stereotype: "Those who can't, teach." This perception thrives when teachers are under-resourced, underappreciated, and unsupported. Perhaps some teachers are so confined in the educational world that they fail to realize there's a whole world outside of it. Teachers should be celebrated, not demeaned, for their dedication and the vital role they play in shaping future generations.

Having seen firsthand the challenges teachers face in America, it's clear that structural reforms are necessary to better support educators and students alike. To improve the American educational system, several specific changes could be made to better support teachers, students, and the overall learning environment. These changes would not only elevate the teaching profession but would ensure a higher quality education for our learners. Here are some of the critical areas where reform could have a significant impact:

1. Increased Teacher Compensation and Benefits

Teachers deserve to be paid what they are worth. In many parts of the U.S., teacher salaries are not aligned with the amount of work, time, and emotional investment required for the job. Competitive salaries would not only help attract and retain high-quality educators but also show society's true appreciation for their work. Comprehensive benefits, including secure long-term contracts, affordable healthcare, mental health support, and retirement plans, would help reduce burnout and ensure teachers' well-being.

2. Professional Development and Ongoing Training

Teachers need access to continuous professional development opportunities. Rather than a one-time certification, there should be ongoing workshops, seminars, and training programs that focus on new teaching methodologies, technological advancements, classroom resources, management strategies, and emotional intelligence. Teachers should also be provided with more opportunities to collaborate with colleagues, share best practices, and learn from one another. This will help them stay motivated, inspired, and at the top of their game.

3. Smaller Class Sizes

Smaller class sizes would allow teachers to give more individualized attention to students, tailor lessons to their needs, and create a more intimate and supportive classroom environment. This would reduce stress for teachers and help them build stronger relationships with their students. Smaller groups would also provide more meaningful connections and offer students the attention they need to develop intellectually, emotionally and socially. This would create an environment where both teachers and students thrive.

4. Increased Support Staff

Many teachers are overburdened with administrative tasks that take away from their time spent teaching. Increasing the number of support staff (like teaching assistants, counselors, and administrative personnel) could help alleviate some of these burdens. This would allow teachers to focus more on instruction and less on non-teaching duties, ultimately leading to better learning experience for students.

5. Improved Teacher Accountability and Evaluation

Instead of relying solely on student test scores to evaluate teachers, there should be a more holistic approach to accountability. This could include peer evaluations, self-assessments, and evaluations based on long-term student growth, engagement, and other qualitative measures. Teachers should be given clear, constructive feedback and resources to improve their practice. It's also essential to trust teachers' autonomy and professional judgment. Rather than top-down evaluations, there should be space for teachers to collaborate, share insights, and take ownership of their professional growth.

6. Mental Health and Emotional Support for Teachers and Students

Teachers often deal with the emotional and behavioral issues of their students, which can be draining. Schools should offer mental health support services, not just for students but also for teachers. Programs focusing on teachers' mental health and stress management could make a huge difference in preventing burnout and ensuring that teachers remain effective in their roles. A mentally balanced, healthy teacher is a more effective teacher.

7. Better Support for Students with Diverse Needs

Special education and English language learners require specialized attention. Schools should ensure that teachers are properly trained to meet the diverse needs of students, and there should be more support in the classroom, such as additional aides or specialized instructors. Every child deserves the opportunity to reach their full potential, and with support, that becomes possible.

8. Curriculum Reform to Focus on Real-World Skills

While academic learning is important, schools should also emphasize teaching practical life skills, such as financial literacy, emotional intelligence, critical thinking, and problem-solving. This would help students better navigate their lives after school and prepare them for real-world challenges.

9. Parent and Community Involvement

Teachers and schools should work in tandem with parents and the broader community to create a supportive learning environment. Schools can implement programs that encourage active parental involvement, including regular communication, workshops, and volunteer opportunities. When parents are involved, students tend to perform better academically and socially.

10. Addressing the Achievement Gap

The persistent achievement gap between students from different socio-economic backgrounds is one of the biggest challenges in the U.S. educational system. Schools must implement more equitable funding models, offer targeted support for students in need, and work to eliminate systemic barriers to education based on race, income, or geography.

11. Increased Investment in School Facilities and Resources

Many public schools lack the resources and facilities to adequately educate their students. This includes outdated textbooks, insufficient technology, and dilapidated buildings. An increase in funding, especially for schools in underfunded districts, would create a more conducive environment for learning and ensure that students have access to the tools and resources needed to succeed.

12. Reform Standardized Testing

Standardized tests should not be the sole measure of a student's success or a teacher's performance. A more balanced approach should focus on long-term student growth — academic, emotional, and social — and evaluate teachers based on their ability to foster this development. By combining standardized testing with assessments of critical thinking, creativity, and practical application of knowledge, we can design a tool for improvement, not as a punitive measure.

Teaching is a labor of love, patience, and perseverance. It plays a demanding and essential role in society yet often goes underappreciated. Teachers have chosen one of the most challenging, yet most impactful, professions in the world. They deserve our respect, proper resources, and the recognition they've long been denied. For the sake of our students, their future, and the future of society, we must give teachers the support they deserve. The time for change is now — teachers deserve better compensation, continuous professional development, mental health support, and a reevaluation of how their performance is measured. Education is the backbone of society, and it is high time we invest in teachers the way they deserve. All in all, the teaching profession is foundational to everything else in the world, and teachers should be celebrated for their dedication. Good teachers deserve the highest recognition, and even those who fall short should be acknowledged as decent human beings with their own flaws. They've chosen a path few would dare to take — and for that, they deserve a resounding 'hurrah.'

Coming to America

By the time I was in my early twenties, I had already accomplished much — earned a master's degree in literature from Taiwan's prestigious Tsinghua University, and was preparing for the next chapter of my academic career at Columbia University in New York City. Coming to America had always been a long-held dream of mine, a vision I'd cherished for years. The dream had been shaped by countless stories, films, and books about the West, and it had driven much of my academic and personal choices. I had chosen to transfer from the Chinese Department to major in Foreign Languages and Literature during my college years. For me, the idea of coming to America, where Western cultures lived and breathed in a way that was different from my own, seemed like an inevitable and exciting next step in my intellectual journey. It wasn't just about education; it was about experiencing another world.

Despite the challenges in my personal life back home in Taiwan, nothing was going to stand in the way of my pursuit. My first love, my boyfriend from Taiwan, had been a significant part of my life for years, but we were going in different directions. He was content with his routine life — a job in sales, a comfortable existence in Taiwan. Meanwhile, I had dreams of a broader life, one filled with the possibility of exploring new cultures, new ideas, and new experiences. I had been waiting for him to finish his mandatory military service so we could continue our path together, but as my plans unfolded, I began to realize that our futures were no longer aligned.

It wasn't my choice to break up; it felt more like a gradual, painful divergence of paths. The emotional wound of our separation was deepened when I discovered, through my sister-in-law's discreet surveillance, that he had already moved on with someone else. The sense of betrayal was jarring, and it left me devastated. To add to that, the physical toll of the breakup was overwhelming — I was so distraught that my body shut down, and I missed my period that month. It was an emotional and physical reaction that made me feel disconnected from the world I had known.

But, as all good journeys do, mine took a new turn. In the midst of this personal crisis, I met Tom — an American expat who was living in Taiwan. Tom was different. He offered me a fresh perspective, a new kind of relationship, and ultimately, he became my first husband. Together, we embarked on a journey to America, but it wasn't a straightforward path. Our journey was filled with detours. First, we traveled through multiple countries, experiencing different cultures, before finally landing in the United States. In many ways, this global journey was symbolic of my larger exploration of the world, one that wasn't just about reaching a destination, but about the experiences and growth that happened along the way.

Coming to America was not merely a change in geographical location; it marked the beginning of my personal transformation. It was the start of a process of self-discovery and cultural exploration. The things I had learned in Taiwan, whether through academic study or personal relationships and experiences, were only the foundation. Coming to America was an opportunity to expand my worldview, to question my identity, and to reshape my understanding of who I was and what the world could offer.

The process of arriving in America was overwhelming at first, like stepping into an entirely new world. I arrived at the airport feeling like a fearless adventurer, dressed in loose, comfortable clothing and carrying nothing but a single carry-on bag. It was the perfect metaphor for how I approached the world: a blank slate, ready to be filled with new ideas and experiences. I wasn't just traveling for the sake of sightseeing; I was driven by a deep curiosity.

For instance, in Thailand, I wondered about the differences in the intonation of greetings between men and women. I marveled at how the temples in Thailand had a distinct architectural style compared to the ones in Taiwan, and I found myself drawn to the intricate details of Buddha images and how they varied from one culture to the next. My curiosity didn't stop there. I thought about the strange and complex ways people lived and worked.

I was fascinated by the Monkey Market in Cambodia, where monkeys were gathered, killed, dried, and cured for various purposes — whether medicinal, recreational, or simply for display. What cultural practices lay behind such activities? Also in Cambodia, I stood in awe at the grandiose Angkor Wat, a sprawling temple complex that stretched across over four hundred acres. The engineering behind it fascinated me. How had King Suryavarman II, who commissioned its construction almost a thousand years ago, managed to create such an extraordinary structure? Was it influenced by other cultural architectural styles, such as those that might have been seen by Zheng He, the Ming Dynasty's famous admiral, during his travels? These were the questions that occupied my mind, as I sought to understand the connections between cultures and history.

In places like Vietnam, I was equally fascinated by the rich blend of culture and history. I found myself wondering why some Vietnamese women, despite their petite stature, were known for their fierce, combat-ready mentality. What social dynamics or historical events had shaped such a unique cultural characteristic?

And then, there were the iconic sights that held a romantic, almost mystical significance in my mind — places like the Charles Bridge in Prague, the Champs-Élysées in Paris, and the Danube River, which flowed through several European countries, each with its own historical and cultural impact. These places seemed to resonate deeply with me, evoking a sense of wonder and longing. I didn't just visit these places; I absorbed them, seeking to understand the stories they told, and to discover my place within this vast, interconnected world.

I entered the United States from the East Coast, traveling westward from Taiwan through several countries before finally landing in Atlanta, Georgia. My first impression was that Coca-Cola truly was one of America's most iconic symbols. From the giant Coca-Cola sign in Atlanta to its constant presence in popular media, it felt as though every corner of American life was infused with the brand. Movies, Coca-Cola, and shopping malls — were the images of America I had seen in the media.

But as I settled into life in New York City, and later in Las Vegas and the D.C. area, I began to see that America was far more than its commercialized image. It is an incredibly diverse country, with distinct cultural, social, and geographical identities that vary not only from region to region but from person to person.

New York City, where I spent over a decade of my life, became my first true American home. It was a city filled with opportunities for growth, exploration, and cultural exchange. It was there that I fully embraced the diversity of the American experience: the different accents, cuisines, traditions, and values that make up this complex country. Moving to the West Coast, then back to the Metro DC Area, I was constantly learning, evolving, and deepening my understanding of America's complexity.

In the end, coming to America was more than just about reaching a destination or pursuing higher education. It was about a personal evolution, about moving beyond my previous understandings of who I was and who I could become. It was about the ever-deepening process of learning from the world around me, while also understanding that some things take time.

I had learned that true understanding of a place, a culture, or even a person, is not achieved through first impressions or surface-level experiences. It takes time, patience, and a willingness to immerse oneself fully in the journey. And for me, America, with all its contradictions, struggles, and triumphs, would forever remain intertwined with the idea of liberty, diversity, and the continuous pursuit of self-discovery.

Coming to America means, in many ways, coming to the Statue of Liberty. Towering above the New York Harbor, she is more than a monument; she is a promise. Without the democratic values she represents — freedom, equality, and hope — America would not be the nation we know today. Her torch lights the way not just for those arriving at its shores, but for anyone striving to find meaning, purpose, and belonging in a complex world.

In my own journey, America has not only been a destination, but a mirror reflecting both my aspirations and my growth. It has challenged me to confront my assumptions, broaden my perspective, and embrace the beautiful, often messy process of becoming. And in that process, I've come to understand that liberty is not a fixed ideal, but a continuous endeavor — one that requires courage, compassion, and an unwavering belief in the possibility of a better tomorrow.

My Christmas Ponchos

The first year we moved to the Metro DC Area from Las Vegas, my husband Bobby and I were filled with excitement at the prospect of a white Christmas. After spending so many years in the desert, where Christmases were warm, dry, and devoid of snow, the thought of celebrating the holidays in a place where snowflakes fell from the sky felt magical. We had dreamt of this for so long, and now, finally, it was becoming a reality again.

In true holiday spirit, we decided to go all out. We bought two "real" Christmas trees — something we had never done in Las Vegas — adding them to our collection of artificial trees. It felt like a nostalgic throwback to the Christmases I had experienced in New York City, where snow covered the streets, and twinkling lights adorned every window, building, and tree. Our suburban DC home quickly became a winter wonderland.

I carefully arranged the trees, placing one fake tree and one real tree on each of the two stories in our home. Then, the decorations went up — an absolute frenzy of festive cheer. A singing Santa stood proudly in the corner, his jolly voice filling the room with holiday tunes. Another giant, battery-powered Santa, whose belly lit up like a Christmas beacon, perched near the entrance. There were nativity ornaments, multi-colored solar lights, angels hanging delicately from the ceiling, and deer figurines scattered about. Even the bed sheets and blankets were Christmas-themed — red, gold, and green, dotted with snowflakes, Christmas trees, and reindeer.

I couldn't contain my excitement, and my enthusiasm seemed to be contagious. Bobby, who was usually more practical about the holidays, found himself swept up in my joy. He watched as I scurried around, creating the perfect Christmas atmosphere, and even started getting into the spirit himself. One day, as I walked past the front door, I noticed a pile of boxes stacked high. I raised my eyebrows in curiosity.

"What else did you order? Why are there so many boxes at our front door?" I asked, trying to suppress my excitement.

With a mischievous grin, Bobby replied, "This one you can open before Christmas, because we'll use it right away."

What could it be? Perhaps a new holiday decoration or something extra special to add to our collection of Christmas cheer. I eagerly tore into the box, my heart racing with anticipation.

When I pulled out the item, I was slightly taken aback. It wasn't what I had imagined. Instead of a shiny new decoration or a gift for me, it was a Christmas base cloth with embroidered snowmen. It was soft and cozy, but not quite the glamorous holiday gift I had envisioned.

Without missing a beat, I tossed it over my head like a poncho and struck a pose, admiring the cheerful colors and embroidered snowmen.' "Look! It's like a Christmas cape!" I said, twirling around, feeling silly but happy. I was clearly having a little fun with it.

But then I noticed something — this wasn't just any random piece of fabric. It was a Christmas tree base cloth, a necessary, practical gift that Bobby had wisely purchased to help tidy up the bases of our Christmas trees. There was one for each tree, and they fit perfectly. It dawned on me that I had misunderstood the true purpose of the gift. I couldn't help but laugh. I had imagined a shiny, extravagant present, but instead, I had received something functional — and hilariously converted it to what I wanted without a second thought.

I kept wearing it as a poncho for a few moments longer, our laughter echoing through the room. What started as an unexpected moment quickly turned into a heartwarming, silly memory we'd cherish for years to come. Our Christmas tree bases, now elegantly dressed in their snowman-adorned cloths, added a touch of whimsy to our festive decor. In the end, the gift may not have been what I had hoped for, but it became one of the most memorable parts of our holiday preparations.

Every time I look at the trees now, with their snowman base cloths adorning them, I'm reminded of that first Christmas in the Metro DC Area — the snow outside, the warmth inside, and the laughter we shared. What had started as a simple, practical gift turned into a cherished, humorous tradition, reminding us that the holidays are not just about the perfect decorations or the fanciest gifts, but about the joy, the laughter, and the unexpected moments that make each and every Christmas truly special.

DC Oh So Green

DC's foliage was so thick that even in the heart of the city, everything felt lush with life. The air was heavy with the scent of nature, and the city's streets were lined with green — thick, vibrant, and unyielding. Moss grew along the edges of buildings, slowly creeping up their sides in a quiet act of defiance against the stone and steel of urban life. Ferns and tendrils reached for the sky, climbing up walls, intertwining with the city's structures, as if to remind everyone that life, in all its forms, would find a way to thrive. It was as though nature itself had claimed the city, weaving a blanket of greenery that softened the harsh lines of the buildings, turning them into something more organic, more closely connected to the earth.

In the spring, I planted sunflowers in the backyard, starting them from seeds. I watched in awe as they shot up from the earth, growing at an astonishing rate, their green stems pushing higher and higher. By summer, they had reached an incredible height — eight feet tall — and their giant, bright yellow heads stretched toward the sky, smiling at the sun in full glory. The sight of them, standing proudly against the backdrop of our suburban neighborhood, filled me with a sense of wonder. It was simply amazing. The vibrant colors, the sheer size of the sunflowers, the way they swayed in the breeze — it all seemed like a small miracle, a reminder that life could still bloom in unexpected places. The city itself seemed to be alive with promise, its parks expansive and green, its streets lined with trees, offering moments of serenity amid the urban sprawl.

In a way, DC felt like a canvas painted with the colors of nature, a living, breathing testament to the resilience and beauty of the earth. There were moments when I walked through the city, my heart racing and my knees buckling, as I saw the greenery everywhere. It was impossible not to feel a sense of awe when confronted with the thick, vibrant foliage surrounding the monuments, the memorials, and the everyday streets of the city. In these lavish, green spaces, there was a sense of wonder and hope, as if the world, despite everything, was still an exciting place to discover, and maybe, just maybe, everything would be all right.

But even amid all this beauty, there was a shadow that hung over the city. The political climate felt increasingly oppressive, and it was impossible to ignore the weight of it. The excitement and energy of the city's natural beauty were often undercut by the turmoil of the times. The stock market was tumbling, trade wars were erupting with Canada, Mexico, and China, and the political discourse was filled with anger and division. Migrants were being deported to South American countries, funding was being cut for many organizations and elite colleges, and federal employees and contractors were being laid off in record numbers. The economic and political instability seemed to seep into every corner of life, and the sense of optimism that DC's greenery inspired was often overshadowed by the fear and uncertainty in the air.

Some people seemed to embrace the changes, viewing the administration's actions as revolutionary reforms meant to tackle the national deficit. They believed that these changes would ultimately bring about a more efficient government, cutting through the fat and making the country stronger in the long run. "The government is doing great things to reduce waste," one conservative friend remarked, her voice filled with enthusiasm. "They also hire many handsome and beautiful department heads." As I listened to her, I couldn't help but think, *This woman is the queen of philistines*, and I found it extremely difficult to agree with her perspective.

Others, however, were far less optimistic. "See what happened to my husband?" another woman said, her voice tinged with bitterness. "He was leaning toward the right, and then he got laid off — given fifteen minutes to gather his things after thirty years of service. A box was sent to us, containing the rest of his belongings." Her story was a stark reminder of how quickly the tides could turn, how precarious stability had become, and how easily someone's life could be upended by the shifting winds of politics. The weight of that reality began to sink in. No one was immune to the effects of the broader political climate, no matter their ideology or status.

At times, I felt utterly speechless in these kinds of discussions. The deep divide in the country, the tensions between different political factions, left me questioning whether I even had the freedom to speak my mind. Was it safe to speak openly at work? In public? Online? At private gatherings with friends? As the political landscape became more polarized, I felt an overwhelming sense of vulnerability. A deep layer of fear and self-censorship had crept into my life, causing me to retreat inward, unsure of how to navigate the complex web of opinions, fears, and uncertainties that surrounded me. I longed for the clarity of those moments when the world seemed simpler, when the beauty of nature and the city could be enjoyed without the constant backdrop of anxiety.

The tension between the outward optimism of the city's greenery and the underlying anxiety of the political climate was palpable. As I walked through the parks and streets, I couldn't help but reflect on the symbolism of the green around me. The moss, the ferns, the towering trees — each of them felt like a metaphor for resilience and hope, for growth in the face of adversity. Despite the political turmoil, nature continued its work, reminding me that growth could still happen, even in chaotic circumstances or difficult times.

It was almost as if nature itself was in conversation with the political landscape. Just as the city's greenery seemed to thrive and flourish despite the human-made barriers that surrounded it, so too did I find myself holding on to hope, even in the face of uncertainty. My own internal struggle mirrored the contrast between nature's distinct persistence and the political landscape's harsh realities. The cycles of change, the ebb and flow of seasons, became a reminder that nothing, whether in nature or in society, was permanent. Change would come, whether through blooming flowers or through political upheaval.

In March, when the trees were still bare, recovering from the winter's grip, the anticipation of spring felt like a promise. The clocks moved forward an hour, and soon, the days would lengthen, and the city would be bathed in sunlight once again. Spring would arrive, and with it, the promise of green — the leaves would return, and the flowers would bloom. DC would once again be a city of color, a city of life, reminding me that even amid turmoil and uncertainty, renewal was always possible.

This tension between hope and fear, silence and action, became the driving force behind my writing. Should I have been more direct? What actions could I take to make a difference in this turbulent world? How could I continue to engage in the world while still preserving my sense of beauty, humanity, and grace? DC had endured many brutal winters, both literal and metaphorical, yet it always returned more vibrant, more magnificent, more alive. There would be uncertain moments ahead, but I knew that the ability to endure, to find beauty and hope in the midst of hardship, was something I could hold onto — calmly, personally, if nothing much else.

For now, and for every resilient moment to come, I longed for blooms — the giant sunflowers I had planted to bloom again, their bright yellow heads turning toward the sky, full of promise. I longed for better times ahead, for a moment when the green of DC would not just symbolize nature's resilience, but also a collective hope for a better, more unified future America.

DC Drivers

Driving in the Metro DC Area feels like a high-speed race — no one signed up, but everyone's forced to participate in. It's a landscape where speed and aggression rule the road, and the concept of driving etiquette seems to be largely forgotten. Many drivers dart between lanes at breakneck speeds, trying to get ahead by any means necessary. The weaving and swerving between vehicles are done with such reckless abandon that it's hard to believe that safety is even a consideration.

In this madness, the use of turn signals seems to be optional at best. Drivers don't bother to signal their intentions, creating an environment of unpredictable movements. Some drivers don't even weave like a snake, attempting to gracefully maneuver between cars. No, these drivers zip across multiple lanes in a single fluid motion, often cutting off others with little to no regard for the safety of those around them. I've seen drivers cross four, five, even six lanes in a matter of seconds, making moves that leave everyone else around them questioning if they're going to make it through unscathed. It's as if the only thing that matters is getting to the destination as fast as possible, no matter the cost.

Then there are the drivers with malfunctioning headlights or overly bright high beams, who inflict more than a little discomfort on everyone else on the road. It's an especially jarring experience at night or in the early morning, when the blinding lights can reduce your visibility to almost zero. It feels like you're being bathed in light so bright it could be mistaken for a floodlight, casting a harsh glare that makes everything else seem out of focus. You find yourself squinting, hoping that it will end soon, but for what feels like an eternity, you're left helpless, feeling more like an obstacle than a fellow driver.

It's strange how quickly the kindness and consideration of others can disappear once people get behind the wheel. You'd think basic driving etiquette, such as using turn signals, respecting others' space, and adhering to speed limits, would be second nature to everyone. But far too often, it feels like people forget the fundamentals of safe driving once they get into their cars. I can't help but feel disheartened when I witness reckless driving — people speeding without regard for others, weaving through lanes as if it's a game. It's frustrating, and I often have to take a few deep breaths to remind myself that safety matters far more than getting ahead.

When I'm faced with these erratic drivers, I try to stay calm. I slow down, keep my distance, and wait for the chaos to pass. There's no sense in joining the madness. Sometimes, I'm honked at for slowing down or not immediately accelerating when the light turns green. Other times, I find myself honking at someone else who has cut me off, just as a warning that their risky behavior might come with consequences. I remind myself that it's better to err on the side of caution. Better to be the one who warns, than the one who stays silent and risks danger.

While many drivers seem to be in a rush to get to the next place, I find myself trying to approach driving with patience and mindfulness. I aim to follow the flow of traffic, speeding up when necessary, but always with a sense of control. My foot is never too heavy on the pedal; instead, I focus on steering clear of distractions, obstacles, and anything that could pose a danger. For me, driving isn't just about reaching a destination as quickly as possible. It's about getting there safely, with my eyes focused on the road and my hands steadily guiding the steeling wheel.

Driving requires a level of mindfulness. My gaze is constantly scanning my surroundings, my peripheral vision alert to the cars around me, to the pedestrians, to the road signs, and to the traffic lights. It's about being aware of everything that's happening around me and adjusting accordingly. If I let my guard down, even for a moment, I risk losing control of the vehicle, just as in life, if you lose focus for even a second, things can quickly spiral out of control. That's why I'm always alert — whether I'm driving or going through my daily routine.

I've often thought about how driving mirrors life itself. In the same way that I carefully navigate the roads, I try to steer through life with the same level of focus and attention. Both require constant vigilance. Distractions are everywhere, whether in the form of speeding drivers around you, unexpected obstacles, or your own wandering thoughts. In life, too, distractions can pull you away from your goals, and if you're not careful, you might end up off course or in a situation you never intended to be in. It's so easy to get caught up in the chaos, but just like driving, you must maintain a steady hand and a clear focus.

Being aware of your surroundings, staying in control, and not rushing — these are all key to avoiding dangerous outcomes. It's not about being the fastest or the most reckless; it's about knowing when to act and when to hold back, when to speed up and when to slow down. Life, much like driving, requires patience, caution, awareness, and the courage to make careful decisions in the face of uncertainty.

Sometimes, I look around at the chaos on the road and think about how easy it would be to get swept up in the madness. But I choose to stay calm, to remain focused, to never let the reckless driving of others make me lose my composure. Life is full of unpredictable detours, just like the roads in DC, but if I stay aware, I can avoid accidents, navigate through challenges, and ultimately reach my destination — safely and with a sense of peace and calm.

Driving in DC reminds me daily of the importance of concentration and enduring patience. I could easily fall into the trap of driving aggressively, trying to keep up with the fast-paced, chaotic environment. But I choose not to. I stay cautious, aware, patient, focused, and deliberate. Life, like the road, is a journey. And in both, it's important to always remember: I have too much to lose, to not stay in control.

A Calculated Risk-Taker

Although people viewed me as calm and collected, I was also quite a risk-taker. I was kooky in that many of my traits seemed contradictory, but they formed an eccentric blend of who I was. Taciturn and introverted, I processed my emotions internally. I rarely talked it out unless it was with someone I felt extremely close to. Instead of speaking, I wrote down the details of how, what, where, when, and why of things or people, dissecting, analyzing, and managing each condition with a survival mechanism that enabled me to handle and overcome challenges in logical and viable ways. I learned and grew from each and every emotional, mental, physical, or intellectual test.

I was adventurous in my own way. I ventured into many areas of study, parts of the world, professional fields, businesses, industries, and job roles. With each exploration, I honed my skills and cultivated new capabilities. Apart from the positive expeditions of the world, the job market, and the career path, I also gambled and smoked cigarettes, taking both monetary and health risks head-on.

People at work often looked to me for solutions or validation in difficult or challenging situations.

"We need you at the gathering. Without you, the conversation is limited," Molly would often say, dragging me to meetings.

"I'm glad I got to be part of the community," I would respond, trying to blend in.

"You're always so calm and funny. How do you do that?"

"There's no point in sweating the small stuff. I process my emotions and try to make sense of things."

I worked for over thirty years in the United States and traveled to numerous countries. What I experienced and learned made me a tough cookie, able to stay calm and collected in the face of adversity and take whatever transpired in stride. For a long time, I was an independent contractor, managing multiple jobs and projects daily. A strong sense of responsibility and discipline was required of me. I learned to prioritize tasks, manage my time, meet deadlines, control the quality of my work, and produce the best outcomes. All that juggling and balancing made me stronger and more capable of living my life with productive introspection and achievable goals.

I was compelled to juggle various aspects of life while embracing new challenges. My calculated risk-taking wasn't reckless — it had to be thoughtful, strategic, and grounded in personal growth. Being calm yet adventurous, introverted yet willing to take risks, I had a complex and multi-faceted personality. To me, being a "calculated risk-taker" wasn't about impulsiveness; it was about knowing when to push forward and when to pause and reflect. This mindful, thoughtful approach is one I've cultivated over time and often suggest others adopt: take risks not just for excitement's sake, but for growth and learning.

I maintained a balance of calmness and boldness, blending careful introspection with adventurous exploration. My life was filled with challenges, calculated risks, and personal growth — experiencing both professional triumphs and personal gambles. My approach to problem-solving relied on analysis: writing down details and mentally dissecting situations. I used a methodical mindset that was proactive, not just reactionary. The blend of adventure and risk-taking, through varied career paths, travels, or even gambling, revealed a key layer of my personality: embracing challenges, not shying away from the unknown, but learning and evolving with each step. My decisions came from a place of cognizance, awareness, and strategy.

Central to my life philosophy is a level of self-awareness and adaptability: balancing my internal process with outward solutions. I didn't just react to the world around me; I was constantly processing and refining my response to it. I took risks, predicted the potential consequences and outcomes, and was mindful of when to step back, halt, wait, or advance. I discovered dynamics and equilibria in my internal processes of understanding myself and the world. I was a calculated risk-taker.

This contradictory nature of mine often confused those closest to me. My husband Bobby would marvel at how I could meticulously plan our finances down to the penny, yet spontaneously suggest a weekend trip to a city we'd never visited. "What a kooky girl," he'd say, shaking his head with a smile. But to me, there was no contradiction — both behaviors stemmed from the same core: thoughtful evaluation followed by decisive action.

My notebooks became "legendary" among friends and family. Filled with observations, calculations, and decision trees, they revealed the inner workings of what appeared to others as intuition. When a coworker once peeked at my open journal, she was astonished by the detailed analysis behind what had seemed like a casual suggestion in a meeting. "You actually mapped out every possible outcome?" she asked. I simply nodded and smiled. This wasn't overthinking to me; it was my natural process.

The gambling that some saw as reckless was anything but. Each bet was calculated, each risk measured against potential reward. I studied patterns, understood odds, and knew exactly when to walk away. The same applied to my career moves — leaving stable positions for uncertain opportunities wasn't impulsive but came after careful consideration of life-work balance and growth potential against security.

My travels reflected this approach as well. While I'd ventured into remote regions or chaotic cities that friends deemed dangerous, I never did so without preparation. My laptop contained meticulously researched maps, contact information for local resources, and contingency plans for various scenarios. Adventure, yes — but adventure built on a foundation of preparedness. I studied each place before my visit.

This mindset served me particularly well during the economic downturn of 2008. While friends panicked, I had already anticipated several possible outcomes and positioned myself accordingly. "You couldn't have known this was coming," one friend said when I quickly downsized into a smaller house. But in my mind, it was simply one of several scenarios I had quietly prepared for. My core approach to life remains: understand thoroughly, plan meticulously, then act decisively.

Perhaps most surprisingly to others, I apply this same methodical approach to relationships. Before opening up to someone, I observe patterns, note consistencies and inconsistencies, and evaluate the potential for mutual growth. Some have called this cold or detached, but those who truly know me understand it's quite the opposite — it's care taken to ensure meaningful, sustainable connections. I'm very particular about who I consider a friend.

What many never realize is that beneath the calm exterior and behind the analytical process lies a deeply felt experience of the world. I feel everything intensely: the risks, the rewards, the possibilities of failure and success. The analysis isn't to suppress these feelings but to channel them productively, to ensure that emotion informs rather than derails crucial decision-making.

I've come to embrace these seeming contradictions as the essence of who I am: methodical yet spontaneous, cautious yet bold, analytical yet intuitive. The calculated risks I've taken have shaped a life rich with experience, learning, and growth — a testament to finding balance between careful thought and courageous action.

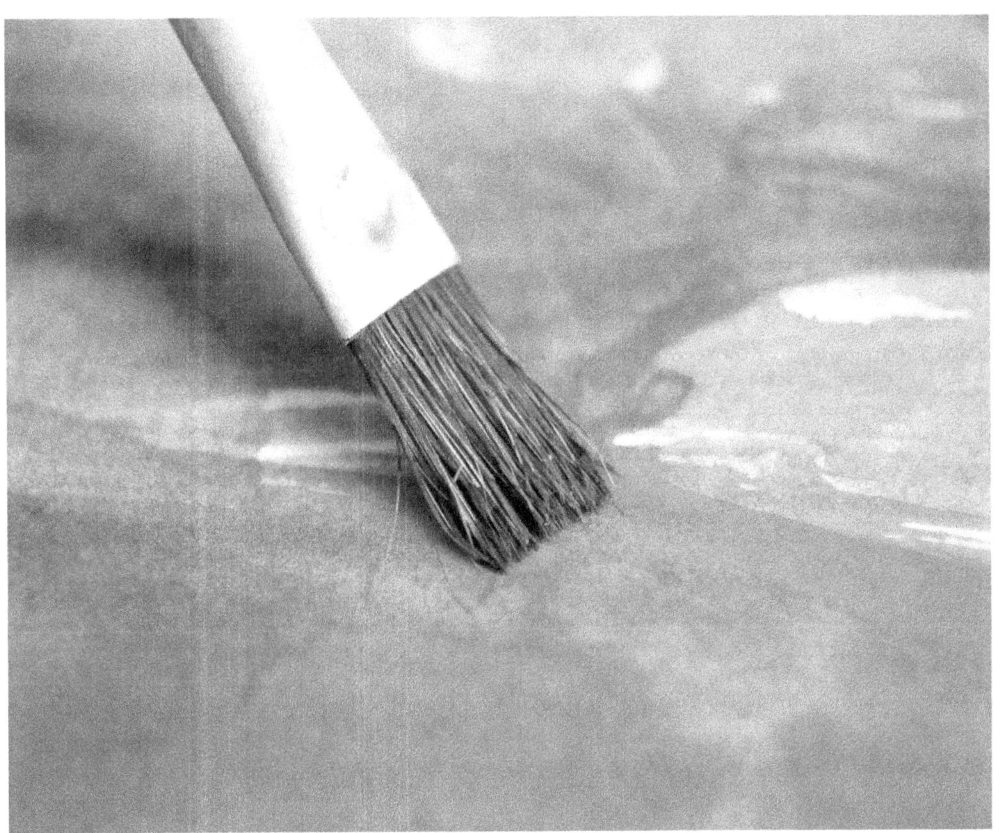

Painting Cy Twombly

I fell in love with painting during my youth in Taipei. It wasn't just the colors or the brushstrokes that captivated me, but the ability to convey emotion, to capture fleeting moments of thought and feeling that were hard to articulate with words. My childhood best friend, Wenlian, grew up to become a gallery curator, and my first American boyfriend, Tom, was an art history major and an aspiring painter. They both introduced me to different facets of the art world, which further deepened my curiosity about its multifaceted nature. Rooted in my curiosity for anything that conveyed the essence of humanity, my love for art has never faded, transcending time and distance.

Wherever I traveled, I felt the overwhelming urge to visit art museums. I sought out the sacred halls of the Uffizi Gallery in Florence, the National Gallery in London, and the Prado Museum in Madrid. I was drawn to the Guggenheim in New York City, Venice's grand palazzos, and Bilbao's strikingly modern architecture. I wandered through the corridors of the Whitney Museum of American Art, the Philadelphia Museum of Art, the Smithsonian American Art Museum, and the Phillips Collection in DC. In Los Angeles, I visited the Getty Center, and at The Art Institute of Chicago, I marveled at works that spanned centuries. Each museum, each gallery, felt like a portal to a different world — a journey into the minds of artists who had captured and immortalized humanity's most intimate thoughts and feelings.

I could feel the textures of oil paintings without touching them. The Mona Lisa's enigmatic smile became a sensation that transcended the canvas, its elusive expression so vivid I could almost reach out and touch it. The paint itself became part of the mystery, thick, tactile, and layered with secrets. The careful composition, so thoughtfully arranged, seemed to defy time and space, allowing her gaze to pierce through centuries, always seeming to shift. I would visit the Louvre and find myself getting lost in the intensity of that painting, transfixed by the lighting that transformed her complex face into a living presence.

I frequented the Museum of Modern Art in New York, where Van Gogh's swirling skies and Salvador Dalí's surreal dreams tugged at the deepest parts of my soul. I made a pilgrimage to Spain, to the Museo Reina Sofía, to stand before

Picasso's Guernica, a brutal portrayal of the violence and chaos of war. The painting felt like a living wound, and standing before it, I could sense the suffering of the Spanish people in each stroke. The sheer scale of it — its visceral energy — was unlike anything I had ever experienced. I marveled at El Greco's masterpieces in Toledo, Spain, and I felt the weight of history in his dramatic compositions. I also spent countless hours contemplating Monet's Water Lilies at the Museum of Fine Arts in Boston. There, the lush colors and soft brushstrokes of the garden seemed to suspend time itself, offering a serene escape from the chaos of the world.

Each of these works taught me something different, and each museum was a world in itself. I found myself drawn to paintings I hadn't yet seen in person, so I read about them, their stories, and the artists behind them. Works like Girl with a Pearl Earring by Johannes Vermeer and The Scream by Edvard Munch gripped my imagination, and I longed to experience them firsthand.

Art, for me, has always been more than just a visual experience. It is a profound language that communicates suffering, emotions, history's violence and struggles, as well as serenity and peace. These sentiments, encapsulated in creative works, spoke to my deepest being, leading me to collect objects with artistic significance — almost like an obsessive collector. My house was filled with knick-knacks, art magnets, and unique creative pieces — each one a tangible reminder of my love for art and its transformative power.

Though I was by no means an art expert or a skilled artist, I dabbled in oil painting. For me, painting was a means of self-expression, a way of processing life's complexities, much like writing. My art wasn't about mastering techniques; it was about capturing feelings, impressions, and moments that words couldn't fully encompass. The act of painting was cathartic, an emotional release, a way to give form to what was otherwise intangible or illusive.

The largest painting I ever created was inspired by Cy Twombly, the American painter, sculptor, and photographer. Twombly's large-scale, abstract works, his calligraphic scribbles and expressive markings, resonated deeply with me. His art felt like a language of its own, indecipherable yet deeply personal. His canvas became a space where emotion and gesture merged, where the absence of clear meaning was, in itself, meaningful.

For my own tribute to Twombly, I chose a monumental ten-foot by ten-foot canvas, determined to create something that would speak to the emotions I wanted to convey. The work I created was a text-like oil composition, with the name "Cy Twombly" subtly integrated into the backdrop, a nod to the master who inspired me. Vibrant colors — pink, yellow, gold, and blue — poured across the canvas, contrasting with Twombly's characteristic tones of gray, tan, and off-white. What started as an imitation of his style soon evolved into something distinctly my own, a unique blend of my love for both writing and painting.

Painting Cy Twombly wasn't just about mimicking his techniques; it was an act of creation, a process of discovering my own voice within his influence. The canvas became an intersection between my admiration for his work and my personal expression, allowing me to infuse it with a sense of both chaos and clarity. I was learning from the masters, but as I stood back and looked at what I had done, I realized that I had also created something entirely new — a piece that was mine, and mine alone.

The experience of painting Cy Twombly, of merging his influence with my own identity, was transformative. It wasn't about perfection, but about the courage to create something, to express myself even in the absence of clear rules or boundaries. And that, in itself, felt like a triumph.

Not a Gossiper

I found myself not joining in the small talk that many of my co-workers engaged in. I'd run into them in the hallway, chatting away about this and that. I'd say my hellos, listen, but often found my mind elsewhere, thinking about topics I'd rather discuss. Conversations that veered toward gossip or the trivial always left me feeling detached, like a spectator observing a world that didn't quite fit.

"You see that Mary and Ben are always taking a walk together!" Wendy shouted with excitement about a potential love affair.

"Yeah, she always clings on to him. Can you tell?" Cynthia asked, eager to know more.

I couldn't help but listen as they shared their musings, but I didn't feel drawn to add to it. It wasn't that I didn't care about the lives of my colleagues; it was more that I couldn't invest in stories that lacked depth, stories where I could only listen but not truly connect. I just felt out of step with everyone around me, deeply and hopelessly different. Still, many of them sought me out for conversations, as though I was someone they could share their gossips and thoughts with, even if I wasn't the type to indulge in idle chatter.

"What do you do when you have too much time on your hands?" One co-worker, particularly talkative and bored, asked.

"Well, I'm never bored. I have so many things I like to do, and so little time," I said frankly.

"If I don't come to work, I'll be bored to tears."

"I'm quite the opposite. If I have more time off, I believe I can achieve so many other things."

"Like what?"

"Like reading, writing, traveling more, gardening, and pursuing art activities and projects…."

I found certain small wonders in the most ordinary things. A spare moment could be a gift — a chance to delve into a book, to write down a new idea, to breathe in the scent of a blooming flower, or to stand still long enough to capture a moment with a camera. I was no gossipmonger, but I loved pursuing my passions and appreciating the beauty around me. It was clear I was more introspective, more connected to the richness of my inner world than the external noise. I didn't feel the need to engage in the typical small talk that many around me enjoyed. Perhaps I sought fulfillment in ways that went beyond surface-level conversation, in ways that allowed me to grow rather than stagnate.

Small talk, especially gossip about others' personal lives, often felt empty or shallow when it didn't align with what I truly cared about. It was like hearing a song you didn't resonate with playing on a loop — eventually, it faded into background noise. That sometimes made me feel disconnected from those around me. I wasn't sure if they even understood what it meant to find joy in quietude, in solitude, or in meaningful exchanges. But despite feeling out of step, my co-workers still sought me out for gossip and casual conversation. And so, I found myself navigating a tightrope between staying true to my desires and participating in social rituals that didn't always align with them.

I tried to find ways to share my passions. Sometimes, I was pleasantly surprised to find a kindred spirit after a deeper exchange. A conversation about an obscure book I was reading, or an upcoming travel destination might spark something in another person, a curiosity they hadn't realized they had. Those moments when someone shared that spark were like little revelations. I always found them stimulating. The conversations became more genuine, more fun, and interesting. It was a reminder that, while most of the chatter was fleeting, deeper discussions could still take place in the most unlikely moments.

Staying silent or withdrawn sometimes felt like a protective measure, especially when it was easier to retreat rather than engage in conversations that didn't agree with my values. But even though I wasn't a fan of small talk, I kept some level of it for balance. After all, interactions are essential. People are social creatures, and maintaining some degree of connection with those around us is part of the fabric of daily life. This is the reality of meeting social expectations. While navigating social dynamics, I also found solace in simple nods, smiles, and a few exchanges of greetings. They were like tiny gestures that allowed me to stay part of the world without having to dive deep into its shallowness.

I'd become animated and happy when any discussion of depth occurred. When a colleague started talking about their passion for a hobby, or when someone asked about a favorite book I'd read, I felt a glimmer of recognition, an acknowledgment that beneath all the surface-level exchanges, something meaningful could take root. It reminded me that these brief encounters had potential beyond the ordinary. I could hold on to my individuality without completely disconnecting from others. I protected my personal space and time while acknowledging the value of interactions. I'd close my office door when I needed to focus, and I'd visit my colleagues' offices when I felt like companionship. I was aware of when to go, where to be, and who to converse with.

The balance I maintained between staying true to my passions and engaging when necessary was the only way I knew how to find my bearings in the world around me. I used a quiet form of resistance against the noise of everyday chatter — retreating inward when necessary, but always aware that those small moments of connection held potential. They weren't meaningless; they were just waiting for the right moment to blossom into something more genuine.

Even though I often find small talk draining, I've come to see it as a bridge, one that may seem shallow at first, but has the possibility to lead to deeper waters if only one is willing to dive in. I've learned that it's okay not to be a gossiper, to be someone who doesn't partake in the latest office blather or talk about others' personal lives. The beauty of life is in the variety of connections we can make, whether they're fleeting or profound. And sometimes, those fleeting moments of small talk are merely the first step toward discovering or developing a deeper connection that might not have happened otherwise.

The Open Sky

America's West Coast is so vast that I often lost myself in its wilderness. Driving across, up, and down the western half of the United States felt like living in the very essence of the boundless freedom this country promises. The endless highways, long and never-ending, wove their way through mountains, deserts, and valleys. The landscape seemed to beckon me forward, daring me to test how far I could go in a single journey. Each mile felt like an entry into a new world, a new chapter. There I was, in my tiny car — a pale beige Beetle that had seen better days, its dashboard adorned with small mementos from previous journeys — often feeling like an invisible dot on the map — drifting through the expanse, yet at the same time, utterly free. The open sky enveloped me, a canopy of deepening blues that stretched from horizon to horizon, making me feel both infinitesimally small and entirely unbound by anything, all at once.

Driving through the barren deserts of Nevada, California, Arizona, and New Mexico, the heat shimmered off the asphalt in waves that distorted the distant landscape like a mirage. I passed lone Joshua trees, their twisted limbs reaching skyward like supplicants, standing like ancient sentinels, watching me move past. The air, thick and dry, carried a stillness that swallowed every sound, leaving only the hum of my engine and the occasional flutter of a bird's wings — perhaps a red-tailed hawk circling patiently above. The silence was all-encompassing, a vacuum that seemed to pull at my ears, compelling me to listen more closely to the rhythm of my own thoughts. In that moment, there was nothing but the endless road ahead, stretching like a ribbon of possibility, and the sun, relentless in its descent across the sky, painting the clouds in shades of amber and gold as day slowly surrendered to dusk.

But the spectacular landscape was not without its perils. The same open sky that made me feel free could also be treacherous, harboring dangers that appeared with little warning. On interstate highways, the speed of traffic far exceeded the 75-mile-an-hour limit, with drivers weaving between lanes as though the rules didn't apply to them — sports cars cutting in mere inches from my bumper, massive eighteen-wheelers barreling past with a gust of wind that rocked my small vehicle. One moment, I'd be zipping down straightaway, radio playing softly as I hummed along, and the next, I'd be navigating winding roads, gripping the steering wheel with white knuckles, feeling sweat bead on my forehead as I maneuvered through sharp curves that seemed to pull at my senses. Scenic routes, often beautiful with their panoramic vistas of canyons and valleys, could also test my patience, especially when oversized trucks would tailgate so closely that their grilles filled my rearview mirror or dart ahead unexpectedly, appearing and disappearing around tight corners like ghosts on the highway.

Then, there were thunderstorms, nature's most dramatic displays of power. Summer storms would hit with almost no warning, transforming tranquility into chaos. One minute, the sky would be a perfect shade of blue, stretching endlessly above me, and the next, dark clouds would gather like an advancing army, swallowing the horizon in ominous gray billows. Suddenly, the sky would explode in jagged streaks of lightning — electric veins illuminating the darkness — and rain would pour down in sheets so thick I could barely see a few feet ahead, droplets hammering on the roof like countless tiny drummers. It felt as though the world had become a whirlpool of sound and water, disorienting, overwhelming, a sensory assault that left me clasping the wheel and squinting through windshield wipers that fought a losing battle against the deluge. I would pull over to the shoulder, sometimes for hours, windows fogging from my breath as I waited for the storm to pass, watching the clouds shift and darken, wondering if they were about to consume me completely. In those moments, I felt a primordial fear, a reminder that for all our technological advances, we remain at the mercy of forces far greater than ourselves.

Winter, too, had its own challenges, its beauty masking potential danger. The snow, which looked so picturesque on postcards, pristine white blankets draped over mountains and meadows — became a silent adversary on the open road. On one trip through the Sierra Nevada mountains, I hit a stretch of freshly fallen snow, transforming the world into a winter wonderland of crystalline branches and white-capped peaks. But that wonderland quickly became a nightmare as visibility dropped to mere yards. The snow and ice slicked the road with a treacherous glaze, and vehicles slid uncontrollably on the frozen surface — spinning, fishtailing, their drivers frantically trying to regain control as they drifted across lanes. What had been beautiful scenery now served as a constant reminder that nature could shift from serene to menacing in an instant, its beauty belying the danger it presented to travelers caught in its embrace.

Despite the risks, the desert landscape offered a unique perspective, one I could not have gained had I stayed confined to the more crowded urban areas with their familiar comforts and predictable rhythms. The dry, barren expanses of the Mojave Desert, where the earth seemed to stretch forever in hues of rust and amber, were a stark contrast to the green, dense woods of the East Coast. The occasional saguaro cactus stood against the backdrop of mountains so distant they appeared blue, monuments to survival in an unforgiving land.

It made me realize how much we, as humans, have created to fill spaces, to give us a sense of security and control: our cities with their grid-like streets, our homes with their walls and roofs — the very infrastructure of civilization itself. The emptiness of the desert, in all its lonely beauty, humbled me. It made me appreciate civilizations even more, the small towns with their single traffic lights and local diners where waitresses knew every customer by name, the sprawling cities with their gleaming towers reaching skyward, and the endless grid of roads that connected every corner of the country — a testament to our determination to link ourselves to one another across this vast land.

And there were the cornfields of the Midwest: endless rows of crops stretching as far as the eye could see, their green stalks swaying gently in the breeze like waves on a verdant ocean. They weren't just fields to me; they were like intricate labyrinths, winding endlessly, their perfect symmetry broken only by the occasional farmhouse or silo that punctuated the landscape like exclamation points. I often wondered what it must have been like for the pioneers to cross this land, to come from places of comfort only to find themselves immersed in this vast, unyielding openness, no landmarks to guide them, no familiar mountains on the horizon, just sky and earth meeting in a distant line. I could almost feel their footsteps in the dirt, see their weathered faces turned toward an uncertain future, the weight of their hopes and fears embedded in the earth beneath me. As I drove through, I couldn't help but think of the people who had made their lives here, working the land with calloused hands, raising families in farmhouses weathered by decades of sun and rain, and finding meaning in a place so far removed from the coasts and established cities. Their stories seemed to whisper in the rustling of the corn, tales of tenacity, perseverance and dignity.

In the evenings, I would stop in small towns, places that seemed almost forgotten by time, existing in a parallel dimension where life moved at a gentler pace. I wandered through ghost towns, their once-thriving streets now abandoned, windows boarded up like closed eyes, and buildings slowly crumbling into the earth — brick by brick returning to the land from which they came. These remnants of past lives stood like monuments to a forgotten era, testaments to dreams both realized and abandoned. The wind would whistle through broken windows, carrying with it echoes of laughter and conversation from long ago — the phantom sounds of saloon pianos and boot heels on wooden boardwalks. I could picture the people who had once lived there, their faces now a ghostly memory in the shadow of the windswept plains: miners seeking fortune, storekeepers serving their communities, children playing in streets now silent save for the occasional tumbling tumbleweed. In one such nameless town Arizona, I found a faded photograph in an abandoned general store, a family portrait from the early 1900s, their solemn faces staring back at me across the decades, asking to be remembered.

But not all was melancholy. The national parks, Yosemite, the Grand Canyon, Sequoia, Yellowstone, the Kaibab National Forest, and the nostalgic stretches of the Old West and Route 66, were places of awe that stretched the limits of human imagination. Standing on the rim of the Grand Canyon at sunrise, watching as golden light spilled over the stratified walls of red and orange rock, I felt the earth's ancient heart, its millions of years carved into the stone beneath me. The sheer size of it was overwhelming, layer upon layer of geological history exposed like pages in a book written by time itself, making me feel both insignificant and deeply connected to everything that had come before. The towering trees of Sequoia, the giants of the forest, stood like silent witnesses to the passage of time — their massive trunks wider than cars, their canopies reaching so high they seemed to touch the clouds. Running my hands over bark that had withstood fires, floods, and the slow march of centuries, I felt a connection to something greater than myself, a lineage that stretched back to times before human memory. In those moments, I felt more connected to the earth than I ever had before, a brief participant in an ongoing story far greater than any single life.

After living on the West Coast for a long time, I ran out of new places to explore. I had seen the West in all its glory, from the snowy peaks of the Rockies to the sun-scorched valley floors of Arizona. I had visited forgotten towns with their dilapidated storefronts and rusty water towers, driven alongside canyons so deep they seemed bottomless, traversed deserts where the heat made the horizon dance, walked through valleys lush with wildflowers that carpeted the ground in explosions of color, stood in forests where sunlight filtered through leaves in dappled patterns, dipped my toes in rivers cold and clear as crystal, gazed at lakes that mirrored the sky so perfectly it was impossible to tell where water ended and air began, and laid beneath star-filled grasslands where the Milky Way spread across the heavens like spilled diamonds on black velvet. And yet, despite all these wonders, the thrill of discovery began to fade like a photograph left too long in the sun. With a melancholy sense of completion, tinged with the bittersweet knowledge that all journeys must eventually end, I made my way back to the East Coast, the familiar skyline of the cities now feeling more like home — their crowded streets and hurried pace a stark contrast to the emptiness I had grown to love.

And occasionally, on quiet nights when the city sleeps, I found myself longing for the open sky, the feeling of driving for miles without encountering another soul, the wind brushing against the window as the sun dipped below the horizon in a spectacular farewell, the stars so close it seemed I could reach up and touch them — each one a distant light beckoning to unknown worlds. That sense of freedom, being so small yet so incredibly free under the vast expanse of the sky, stays with me, no matter where I go, a phantom sensation that returns to dreams. It's a memory of a time when I wandered through a land both harsh and beautiful, a land of extremes where danger and wonder walked hand in hand, always open, always waiting for the next adventurer. Sometimes I think I can still feel the desert heat on my skin, still taste the dust of those lonely roads, still see the endless horizon stretching before me like a promise of what might lie beyond the next turn. And in those moments, I know that a part of me remains there still, driving endlessly under that open sky, forever seeking what lies just beyond the horizon.

The Pigs in the Pigsty

Growing up, I was never around pets or animals. My mother was a neat freak who didn't allow any cats or dogs in the house. To this day, I flinch when a dog sniffs me or barks at me. Even the tamest of animals make me recoil to a safe distance. I remember the occasional encounters I had with animals: an owl my father caught and tied to the ceiling beam, and a deer he hunted and kept alive in an enclosure near our kitchen — one that never became venison. But what I remember most fondly are the pigs in the pigsty at my childhood neighbor's place, just down the back road from my family home.

The pigs in my neighbor's pigsty were cute, smart, and funny. I often stopped by to visit them, bringing handfuls of leftovers from our dinner table. They eagerly devoured my scraps, their "oink, oink, oink" echoing between bites as they looked up at me, waiting for more. Their eyes, framed with long lashes, sparkled with curiosity, and their snouts wiggled as though they were sensing the world around them with some hidden intelligence.

Sometimes, when I visited, the pigs were sleeping, piled together in a corner near their feces, looking peaceful and docile. Though they had a strong smell and happily ate our stinky leftovers, I never recoiled from them. Instead, I invited them to join me for a chat. I'd rouse them from their lazy slumber to play with me, craving their companionship.

The pigs in the pigsty became more than just animals to me; they became friends, offering comfort and warmth in a world that often felt too structured and controlled. I had no concept of boundaries when it came to their world. The smell of the pigsty, while unpleasant, became something I grew used to — almost like a reminder that life, even in its messiest forms, had its own charm.

Unlike the owl my father had once caught — something foreign and untouchable — or the deer that symbolized control and ownership, the pigs were simply there, existing in their own space with no pretense. They were so unpretentious, so comfortable in their own skin, that it never occurred to me that they were raised to become bacon or pork chops someday.

There was something honest about their behavior, something endearing in the way they nudged each other for space or rolled in the mud with contentment. They didn't need to impress anyone, and perhaps that's why I felt so at ease with them.

I sometimes wondered if they enjoyed our time together as much as I did. When I'd leave, they'd grunt in a way that felt almost like a thank you, and I'd wave goodbye, knowing that tomorrow, I'd return with more scraps and a new story to tell them. These pigs, in their quiet and simple way, taught me something about the world: the value of presence and companionship, even in the most unlikely of forms.

Looking back, I realize those pigs, in their small, humble pigsty, gave me more than any cat or dog ever could. Their acceptance was unconditional, and their joy in life's simple pleasures taught me to appreciate moments of stillness and tranquility — something I still cherish today. Although I didn't grow up with traditional pets, those pigs remain the animals I felt closest to — a gentle reminder that true companionship can come from the most unexpected places, offering comfort in ways we don't always anticipate.

Crushes

My childhood crush was the class leader, a boy who hung out with us, a group of girls who gathered after school all the time. He joined us while we girls spent our time playing dress-ups, dollhouses, and collecting bookmarks with flowery designs and sentimental maxims.

"Come to my house at three after school," Wenlian would say. Her house was our usual gathering place, where we exchanged countless secrets and treasures like bookmarks, paper dolls, trinkets, and charms.

"I'll bring two blankets to contribute to our playact," the class leader offered, eager to be part of the girls' group.

"Great! We need someone to play the King of Merryland," I replied, excited to play his queen.

We played, studied, and walked together everywhere. Outsiders might have thought our group was exclusive, made up of the leaders and high achievers of the grade. I was the commander of the school drum and bugle band, hugely popular in the community; my friends were top students with the best grades. And my crush, the class leader, was tall, gentle, and handsome — every girl wanted to be with him.

I didn't get to be his girlfriend, but no one did. Even as we moved into senior high school, no girl ever became his girlfriend. I felt special, though, because he always sought me out to chat and discuss "important" school matters.

Then, when we all went to college, Wenlian, who attended the same university as the class leader, discovered that he dressed like a woman. She called me, exclaiming in a high-pitched voice, "Guess what, he has a boyfriend!" I was as shocked as she was, but then everything became clear. My first crush was gay, and it took me all the way into my college years to fully understand it.

Looking back now, I see the signs that I missed in my youthful innocence. The way he gravitated toward our female friend group, how comfortable he was playing dress-up with us, his natural affinity for activities that most boys our age would have scorned. At the time, I interpreted his attention as interest, his kindness as potential romance. But there was something deeper happening: a young man finding sanctuary among friends who accepted him without question, even before he fully understood himself.

I wonder now if our little group was the one place where he could truly be himself, free from the expectations that followed him as the "perfect" class leader. When he played the King of Merryland in our elaborate games, was he simply fulfilling a role that was expected of him? Or was there joy in the playacting, in being able to explore different sides of himself in the safety of Wenlian's home. The revelation in college didn't diminish my fondness for him. Instead, it transformed my understanding of our shared childhood. What I had experienced as unrequited love was something equally precious and valuable — a friendship built on mutual trust and acceptance. He had chosen us, chosen me, not as romantic prospects but as safe harbors in the confusing waters of adolescence.

The deep admiration I had for him, shaped by our shared experiences, turned into a bittersweet mix of innocence, longing, and self-discovery. I learned that love comes in many forms, and sometimes the crushes that don't bloom into romance teach us the most about ourselves and about compassion for others.

In college, I developed a crush on a bass singer in the choir whose vocal range stretched from the second E below middle C to the E above. His voice was rich and deep, with a full, resonant timbre — so beautiful it gave me goosebumps every time he sang.

I would go to the school church just to watch him rehearse.

"You should join the choir," he suggested one day.

"Ah, I'm too shy to sing like you. You're wonderful," I blushed.

"Come join us; you'll be just fine," he encouraged. After that, he kept me informed about every school event where he was performing. He was not only a talented singer, but also an exceptional modern dancer and actor. I fell in love with every artistic presentation he was a part of: concerts, plays, dances, and historical enactments. He even mentioned concerts and artistic events outside of the college, as though he was inviting me.

I attended all the interesting events he shared with me, but we never went together. It felt as though we had an unspoken agreement that our connection was best kept in the stars — connected but distant, silent yet strong. At least, that's how I felt.

There was something almost sacred about our arrangement. I'd sit in the audience, often alone, feeling both completely isolated and intimately connected to him as his voice filled the space between us. Sometimes, when he performed solo parts, I'd imagine he was singing just for me, his voice carrying messages his words never did. During curtain calls, our eyes would meet briefly across the crowded auditorium, and a subtle nod or smile would pass between us — acknowledgment of our peculiar bond.

I never told my friends about the depth of my feelings. How could I explain this relationship that existed primarily in shared glances and musical notes? They wouldn't understand the thrill I felt when he mentioned a new performance, or how I'd spend hours choosing what to wear to these events, hoping he might notice me in the sea of faces. I kept a program from each performance in a box under my bed, a collection of moments that mapped the geography of my heart.

Once, after a particularly moving rendition of a Bach cantata, I waited behind the church, gathering courage to congratulate him properly. When he emerged, still flushed from the performance, he seemed surprised but pleased to see me there.

"Your voice was transcendent tonight," I said, the words tumbling out before I could polish them.

He smiled, a genuine smile that reached his eyes. "It means a lot that you were there," he replied. Then, after a moment's hesitation, he added, "You know, you have a particular way of listening. I can always tell when you're in the audience."

We stood there in the cool evening air, surrounded by the muffled sounds of the departing crowd, locked in a moment of perfect understanding. Neither of us moved to change our relationship, to define it with words or actions that might break its delicate magic. It was enough to exist in that shared space of unspoken connection.

The bass singer traveled the world after graduation. The last time he came back to our home country, he attended famous artists' gatherings, and I saw his photos on social media. I still felt the compelling pull of this crush, even with time and distance between us. I also felt fine with this unspoken bond that never evolved into anything more tangible.

Now, years later, I sometimes find myself at concerts, closing my eyes when the bass section begins, searching for the particular resonance that his voice had. I follow his career from afar, taking private pride in his accomplishments as though I have some small claim to them. Sometimes I wonder if he remembers me as clearly as I remember him — if in some distant concert hall, he ever scans the audience hoping to find my face.

We both existed in parallel worlds, connected by admiration, but never quite crossed into something more. Sometimes, the distance between two people can create a beautiful, platonic bond, even if it's not romantic or passionate. Perhaps what makes this crush so enduring is precisely that it remained unrealized — a perfect possibility that reality never had the chance to disappoint.

The connection I shared with my college crush was pure and powerful. We communicated through mutual appreciation without ever needing to define it. Even though we never really courted, our bond was fulfilling in its own way. And in the end, that unspoken connection, full of respect and admiration, was enough. Some loves are meant to be lived; others are meant to be cherished from afar — each teaching us different lessons about the capacity of our hearts.

My Ideal Husband

An ideal husband? I never really thought about it until now. When I was younger, I fell in and out of love with the wrong guys: an engineer who pampered me, only to run off when our paths diverged; an artist who was never meant to start a family; an investment banker who fled when I told him my life's purpose wasn't to work a nine-to-five job; a Hollywood producer who took too many different girls to the Oscars; a tall, funny East Village misfit who had Hepatitis B; a corporate leader in a highly visible position, too absorbed in himself to truly love me; a school district PR guy who assumed too much white male supremacy; a college professor who prematurely envisioned our happily-ever-after; an out-of-towner who couldn't commit to a long-distance relationship; a pious, spirited bipolar man more into himself and metaphysics than into me; a blue-collar biker who seemed like a knight in shining armor, but snored too loudly to be a true gentleman; and a county hospital accountant who retired early and had too much time on his hands. I was drifting, lost in the sea of failed relationships, until I met my second husband, Bobby.

What is an ideal husband, anyway? Is it someone who provides for you, ensures your independence, and manages to be your spouse, friend, lover, brother, father, and companion all at once? Bobby gave me a sense of care, a care so profound it felt like he was anchoring me, like my life was centered yet free, free from imposed insecurities, limitations, bondages, or struggles. With him, I felt I could breathe, explore, and grow without fear of being held back. I was able to live a comfortable life with a partner by my side, yet still pursue my own ambitions and dreams, living a life that was fulfilling in my own eyes. In his presence, I was not just a wife; I was a woman with her own identity, and he supported that.

Bobby and I experienced passionate love, full of sparks and fireworks, but we also faced the challenges of blending our families, navigating the complexities of life. No matter what we did, where we were, or how we faced the world's difficulties, we always found a deep sense of belonging in each other. Perhaps the essence of an ideal husband isn't about checking off a list of traits or expectations, but about someone who can face the world with you. Someone who grows with you, for you, but never grows apart from you. He is your partner in the truest senses, steadfast and evolving, yet never leaving you behind.

The qualities that made Bobby "ideal" weren't about perfection; they were about security, mutual growth, and a connection that went beyond the surface. My ideal husband wasn't a man who adhered to a rigid framework of characteristics; he was someone who supported my autonomy, encouraged my growth, and allowed me to have a sense of belonging — both as his partner and as an individual. The balance he provided between partnership and individuality was something I needed and wanted. There was a beautiful symmetry between us: an understanding that we could stand together, side by side, without sacrificing our individuality or each other's dreams.

In many ways, Bobby represented a departure from all my past relationships. Each one had their own set of qualities, but none of them quite measured up to the fullness of what I wanted in a partner. They had their flaws, certainly, some more than others. But Bobby, with his understanding, his patience, his humor, and his unwavering love, demonstrated that the right partner isn't someone who fits into a neat box of descriptions. It's someone who doesn't just accept you, but encourages you to be the best version of yourself. He is not flawless, but his imperfections are never a burden — they are simply part of the whole person he is. Yes, Bobby could be quick-tempered at times, but it was his passion that also made him an endlessly fascinating companion.

Bobby is the kind of man who plays the guitar beautifully, effortlessly blending his love for music with his ability to crack jokes like a seasoned comedian. He is well-read, but also street-smart, capable of navigating both formal knowledge and practical life situations with ease. He can fix our cars, our houses, and can make us laugh while doing it. What I admire most is how well he connects with everyone around him — from family to friends — because he is genuinely interested in the lives of others. His empathy and kindness extend beyond just me, but to everyone who crosses his path. And above all, Bobby loves me in a way that makes me cherish life.

An ideal husband isn't defined by a set of ideals or perfect merits — it's about the ability to walk through life together, hand in hand, no matter what the world throws at you. A true partner supports you, challenges you, and grows with you, but never leaves you behind. He sees you, all of you, and still chooses to stay. Bobby taught me that love isn't about perfection; it's about a connection that runs deeper than the surface. It's about feeling supported, valued, and loved through every phase of life, from the heights of joy to the depths of struggle.

My ideal husband, Bobby, stood with me through it all, offering love and support in ways I had never experienced before. He didn't just fill a role; he created a partnership where we both contributed uniquely, shaping a life together that was fulfilling and deeply meaningful. Our bond was grounded in trust, respect, and love, and that was what made our relationship truly ideal — not because it was flawless, but because it was real. Together, we built a life rooted in shared purpose, growth, and mutual support. The essence of our relationship is not in the perfection of each individual, but in the strength of our connection and the beauty of the journey we take together.

The Journey Continues.

We met on a quiet, sunny Sunday afternoon at a small café downtown. It took six months before we had our second date. I was initially hesitant about giving another tall, handsome corporate executive a chance, but everything changed when I heard him sing and play rock music on his guitar. As the music flowed, something inexplicable happened between us — a silent connection, like two kindred spirits recognizing each other in the most ordinary of places. In that moment, I knew something significant had just begun.

Born in a small inland town, Bobby grew up to the rhythm of city life, surrounded by four brothers and one sister. His father, a heavy equipment operator and salesman with calloused hands and a gentle heart, also carved decoy wooden ducks as a hobby. He taught Bobby the value of creating something with his own hands. His mother, a nurse and piano teacher with a passion for fantasy literature, instilled in him a love for words and stories. This unique blend of influences shaped Bobby into a man who could build a bookshelf from scratch and then fill it with his favorite epic fantasy novels, quoting passages from memory as he worked.

After a few dates, I began to truly see the depth of Bobby's character. He had this remarkable ability to be fully present and observant. While watching a movie, he'd catch inconsistencies or details most would miss. Sharp as a tack, he asked questions not out of curiosity, but to engage in the moment. There was no pretense with him, no facade to uphold. What you saw was exactly what you got: a man completely comfortable in his own skin, with nothing to prove to anyone in the world.

Our relationship wasn't without its challenges. Six months after we started dating, Bobby's children from his previous marriage visited, and his son was moving in with him. We learned to navigate these changes together, finding moments of joy amid the complexities of life. Bobby taught me that strength wasn't about stoicism or hiding emotions; it was about facing life's difficulties with an open heart and the courage to be vulnerable. When he finally proposed, it wasn't a grand, elaborate gesture. Instead, he knelt down in my living room and asked me to build a life with him — a life filled with stories, ones we would write, and write, and write together

Our wedding reflected who we were: intimate, meaningful, with personal touches that spoke to our journey. Bobby surprised me by playing a song he had written, his fingers moving confidently across the guitar strings as he sang words that traced our story from that Sunday afternoon to this moment of commitment. His voice, usually confident and steady, cracked with emotion during the chorus, and there wasn't a dry eye in the small gathering of our closest friends and family.

The early years of our marriage were about finding our rhythm together, creating traditions that were uniquely ours. Sunday mornings became sacred — Bobby would make his famous blueberry pancakes while I brewed coffee, and we'd watch the news and planned adventures. He taught me to appreciate the simple pleasures: the feel of sand between toes during beach walks, the satisfaction of growing our own herbs, the joy of spontaneous road trips to nowhere in particular.

Bobby's greatest gift to me was his belief in my abilities, especially during the times I doubted myself. When I decided to move back to the East Coast to teach Mandarin to foreign service officers, Bobby rearranged his life to support mine, celebrating every joy we discovered in our new home in the Metro DC Area. What makes Bobby truly extraordinary is how he balances strength with tenderness. He's the kind of man who can spend the morning chopping wood for our fireplace, his muscles straining with each swing of the axe, and then gently nurse a fallen baby bird back to health in the afternoon. His hands, rough from his love of car mechanics, can fix a broken sink and then gently wipe away my tears with equal care.

His sense of humor has been our lifeline through difficult times. Bobby has this remarkable ability to find lightness in even the darkest moments. When I lost my dear friend in a car accident, he held me through nights of sobbing. And when the acute pain began to subside, he found ways to make me smile again, not to diminish the loss but to remind me that joy could still exist alongside grief. His humor is never at someone else's expense; instead, it comes from a place of keen observation about the absurdities of life and human behavior.

One of the qualities I admire most in Bobby is his ethical compass. In a world that often rewards cutting corners and self-interest, he stands firmly by his principles. I've watched him turn down lucrative opportunities because they didn't align with his values, speak up against injustice even when it was uncomfortable, and extend kindness to those society often overlooks. His moral code isn't rigid or judgmental; rather, it's rooted in empathy and a genuine desire to leave the world slightly better than he found it.

Bobby's relationship with his children revealed new dimensions of his character. Fatherhood brought out a patience and gentleness in him that seemed limitless. He approached parenting with the balance of guidance and freedom, instilling values while allowing his children to find their own paths. Though his teenage son came to live with us, I had never raised children with my husband. Still, I could easily imagine how he had spent time building treehouses, exploring tide pools, conducting backyard science experiments, or simply lying on a blanket, identifying shapes in the clouds.

As we've grown older together, our love has evolved from the passionate intensity of youth to something deeper and more sustaining. Bobby's hair has started to gray at the temples, and laugh lines frame his eyes — physical reminders of a life filled with joy. We still discover new things about each other, small revelations that keep our connection fresh and dynamic.

What makes our relationship work isn't that we're perfectly matched or that we never disagree. We have our differences: Bobby is an extrovert who draws energy from social interactions, while I need solitude to recharge. I am spontaneous and comfortable with change, whereas he prefers planning and routine. These differences could create friction, and sometimes they do. But we've learned to approach conflicts with curiosity rather than defensiveness, seeing them as opportunities to understand each other better.

Bobby taught me that love is active — it's something you do, not just something you feel. It's in the small, daily choices: choosing kindness over being right, choosing presence over distraction, choosing to see the best in your partner even on their worst days. It's making coffee exactly the way I like it every morning, not because it's a chore but because it's an expression of care. It's the way he still reaches for my hand when we walk together, a simple gesture that says, "I choose you, still and always."

After fifteen years together, what strikes me most about Bobby is his capacity for growth. He isn't the same man I married, and I'm not the same woman. We've changed, shaped by life's joys and sorrows, by our blended family, by professional successes and failures, by health scares and healing. Yet through all these transformations, our connection has remained constant — not because we've stayed the same, but because we've learned and grown together, always making room for who the other is becoming.

Love is like tending to a garden; it requires daily attention, protection during storms, and the wisdom to know when to prune and when to let things grow wild. Some seasons bring abundant blooms, others seem dormant, but beneath the surface, roots continue to deepen and strengthen. This philosophy has guided our marriage through its various seasons, teaching us patience during the sparse times and gratitude during the plentiful ones.

As I look toward our future together, I feel a deep sense of peace. There will be more challenges ahead — aging parents, children forming their own families, our own inevitable physical changes — but I face them without fear because Bobby will be beside me. Not as a perfect husband, but as my ideal one: imperfect, evolving, deeply human, and completely mine. Together, we'll continue writing our story, adding chapters filled with ordinary days and extraordinary moments, creating a narrative of a love that isn't perfect but is perfectly real.

I Kill Things

When I lived alone, I liked to think that I could raise things, make them grow, watch them bloom, and transform into magical beauty — because all living things, I believed, had the potential to do so. There was something deeply satisfying about nurturing life, whether it was a fragile seed sprouting into a tender plant or a delicate creature blossoming into something full of vibrancy and energy. I always believed that with time, care, patience, and nourishment, anything could flourish.

One afternoon, I decided to bring my vision of a thriving home to life. I went to PetWorld, hoping to create a lively, colorful space filled with the sweet songs of creatures that would fill the air with life and energy. After much deliberation, I chose two green-yellowish parakeets, tiny but spirited birds with bright eyes and vibrant feathers. Their personalities were so full of curiosity and joy that I could already picture them playing and chatting away, a perfect addition to my little ecosystem. To house them, I purchased an extra-large birdcage, elegant in design and sturdy enough to provide ample room for both parakeets. It had three feeder compartments and two rolling stands that could be moved around, allowing the birds to perch and play wherever they pleased. I imagined them hopping around the cage, exploring, engaging with the world around them.

My love for life didn't stop at the birds. I also ventured to local nurseries, eager to find plants that would thrive in my home and become part of the living tapestry I was trying to create. The air was fragrant with the scent of earth and fresh greenery as I explored rows of vibrant plants. I picked up a Juniper Bonsai tree, its small, intricate leaves folding into a perfect shape like a miniature forest. I also found a Palm tree, its long, graceful fronds swaying in the soft breeze of the store, and a sturdy Philodendron tree that would add a touch of wild, unruly charm to my collection. There were also many small pots of greens, all unique in their own ways, as well as some cacti —

each one a miniature marvel of resilience, thriving in an environment where other plants would falter.

Back at home, I carefully arranged my plants, placing them by windows where they could bask in the sunlight. I played music for my parakeets — soft melodies I hoped would soothe them and make them feel at ease in their new surroundings. I talked to them, too, offering them my company as I refilled their food dishes, making sure they had everything they needed. I wanted to be part of their lives, to offer them the same care and attention I gave to the plants.

For a while, things seemed to fall into place. The birds chirped happily, and the plants unfurled their leaves, reaching for the sun. I found peace in the routine of caring for them, watching them grow. Each morning began with the soft rustling of feathers as the parakeets stirred in their cage, greeting me with cheerful tweets that made my house feel more like a home. They flitted between perches, their movements quick and delicate, sometimes pausing to preen their feathers or nuzzle against each other. I named them Bip and Mip, and found myself talking to them as if they understood every word, telling them about my day while they tilted their heads in what I imagined was genuine interest.

The plants became characters in my home, too. The Juniper Bonsai stood proudly on my coffee table, its miniature branches creating perfect shadows across my notebooks when the afternoon sun streamed through the window. The Palm stretched taller each week, its fronds creating a gentle whisper when the air conditioning switched on. My Philodendron seemed the most responsive, unfurling new leaves that curled outward like tiny green hands reaching to touch the world. I took photos of their progress and documented their growth in a small green journal, feeling a sense of accomplishment with each new leaf or vibrant feather.

I established rituals around their care: Sundays were for rotating the plants to ensure even sun exposure, Wednesdays for changing the parakeets' water and replacing the paper at the bottom of their cage. There was something meditative about these tasks, the way they anchored my weeks and gave structure to my days. I found myself rushing home from work, eager to check on my little ecosystem and witness the subtle changes that occurred in my absence.

But there was a stark truth, something I hadn't anticipated when I embarked on this journey: life, no matter how carefully tended, doesn't always follow the paths we imagine for it. Living things require consistent attention, a steady hand, a reliable presence. They exist in their own reality, with needs that don't bend to our schedules or align with our human preoccupations. They cannot pause their requirements when we become distracted, preoccupied, or overwhelmed.

Life, as it turns out, doesn't run on sentiment or hope. It requires more than attention; it demands consistency. What I didn't realize was the complexity and unpredictability that came with tending to life in all its shapes or forms.

I had a hectic few weeks working on a project that consumed all my waking hours. The deadline loomed, and I found myself staying late at work, sometimes into the night, my mind so focused on my project that everything else faded into the background. Then came the time for me to get away on a vacation. I arranged for a neighbor to check in occasionally, but she admitted later that she had only stopped by once, assuming everything was fine when she glanced through the window. I didn't blame her — I was the one who had taken responsibility for these lives, not her.

When I finally returned home, exhausted but satisfied with my completed project and holiday, the silence in my house struck me immediately. No cheerful greeting from Bip and Mip, no rustling of feathers or scratching of tiny claws against perches. I rushed to their cage, my heart already knowing what I would find. They sat side by side on the bottom perch, no longer the vibrant creatures I had brought home, but small, still forms. Their feathers were dulled, their bodies stiff. I tried to wake them, my hands trembling as I used a soft cloth to moisten their beaks, hoping against hope that they were merely dehydrated, that I could somehow revive them. But they were gone, had been for days, perhaps, while I was lost in my work and a much-needed break, forgetting the fragile lives that depended on me.

My plants had suffered similar fates. The Juniper Bonsai, which required such specific watering — not too much, not too little — had drowned in my overzealous attempt to compensate for my absence. Its needles had turned brown, and the soil was a soggy mess that smelled of rot. The Palm drooped lifelessly, its once-proud fronds now yellowed and brittle, while the Philodendron, the hardest of them all, showed only the faintest signs of life — a single green leaf among the withered brown ones. The cacti, which I had chosen specifically for their resilience, had paradoxically fared the worst — I had overcompensated for their drought-resistant nature by drowning them in guilt-driven watering.

I stood amid the carnage of my neglect, the evidence of my desertion surrounding me. I kill things. Not through malice or even indifference, but through a fundamental inability to maintain the consistent care that life requires. I am overly attentive but easily become negligent when I get too busy or over-obsessed with my creative projects. The intensity that serves me well in my work and travel becomes a liability in nurturing life — I either smother with excessive attention or abandon when distracted by the next consuming idea.

I gathered the parakeets gently, wrapping them in a soft cloth before placing them in a small cardboard box. I thought about burying them in the park nearby, giving them some dignity in death that I had failed to provide in life. As I cleaned out their cage, removing the untouched food, the soiled paper, I wondered if I had been selfish to bring them home at all. Perhaps I do not have what it takes to nurture lives, or maybe these creatures and plants simply weren't meant to be raised by me.

That night, I sat in my living room, returned to its lifeless state — no chirping, no rustling of leaves, just the refrigerator's hum and occasional passing cars. The remains of my houseplants lined the windowsill, their once vibrant leaves now brittle and brown. *I kill things.* The thought settled over me like a shroud, a truth I must reconcile with my desire to be surrounded by life. The contradiction has haunted me for years: craving vitality while being unable to sustain it.

Perhaps it's about choice, or rather, the freedom to choose. I need the ability to move unencumbered, to not be tethered to living things — pets, plants, children. This explains my peace with not having children with Bobby, my husband who brought two from his previous marriage. His daughter and son visit every so often. I lived with my stepson when he was fifteen. I cared deeply during those precise windows of time, when I could muster my full attention, knowing there's an endpoint. Bobby handled the daily grind of adolescent mood swings and schoolwork battles, and up until now, he remains the go-to for his son's monetary issues, girlfriend problems, and unsteady career moves — the sustained care I know I cannot and will not provide.

Bobby understood this about me from the beginning. "It's OK for you to stay out of it when it comes to my children. You could be like a brilliant thunderstorm," he once said, "intense and nourishing, but does not have to linger indefinitely." He didn't mean it unkindly. He saw my need for solitude, my capacity for ardent but limited engagement. That's why we work. He doesn't expect me to be what I'm not.

My acceptance came after years of struggling to balance self-care against responsibility for others. Three therapy sessions, countless stepfamily research books, and the withered remains of numerous relationships later, I finally understood: my emotional bandwidth isn't infinite. I like to be socially mobile and intellectually limber. I constantly explore new domains of knowledge and interests, and in doing so, I choose not to be burdened by life's pettiness or others' dramas.

Life's impermanence often stems from neglect or nature's indifference — I've resolved to face this squarely rather than disguise it with good intentions. I kill things not through cruelty but through the inevitable waning of my attention. The houseplants died not in a day but gradually, as my initial enthusiasm drained away, replaced by a vague guilt that itself eventually evaporated. I am not responsible for others' lives.

People must grow responsible for themselves. Independence isn't merely desirable — it's essential. The greatest gift one person can offer another is the capacity to stand alone: self-sufficiency, emotional discipline, the strength to carry one's weight without leaning on others. I've watched Bobby's son develop this strength, partly through my deliberate withdrawal when he reached for help he didn't truly need. Bobby calls me instructive. I call myself honest.

Life doesn't pause for handholding, and the world remains unmoved by unpreparedness. When my stepson failed to pay his rent after mismanaging his spending, I refused to send him money — whether from Bobby's retirement funds or my hard-earned wages.

I couldn't justify condoning recklessness while I was commuting and working twelve-hour days, while I was the one furnishing every household item, every meal, every vacation trip after Bobby retired. I was also the one spending most of my life savings to purchase our homes, while Bobby was always broke from constantly supporting his children, putting out fires.

So instead of rescuing his son, I suggested he teach him financial planning. "This feels terrible now," I told him, "but life skill is worth ten times more than handholding for life"

That moment hurt — but it worked. My stepson rarely had to borrow money again.

I've learned to do what needs doing and expect no less from others. I kill things — literally and metaphorically — but I also know how to step back and let others nurture what I cannot. Bobby tends to his son's life journey. That is not a responsibility I am to take on.

What I cannot tolerate are children in adult bodies, people expecting rescue when they should be rescuing themselves. I watched Bobby drain himself caring for his children, who've not yet learned to manage their own emotions. I watched friends disappear into relationships where they became caretakers rather than partners. The cycle of dependence kills more than my intentional neglect ever could — it kills potentials, spirits, ambitions, and possibilities.

The tension between caring for myself and caring for others isn't really a tension at all, but a necessary balance. By recognizing my limitations, I offer more authentic care — bounded, honest, and sustainable. I don't promise unconditional care. I don't pretend to be inexhaustible. Instead, I offer what I can, when I can, and make no apologies for the rest.

I kill things. But I also recognize life's resilience. New plants will eventually occupy my yard where they will live more happily than on my windowsill, sustained by rain and natural cycles rather than my inconsistent care. The ferns I couldn't keep alive indoors now thrive in the shadowed corners of the garden, unfurling their fronds without my daily attention. Perhaps my touch isn't deadly after all — just misplaced in its application.

Bobby's children will grow; they don't need my constant attention. His son already calls less frequently for money, finding his own solutions to the problems that once seemed insurmountable. His daughter has inherited her mother's practicality and skepticism — a combination that serves her well in navigating adulthood. They've learned to seek me out for what I can offer: perspective, honesty, and the occasional burst of unconventional wisdom. They've learned not to expect what I cannot give: unwavering patience, predictable routines, and emotional scaffolding. In this mutual understanding, we've found something more valuable than traditional bonds — we've found respect.

The rhythms of intermittent engagement suit me. I've come to see myself not as a permanent fixture but as a catalyst, appearing at critical moments, offering what insight I can, then receding to allow natural development. Like a thunderstorm that waters the earth and then moves on, I contribute most effectively when I honor my nature rather than forcing myself into patterns that deplete me.

And I will continue to contribute in my own way, illuminating what I can before retreating to replenish my light. My intensity, though fleeting, has its place. I've watched students transform after a single conversation, colleagues pivot careers following a brief collaboration, friends find courage after a moment of my unfiltered truth. These weren't sustained efforts but concentrated ones — all the more powerful for their brevity.

I've made peace with my limitations. I no longer apologize for the kind of attention I can give — intermittent but intense, like lightning in a thunderstorm. Those who thrive under such care and attentiveness find something rare in it: freedom from expectation, permission to stand alone, encouragement to find strength in self-reliance and independence, rather than continuous babysitting.

I kill things. But that doesn't mean I don't also, in my own limited fashion, help things grow. Sometimes growth happens precisely because I wasn't there to interfere, because I created the space for self-sufficiency, because I refused to rescue when struggling was necessary. The plants that survive my neglect emerge taller, the people who weather my temporary absence return stronger. Perhaps that's my contribution: not the steady hand of nurturing but the challenging gift of absence — the void that compels others to fill their own spaces, tend their own gardens, and ultimately, find their way back to themselves.

Something New

I had been driving my convertible Beetle for almost twenty years. From the moment I got behind the wheel, I felt like we shared a bond. I knew every curve of her body, every squeak of the brakes, and every quirk in the way she handled. Over the years, I came to think of myself as a sort of expert on my little car. From the engine's hum to the way the wind tousled my hair when I drove with the top down, I thought I understood her inside and out. But little did I know there were still mysteries hidden beneath her familiar curves.

One afternoon, as the sun dipped low in the sky and the highway stretched out before us, Bobby, my car-enthusiast husband, turned to me with a puzzled look.

"Why are you driving with the rearview mirror set for nighttime?" he asked, his voice laced with curiosity.

I blinked, confused. "What are you talking about? What do you mean?" I replied, genuinely perplexed.

He pointed to the mirror, slightly tilted, its edges tinged with a faint, tinted hue. "See, if you hold the bottom of the mirror and push it back, it gives you a clearer, wider view of what's behind you. But if you pull it forward, like you've got it now, it deflects the high beams from the cars behind you, making it easier to see at night without glaring."

I stared at him, then glanced back at the mirror, testing his explanation. Sure enough, with a simple push, the mirror adjusted, and suddenly, the view behind us sharpened, clearer, more focused. It was such a small adjustment, yet it made a world of difference.

"Really? I never knew that!" I exclaimed, a mix of embarrassment and amazement flooding over me. How had I driven all these years without ever realizing this simple tweak could improve my experience? It seemed so obvious, but for all the time I spent with my Beetle, I'd never noticed that tiny feature.

Bobby chuckled, his laughter warm and light, a sound that told me he wasn't judging, but enjoying the moment of revelation. "It's one of those things most people never think to look for, especially if they've been driving a car for so long. But hey, you know it's never too late to learn something new."

That was the moment it hit me: no matter how long we'd spent with something, there was always something fresh to discover. The experience wasn't just about the mirror. It was a reminder that, no matter how well we think we know things, there's always more to uncover, more to learn, more to discover, and more ways to improve.

As the wind carried us along the open road, I marveled at how a single, simple moment, a new perspective could reshape my view. It wasn't just about the mirror; it was about how, sometimes, life offers us fresh insights when we least expect it. We often take things for granted, thinking we know them inside and out, only to find new details we hadn't noticed or considered before.

Life constantly offers new perspectives. Learning never truly stops, no matter how much time we've spent with something or someone. This truth has become something of a personal philosophy for me over the years — a lens through which I've come to view not just objects like my beloved Beetle, but relationships, places, and even myself.

There's a certain comfort in familiarity, in believing we understand the contours of our world completely. It gives us a sense of mastery, of control. But there's also a danger in that comfort; it can lead to blindness. We stop looking, stop questioning, stop wondering, convinced that there's nothing left to see.

The Japanese have a concept called "shoshin," or "beginner's mind." It's the idea that we should approach even familiar subjects with the curiosity and openness of a beginner, free from preconceptions about what we already know. When we cultivate this mindset, people, everyday objects and long-term relationships transform into landscapes ripe for exploration.

I thought about this one evening as Bobby and I sat in our gazebo, watching the sunset paint the sky in a captivating blend of red, orange, and yellow. We'd watched the sunset countless times over our fifteen years together, yet somehow, each evening sky felt new — the colors never quite the same, the clouds never arranged in quite the same pattern. The familiarity didn't diminish the beauty; if anything, it enhanced it. We had learned to see the subtle differences, to appreciate the unique fingerprint of each day's end.

"You know," I said, leaning my head against his shoulder, "I think that's what keeps life interesting. Finding the new in the familiar."

Bobby nodded, his arm tightening around me. "It's like us," he said simply. "Know that you'll never grow tired of me."

Yes, Bobby and I had been together for almost two decades, and even after all that time, we were still discovering new things about each other. He never knew I could sing like Celine Dion until we spent an afternoon with my family, laughing and belting out classic hits on a karaoke night. It was such a fun and unexpected moment, and it felt like a new layer of me unfolded before him, one that he hadn't had the chance to see before. I could tell he was impressed, maybe even a little shocked — but he loved it. It was one of those moments when it felt like we were both rediscovering each other in the best possible way.

On the flip side, I never knew Bobby could skate so gracefully, like a ballet dancer gliding across the ice, until one crisp winter afternoon when we decided to go ice skating together. I was used to seeing him with a hockey stick in hand, charging down the rink with all the intensity of a fierce competitor, but this was something entirely different. On the ice, he was light, fluid, and elegant, showing a soft side of himself that I'd rarely seen before. I had always known he was strong and athletic, but this effortless grace caught me off guard. There's so much more to a person than what you first think you know.

I remember another instance, about fifteen years into our marriage, when we were caught in an unexpected downpour during a hike in the mountains. The rain came suddenly, turning the dirt path into slick mud beneath our boots. Most people would have been frustrated, maybe even angry at the ruined outing, but Bobby surprised me. He took my hand with a big smile, pulled me into a clearing, and began to dance with me in the rain, twirling me around as cascades of water streamed down our faces and soaked our clothes.

"I didn't know you were such a romantic," I laughed, breathless from spinning and giggling.

His eyes crinkled at the corners as he smiled down at me. "There's a lot you still don't know about me, sweetie pie," he said, calling me "sweetie pie" in that way he did when he was being particularly sincere.

And he was right. That day, I discovered a spontaneity in him I hadn't fully appreciated before, a willingness to find joy in the unexpected. It was like uncovering a hidden room in a house I thought I'd explored completely.

Then there was the time I fell ill with a nasty flu that kept me bedridden for a week. Bobby, who had mostly relied on my cooking, suddenly revealed himself to be remarkably resourceful in the kitchen. He appeared at my bedside with a bowl of homemade chicken soup that tasted surprisingly authentic.

"Where did you learn to make this?" I asked, savoring the warmth and comfort of the broth.

He shrugged, a shy smile playing on his lips. "I looked up the recipe. Figured it was time I learned."

That small gesture — his willingness to step outside his comfort zone, to learn something new for my sake — showed me yet another facet of his character. All these years in, and he was still capable of surprising me with his depth of care.

Our house sits near a small wooded area, and for years, we'd looked out at the same view from our kitchen window: the edge of the forest, a few bird feeders Bobby had hung from the lower branches, a simple stone path leading to a bench where we sometimes sat in the evenings. Familiar and lovely, but unchanging.

Then one spring, without telling me, Bobby began a project. Each day while I was at work, he would disappear into the woods for hours. When I asked what he was doing, he would just smile mysteriously and say, "You'll see."

After three weeks of this secrecy, he blindfolded me one Saturday morning and led me carefully down the stone path. When he removed the blindfold, I gasped. He had cleared a small area among the trees and created a hidden garden, complete with a fire pit, a bubbling fountain, flowering plants arranged in concentric circles, and a new bench carved from a fallen oak tree.

"I never knew you had such an eye for design," I said, touching the smooth curve of the bench in wonder.

"Neither did I," he admitted. "I just started and let it evolve. Something about this space called for beauty."

That garden became our sanctuary, a place we returned to again and again over the years. But what struck me most was not just the garden itself, but the revelation that after almost two decades together, Bobby still contained multitudes I had yet to discover — habits, talents, passions, and depths I hadn't yet glimpsed.

And it wasn't just Bobby who continued to unfold in new and unexpected ways. I surprised myself too.

At fifty-five, I discovered a passion for pottery, my hands finding a natural rhythm with the clay that I never would have predicted. Bobby came home one evening to find me covered in clay slip, utterly absorbed in shaping a bowl on a wheel I'd impulsively purchased that afternoon.

"Where did this come from?" he asked, gesturing to the wheel and the several misshapen but earnest attempts at pottery that surrounded me in my office.

I couldn't really explain it. "I saw a demonstration at the arts festival downtown and something just... clicked. I knew I needed to try it out."

He nodded, understanding immediately. "I love that you still find new parts of yourself," he said, kissing the one clean spot on my forehead.

Who said "there's nothing new under the sun"? This phrase is famously attributed to King Solomon, as found in the

Book of Ecclesiastes, Chapter 1, Verse 9, in the Bible. Solomon, reflecting on the repetitive nature of life, expressed the notion that everything we encounter or experience has already happened before in some form, making it feel like there's nothing truly original or new under the sun. This sentiment highlights the cycles of life, work, and human behavior.

But there is something new for us to savor in every turn. While it's true that many aspects of life are cyclical, and history often seems to repeat itself, the human spirit, creativity, and innovation continue to prove that new things emerge over time, under the sun or elsewhere.

I've come to believe that newness exists not just in the creation of things that have never been before, but in our evolving relationship with the familiar. The same sunset viewed through eyes that have aged and experienced more becomes, in some essential way, a different sunset. The same person, known deeply over decades, continues to reveal new facets when seen through the lens of our own growth and change.

One evening, as Bobby and I walked along the beach across our Belize vacation house — a tradition we'd maintained for fifteen years — I noticed how the sun illuminated his profile differently than it had when we were younger. The light caught on the silver threading through his dark hair, highlighted the laugh lines that had deepened around his eyes. He was the same man I'd always loved, yet transformed by time and experience, revealing new beauty I hadn't seen before.

"What are you thinking about?" he asked, catching me staring.

"About how you're the same and also different all at once," I answered honestly, smiling.

He smiled back, squeezing my hand. "That's the trick to staying together this long, isn't it? Recognizing that people aren't static. We're always becoming."

I nodded, struck by the simple wisdom in his words. We had both changed over the years — our bodies, our interests, our perspectives. But we had done much so together, witnessing each other's transformations with curiosity and wonder rather than resistance.

Throughout history, humankind has continually created, discovered, and imagined things that had never been seen before. From groundbreaking scientific discoveries like electricity and space exploration to artistic revolutions in music, literature, and the visual arts, there have always been people who found new ways to think, create, and inspire. The phrase "there's nothing new under the sun" might highlight the repetition of basic human nature and recurring patterns in society, but it doesn't account for the constant advancement of ideas, technologies, and worldviews. Every new generation builds upon the past, pushing boundaries and inventing things that change the course of history. Think of the internet, for instance, or smartphone, concepts that didn't exist in any tangible form in Solomon's time. In this way, while some truths and behaviors remain constant, the world continues to offer innovations, ideas, and possibilities that were once unimaginable.

But beyond these grand innovations, I've found that the most profound discoveries often happen in the quietest moments, in the spaces we think we know completely. Like finding a hidden feature in a car I'd driven for two decades, or witnessing a new expression across my husband's face — one I'd never seen before despite years of studying his every mood.

So, while there may be familiar patterns that repeat themselves, the world we live in constantly finds new ways to surprise us. The beauty of human existence lies in our capacity for reinvention: seeing old things in a new light and bringing entirely new ideas into being. The world, though shaped by history, is always evolving in ways that prove that, indeed, there is always something new under the sun. And Bobby's and my journey together will never be trite or banal, because we will evolve and grow constantly, individually, and as lifelong partners, facing the world together as a team.

Perhaps the greatest discovery of all is that familiarity, rather than breeding contempt as the old saying goes, can instead deepen into a rich tapestry of understanding, one that continues to reveal new patterns and colors the longer we look. In everyday routines, in ourselves, in the shared moments together, in the landscape of a face we've known for decades, there is always something new to be found if we approach life with eyes willing to see freshly and hearts open to wonder.

"Look," Bobby whispered one night, pointing up at the sky from our backyard. We'd stargazed countless times before, but that night, a meteor shower painted streaks of light across the darkness, ephemeral, stunning, gone in an instant.

"Imagine how many people throughout history have looked up at the same stars," I mused.

"And yet," he said softly, "no one has ever seen exactly what we're seeing right now, in this moment."

And that, perhaps, is the truest magic of all. Yes, in the most familiar experiences, in the most well-worn pathways of our lives, there is always something new waiting to be discovered. It's easy to overlook the beauty of the ordinary, the small moments that pass by unnoticed, but with a deeper sense of curiosity and mindfulness, we can begin to see the world in a different light. Every corner of our lives holds potential for growth, transformation, learning, and understanding if we allow ourselves to truly engage with it.

In the most routine interactions, the simplest actions, there is an infinite well of possibility. A walk down a familiar street may reveal something we've never noticed before, a shift in light, the way the wind dances through the trees, or the laughter of children echoing in the distance. Even the humdrum of daily chores can take on a new depth when approached with an open heart. What we thought was mundane becomes sacred when we stop to fully appreciate it, when we allow ourselves to be present in each moment rather than rushing through them in search of something more exciting or more extraordinary.

In this constant journey of discovery, the key lies in our willingness to shift our perspective. Just as a slight turn of the mirror can reveal a different view of the same scene, adjusting the lens through which we see our world can unveil hidden wonders. It's not always about seeking out grand adventures or dramatic changes, but rather about embracing the subtle nuances that already exist. The magic lies in the way we choose to perceive what is already around us.

Curiosity, then, becomes a powerful tool, a crucial force that invites us to see with new eyes. Mindfulness helps us slow down, allowing us to notice the intricate beauty of the world that often eludes us in our haste. And when we allow ourselves to be open to wonder, we create space for new connections, new insights, and a deeper appreciation for the richness of the life we are living. The most profound magic is not necessarily in the extraordinary, but in our ability to discover the extraordinary within the ordinary. The trick is to believe that it is there, waiting, always, just beyond the surface of what we think we already know.

Vignettes of a Collected Kook by Alicia Su Lozeron

About the Author

Asia-Literacy and Global Competence Mentor | AACS Author | Interpreter| Translator |Licensed English Language Arts and Chinese Mandarin Educator

Think Global Live Noble

Alicia Su Lozeron is an accomplished author, educator, and cultural advocate who has written a diverse body of work, including numerous articles, short stories, and novels. She holds multiple graduate degrees, including a master's degree in English and Comparative Literature from Columbia University in New York City. She is also a licensed secondary-school

English Language Arts and Mandarin Chinese teacher across several states, including Nevada (NV), California (CA), Michigan (MI), Pennsylvania (PA), Texas (TX), and Arizona (AZ). She has taught literature as well as English and Mandarin language courses to students of various ages, including at secondary public schools, colleges, and, most recently, adult learning institutions such as the Foreign Service Institute, a State Department–affiliated school, where she taught Mandarin Chinese to U.S. foreign service officers.

With a passion for global understanding, Alicia Su Lozeron has combined her academic background and teaching/travel experience with a deep commitment to cultural exchange and communication. Through her career as a writer and the communication management company she founded, Asia-America Connection Society (AACS | 亚美合作协会), she works tirelessly to raise awareness about global competence, facilitate cross-cultural communication, and bridge the gap between the West and the rich cultural and economic contributions of the Asian world.

Alicia Su Lozeron's work explores the complexities of cultural interactions, the impact of globalization, and the deep importance of understanding and embracing diverse perspectives. Her essay collections *Asia-Literacy and Global Competence* (2017) and *Global Competence Revisited* (2019) dive into the challenges and rewards of navigating cultural differences, offering readers an opportunity to reflect on how interconnected the world truly is. These works represent not just her professional insights but her personal musings on the evolving landscape of global literacy, setting the stage for her subsequent creative and advocacy endeavors. In *Writings in the Time of Coronavirus* (2021), she continues to explore these themes in the face of global uncertainty, focusing on human justice, ethical values, and the importance of resilience during difficult times. Her reflections call for a renewed focus on upholding integrity, understanding, and kindness, reminding readers of the enduring importance of shared humanity, especially in times of difficulty or crisis.

Her debut novel, *The Un-death of Me* (2016), is a poignant exploration of identity, alienation, and self-discovery. The novel tells the story of a world-traveling, immigrant Asian American woman who navigates the complexities of cultural assimilation, personal growth, and the search for belonging. Set in a world where contemporary global issues intersect with the timeless struggles of the human condition, *The Un-death of Me* challenges readers to reconsider their perceptions of cultural identity, love, marriage, and personal fulfillment. It is a work that not only explores the individual's quest for meaning but also addresses societal biases and prejudices, using the personal experiences of the protagonist as a lens through which to view broader issues of alienation and discrimination.

In *A Man with Immense Love* (2022), Alicia Su Lozeron continues to expand her exploration of humanity through the character of Aiden William Melone, a man whose emotional and spiritual journey offers profound insights into human complexity. The novel is not just a story of love but a prayer for understanding, compassion, and kindness. It invites readers to reflect on the power of a good soul, the transformative effect of love, and the potential for growth and healing in even the most challenging of circumstances. Through Aiden's journey, the author challenges us to look beyond surface-level differences and explore the deeper, often hidden, layers of the human experience. The novel subtly critiques human flaws while also offering a hopeful vision for the future — a future in which compassion, understanding, and kindness create the possibility for personal and collective healing.

Alicia Su Lozeron's most recent book, *Vignettes of a Collected Kook* (2025), is a thought-provoking and deeply personal work. This collection of reflections, narratives, and insights is drawn from her own life expericnces, offering readers a glimpse into the complexities of her journey. The narrator, a self-described "collected kook," represents a person who embraces both eccentricity and mindfulness — a unique individual who seeks meaning in the contradictions of life. These mini-stories not only offer glimpses into the author's personal evolution but also serve as an invitation for readers to examine their own paths and personal growth. The collection celebrates the beauty of imperfection and the richness of human experience, showing that embracing both the joys and struggles of life can lead to much deeper understanding and personal fulfillment.

Across her body of work, Alicia Su Lozeron has consistently focused on themes of personal growth, self-reflection, and emotional connection. Her writing encourages readers to examine their relationships with themselves and others, offering practical wisdom on how to navigate life's complexities. Her exploration of cultural competence, family dynamics, and conflict resolution reflects a holistic approach to improving both individual well-being and societal harmony. Her work is not merely about storytelling; it is a tool for self-improvement and understanding, urging readers to consider their role in fostering empathy, compassion, and social change or reform.

One of the most consistent threads throughout Alicia Su Lozeron's writing is the theme of self-reflection. Her stories encourage readers to look inward, challenge their assumptions, and actively engage in the process of self-discovery. She believes that the path to a happier, more meaningful life begins with the ability to understand one's own emotions, motives, and actions. She advocates for the importance of effective communication and empathy in resolving conflicts and fostering deeper connections with others. Her stories offer not only narrative pleasure but also a practical guide to navigating the complexities of modern life with grace.

In addition to her literary contributions, Alicia Su Lozeron has dedicated herself to promoting lifelong learning and global competence through her communication management and translation/interpretation company, Asia-America Connection Society (AACS | 亚美合作协会). She works to facilitate cultural exchange and ensure that global conversations are inclusive and informed. Her company's work extends beyond traditional translation/interpreting services — it is a platform for sharing knowledge, fostering understanding, and promoting cross-cultural dialogue. Alicia Su Lozeron's dedication to these ideals has made her a valued advocate for global competence, helping individuals and organizations navigate an increasingly interconnected world with sensitivity and awareness.

Her work is not just a career; it is a cause and a calling. She finds deep satisfaction in the process of creation and in the opportunity to contribute to the global community. Her efforts aim to elevate people of all cultures and backgrounds, celebrating the shared humanity that connects us all. By advocating for mutual understanding, collaboration, and respect for diverse perspectives, Alicia Su Lozeron seeks to foster a world where individuals and cultures can thrive together, creating positive changes in people, business, culture, education, and beyond.

Readers have shared how Alicia Su Lozeron's work has had a profound impact on their lives:

- It has helped them remain calm and composed in the face of adversity, offering strategies for resilience and emotional balance.
- It has inspired them to strive for self-sufficiency, independence, and a lifelong commitment to personal growth and learning.
- It has provided them with the tools to process emotions in healthy ways, encouraging self-awareness and emotional intelligence.
- It has empowered them to overcome difficulties or fears, showing them how to find beauty in human interactions and see the potential for positive change or outcome.
- It has broadened their understanding of people from diverse backgrounds and encouraged them to appreciate the rich tapestry of the world around.
- It has helped them strengthen relationships, particularly within interracial or blended families, by promoting empathy, as well as open and honest communication.
- It has allowed them to savor the complex emotions tied to important life experiences, fostering deeper self-reflection and self-awareness.
- It has inspired them to see the world with renewed hope, courage, and respect for others, reinforcing the importance of respect, kindness and understanding.

- It has increased their awareness of cultural competence, helping them navigate global conversations with sensitivity and respect.
- It has nurtured a well-rounded worldview, encouraging them to learn about life from multiple perspectives and embrace diverse viewpoints.
- It has helped them develop the ability to express genuine love, empathy, and care, contributing to healthier and more harmonious relationships and lives.
- It has provided guidance on reducing conflict and building trust, offering valuable insights into effective communication, positive interaction, and conflict resolution.

Through her literary work and advocacy efforts, Alicia Su Lozeron continues to inspire readers and individuals around the world to embrace their shared humanity, foster understanding, and work toward a more compassionate, just, and interconnected world.

Alicia Su Lozeron
Asia-America Connection Society
Think Global Live Noble
Phone 702-577-0700
E-mail aliciasulozeron@gmail.com

Detailed Information:

https://www.linkedin.com/in/alicia-su-lozeron

http://amazon.com/author/aliciasulozeron

www.ingramcontent.com/pod-product-compliance
Lightning Source LLC
Chambersburg PA
CBHW081128300726
48982CB00005B/881
* 9 7 8 1 7 3 3 2 0 3 9 8 2 *